PET WHISPERER P.I.:

BOOKS 13-15 SPECIAL COLLECTION

MOLLY FITZ

Editor: Jennifer Lopez, Mistress with the Red Pen
Cover: TM Franklin

PO Box 873543
Wasilla, AK 99687

GRIZZLY GRIEVANCE

PET WHISPERER P.I.

Life has been kind of hectic lately, so Charles and I have decided to fill our weekend with the three Rs: Rest, Relaxation, and Romance, courtesy of a private weekend away.

Unsurprisingly, two furry stowaways manage to sneak aboard our rental RV, which means we're stuck with one very bossy talking cat and a raccoon who's decided to role-play the weekend as some kind of big rig trucker.

And if that wasn't enough to put a damper on things, the dead body that shows up in the communal picnic area surely does the trick.

Throw in a grizzly mama with a desperate plea for us to help find her cubs, a budding reality TV star who's desperate to be liked by everyone she meets, and a couple secrets of our own, and the four of us are in for one wild, wild weekend!

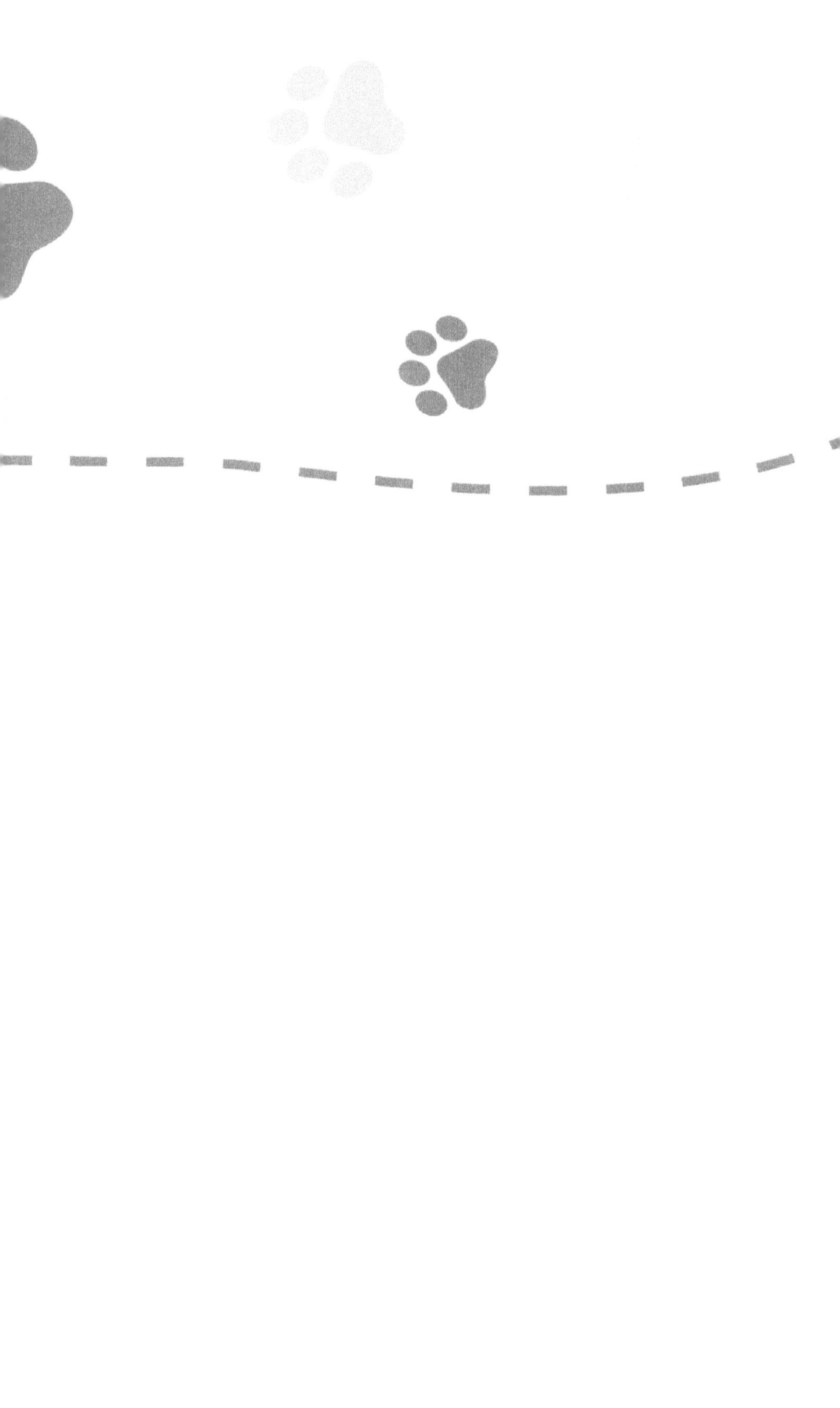

1

I'm Angie Russo, and lately my life has been one train wreck after another. And, yeah, I do mean that literally. First my cat and I found ourselves aboard a derailed train about six months back, and then just a couple weeks ago, my nan crashed her sports car on the highway with us in it.

I've started to fear various modes of transportation just as much as I've feared electric coffee makers for a while now. In my life, both have only led to trouble.

And that's how it all started, too.

I got zapped by an old coffee maker and woke up with the strange new ability to talk to animals. And those talking animals have led to most of my problems, like the aforementioned vehicle wrecks. I've also dealt with more than anyone's fair share of murders, thefts, kidnappings, and other nefarious crimes. Then again, I guess that's what I get for setting up shop as a private investigator.

Still...

I could really do with just a week or two where nothing life-altering comes around and rocks my world.

I can't even remember the last time I enjoyed a good old-fashioned Netflix binge or spent the full day in bed reading. Also, I almost never get paid for my investigative work, which begs the question: Why do I keep signing myself up for more and more?

My partner at Pet Whisperer P.I. has zero issues saying no. Of course, he's not the one doing any of the talking. He wouldn't miss napping in a sunbeam or giving himself a slow, leisurely tongue bath for anything... Oh, did I mention my partner is a cat?

He's a standard tabby with an oversized attitude, but don't tell him I said that. His full name is Octavius Maxwell Ricardo Edmund Frederick Fulton Russo, Esq, P.I. (a name he freely and regularly adds to). I prefer to call him Octo-Cat. He's not a fan, but at least he's stopped arguing with me about it.

The trust fund his previous owner left him pays all our bills, and those rare moments when he offers me genuine displays of love and affection are the brightest spots in my day.

We also live in our—or rather his—giant manor house alongside my nan and her rescue Chihuahua, Paisley. Pringle the nosy reality TV addict lives in a treehouse in our backyard; he's a raccoon. And then we have Charles, my big-time lawyer boyfriend, to round out our motley crew.

Our latest adventure took Nan, Octo-Cat, Paisley, and me on a cross-country trip to visit my cat's girlfriend, a former show Himalayan named Grizabella. On the way, I learned that Nan has been blabbing what is meant to be a secret ability to random friends of hers on the Internet.

While that was going on, a militarized flock of seagulls bribed me into helping with their turf dispute, a case that mainly fell to Charles and Pringle since the rest of us were out of town.

And even though we held up our end of the bargain, the seagulls needed more time to deliver on theirs. I trust them, though. Any day now, they'll lead me to my long-lost grandmother and I'll finally learn the truth about my lineage.

Until then, I've been doing my best to focus on other things. It hasn't been going well…

Mainly because my cat makes non-stop demands, and I'm just too tired to argue with him anymore. That's why I'm driving more than thirty minutes out to Misty Harbor to purchase a lobster roll from his preferred venue, the Little Dog Diner. And when I get home, he probably won't even say thank you for sending me to another far-flung end of Blueberry Bay to fulfill his latest request.

Yeah…

Have I mentioned just how badly I need a break from my life?

* * *

When I returned that afternoon with a bag of lobster rolls in hand, I found a pair of seagulls roosting on my porch.

"Bravo?" I asked as I parked my car and ambled over to greet them. "And is that Abigull? No way."

The smaller of the two birds puffed out her feathers and let out a tinkling giggle. When I last saw her a few weeks back, she'd been little more than a hatchling. Now she was almost as large as her adoptive father—and a very happy-looking bird at that.

"We've finished our search for your grandmother," Bravo informed me without further pretense. He'd promised to put me in touch with my long-lost biological grandmother in return for Charles, Pringle, and me assisting in a land dispute with another flock. And I knew he was trying his best to deliver on his end of the deal, but the more that time passed, the less I believed any of us would be able to find her.

I never should have doubted them, I realized now as an enormous smile stretched across my face. "That's wonderful. Can you take me to her now?" I moved back toward my car, but the seagulls didn't follow.

"She's not here anymore," Abigull said with a sad shake of her head.

Bravo picked up where his ward left off. "She was here in the Bay for a long time, but now we can't locate her."

"Did she...?" I swallowed hard, unable to believe the horrible timing. "Did she die?"

"Oh gosh no!" The little bird chirped and shifted her weight from foot to foot. "Nothing like that."

"I've put my best gulls on scouting duty, but so far we're unable to locate her new residence," Bravo added, all business, while Abigull seemed much more concerned about tending to my feelings.

"So what now?" I asked with a sigh. I appreciated that they'd tried but also felt terribly heartbroken that I may never get to meet my missing family member after all.

"We'll keep searching, but we'll need to expand the radius. She may have left the state. It's no problem, really. We will find her, but it's just going to take a little longer than originally estimated."

"Thank you," I said, working hard to show them a smile even though the news they'd just brought me had ruined my whole day. "Thank you for not giving up."

"Nothing can stop a bird on a mission," Bravo informed me with a narrowed gaze.

"Yeah," his adoptive daughter chimed in.

"Now we must be off." Bravo immediately launched into the sky with Abigull at his tail.

"Bye, Angie," the girl gull called as they soared away on the winds.

I slumped down onto the worn oak porch steps and sat there for a while, just me and the dwindling warmth of the setting sun.

What would I do if the flock failed to find my grandmother? I'd already questioned my remaining family in Larkhaven, searched every nook and cranny of the Internet... I'd even tried the genealogy route but had come up with absolutely nothing.

Somewhere out there, I had a grandmother I hadn't even known existed until last year. Her entire family had been stolen from her when my grandpa took their baby—my mother—and asked Nan to take her somewhere far away.

None of us knew why, and my grandpa had already passed by the time I learned of his existence. And now these two huge players in my personal history were nothing more than a giant question mark, and I doubted I'd ever really be whole again until I could find her.

2

Octo-Cat found me on the porch a while later. I wasn't sure how much time had passed since the pair of seagulls delivered the news of their delay in finding my family. It must have been a while, though, because the light had faded and a chill that hadn't been there before now hung in the air.

"What are you doing out here?" Octo-Cat asked after pushing through the automatic pet door and coming to sit at my side.

I would have thought he was showing a rare moment of affection, except the next words out of his mouth were, "And where is my lobster roll?"

I sighed and pushed the almost transparent paper bag over to him.

"It's almost all the way cold," he whined as he crinkled his way into the sack, but he accepted the food nonetheless.

I sat and watched the branches of the white ash trees that lined our property as they blew in the wind.

"Do you—uh—want some?" my cat offered hesitantly, his face a distorted mask of concern through the oily paper. His eyes remained glued to the food, daring me to accept the offer.

I shook my head. "All yours."

"You seem..." The bag broke open, spilling the cat and his lobster roll onto the porch with me. He grabbed the food with his paws and tried to regain his normal, dignified air. With a twinkle in his eyes, he turned his head to one side then the other as he examined me. "Less irritating than usual," he decided at last. "What's wrong?"

"Bravo is having a hard time finding my grandmother." I shrugged, trying to play off my devastation.

"So what's the big deal? You've lived without her this long. Besides, I haven't seen my mother or any of my brothers or sisters since I was a kitten. And you're well past your youth now, Angela."

I chuckled at his logic. "Cats and people aren't the same. I think you know that better than anyone."

"I've been thinking about that," Octo-Cat said, bits of lobster hanging from his chin and whiskers. "And I spend way too much time with humans and other lesser creatures these days..."

He paused to let this sink in. I assumed the other lesser creatures referred to Paisley and Pringle but knew better than to ask for specifics.

"It might be nice to know what happened to my litter mates," he continued, running a paw over his face. "Ever since we found those kittens, I got to thinking. What if all my brothers and sisters turned out almost as awesome as me?"

"That's hard to believe," I said with another laugh. Leave it to Octo-Cat to make my personal tragedy all about him.

"You're right. It would be almost too amazing, but that's a chance I'm willing to take."

I turned to look at him, cupping my cheek in one palm and resting my elbow on my thigh. "What do you mean?"

He finished chewing his bite and swallowed hard. "We're searching for your family. I want to search for mine, too."

"But—"

"But nothing. I think it's fair to ask, since it is my trust fund that pays all our bills."

"Remember how curiosity killed the cat?" I asked with one eyebrow raised, a slight smile playing at my lips.

Octo-Cat scoffed at this. "That's just a vicious generalization, and you know it. But fine, I am curious. What's so wrong about that?"

He had me there. It was only natural that with all the focus on my family Octo-Cat would also wonder about his.

"Okay," I said, nodding for emphasis. "I'll help you."

"Don't make me pull out my—" He stopped suddenly. "Wait, you'll help? That easily?"

"That easily," I confirmed, my smile widening now.

"Well, okay, then. Thank you." He returned to his lobster roll, making such fast progress of it that I was worried he may choke.

Just then, a raccoon skittered up the porch steps and grabbed the remaining sandwich with greedy black fingers.

Octo-Cat growled and took a swipe, but Pringle had already managed to climb up onto the railing and out of reach of the irate tabby.

"For me?" the raccoon crooned. "Why, Angie, you shouldn't have."

"She didn't!" Octo-cat yelled and flicked his tail wildly behind him.

Pringle stuffed the entire thing in his mouth, cheeks bulging, then swallowed it down and slowly licked each of his fingertips.

"I hate you," Octo-Cat muttered before running back in through the pet door.

I let out a long sigh. "Why do you have to get him riled up like that?"

"That cat has never liked me. So, frankly, I don't trust his taste. Although that lobster roll was delicious. Would have been even more delicious without the cat spit on it, though." Pringle chuckled to himself, then clambered down from the railing and came to sit at my side. "So when do we start our next case?"

I sighed again—something I did often in my raccoon neighbor's presence. "When someone hires us."

"Hey, not being hired hasn't stopped you before. You've gotten involved in plenty of cases just because you happened to stumble upon them. Let's go for a nice walk through downtown, see what trouble we can stir up there."

I stared at him for a moment, but when I realized Pringle had no idea why this suggestion would be problematic, I attempted to explain. "If I show up with a raccoon in broad daylight in the middle of a crowded street, there will definitely be trouble. And not the kind either of us would enjoy. Besides, maybe I don't want another case right now. Honestly, I could really use a break."

"Level with me here. I'm going stir crazy. I've almost finished my second watch-through of all forty-ish seasons of Survivor. What am I supposed to do when I'm through with that, huh?"

"Start a third watch-through," I suggested with a shrug.

His jaw fell open as if I'd just made the most shocking and offensive recommendation of all time. It looked like he wanted to say something more, but before he could a car pulled onto our long driveway and began its approach to the house.

Pringle scurried off to hide, because as much as he liked bugging me and Nan, he was still wary of other humans. If he would have waited just a couple seconds longer, though, he would have seen that the new arrival was someone he'd come to trust, thanks to our recent adventures forcing them to work together while the rest of us were out of town.

"Hi, Charles," I said when my boyfriend parked and got out of his car. He wore his button-down shirt with the sleeves rolled up to the elbows and still wore his suit pants, although he'd ditched the jacket and tie.

"Ready to go?" he asked, waiting at the car door and eyeing me suspiciously.

I stood and brushed away the crumbs that had fallen to my lap while Octo-Cat and Pringle battled over the lobster roll.

"Angiiiie," Charles ground out. "Don't tell me you forgot!"

Somehow "forgot what?" didn't feel like the right response here, so I just smiled and batted my eyelashes.

"About the movie," he prompted. "It was your idea for us to see it tonight."

"Oh! Oh, right! I am so sorry, Charles. Things have just been…" I popped to my feet as I searched for the right word. Busy wasn't accurate, but I was still very overwhelmed, regardless. "They've been a lot lately. If you give me five minutes, I can run a brush through my hair and then we can go."

He shook his head and trotted up the steps, taking me in his arms before I could slip away. "Let's stay in tonight," he said, pressing a soft kiss to my forehead and reminding me all over again why I was crazy about this particular man.

I looked up at him with half-lidded eyes. "You don't mind?"

"Nah." He pulled me to his chest and held me tight. "As long as I get to spend time with you, it doesn't really matter what we do. How about you choose tonight, and I'll choose what we do next time around."

We shared a slow kiss. I practically melted into him as he held me.

That is, until Octo-Cat rushed back through the pet flap and shouted, "Gaaah! You know I hate it when you two groom each other in my presence."

I laughed and kissed Charles again. Octo-Cat would just have to deal with it.

3

Charles and I ended up watching a made-for-TV movie on the Disney channel, which offered just the right amount of wholesomeness mixed with campiness to lighten my mood—and to send me drifting to sleep early.

The next morning, I woke up and took a quick shower, hoping it would help make me more alert for the day ahead. It didn't.

So I pulled on my favorite ratty polka-dot bathrobe and padded down to the kitchen, where I found Nan at the sink, rinsing some mixed berries in a colander.

"Good morning, sleepy head," she sang out. "I'll have you know, ten o'clock has already come and gone."

"Sorry," I said around a yawn. "I don't know why, but I've just been so exhausted lately."

Nan finished with the berries and patted her hands dry.

"There's some vanilla yogurt in the fridge and granola in the cabinet, if you'd like to help yourself to a parfait."

"Right now I just need coffee," I mumbled, removing my French press from the dishwasher and setting to work. This was the latest in my attempts at satisfying my caffeine cravings without having to rely on an electric coffee maker. It took a bit more work, but I'd started to prefer the taste of the fresher brew that this process yielded.

"Any big plans for today?" I asked while I waited for the water to heat up.

Nan popped a particularly plump raspberry into her mouth and sighed with pleasure. "Grant and I are going to take the ferry out to Caraway Island and do some window shopping."

I'd never quite understood the older generation's obsession with window shopping. Was it really shopping if you went knowing you wouldn't be buying anything? I was pretty frugal with my money, but even I couldn't see the appeal of that activity.

"Sounds like a nice, relaxing day," I said with my lips pressed into a tight smile.

"Oh, my dear grandchild, it's boring, and you know it." Nan winked at me, and we both giggled.

"Then why are you doing it?"

"That's how love works sometimes, sweetie. I agree to one of Grant's activities knowing that next time I'll get to make the plans for the day."

Nan and Mr. Gable, the owner of the local jewelry shop and

head of the downtown commerce committee, had been dating since the holidays, and they made the sweetest couple, too.

Nan's chihuahua Paisley had recently become good friends with Grant's rabbit, E.B.—short for Easter Bunny. At first the little thing was terrified of our pets, but even she could see that sweet Paisley would never harm a soul. Octo-Cat, on the other hand, give him opposable thumbs and he would have gladly used them to assist in making rabbit stew.

"Charles said something like that last night, too," I mumbled, searching through the cupboards to select a coffee mug. Call me superstitious, but I tended to believe that the choice of coffee cup could impact one's entire day. I bypassed the #1 Private Investigator mug Charles had gifted me for Valentine's Day in favor of a fun color-changing mug inspired by one of my favorite book series. Every time I used it, I made another solemn promise that I would be up to no good. And that always made me smile.

I took a slow glorious sip of mid-morning bliss just as a knock sounded on the front door. I turned to Nan, but she simply shrugged and returned to fiddling with the berries.

So I went to answer the door, bleary-eyed, in a ratty bathrobe, and with zero percent blood-coffee ratio.

And there on the other side of the door stood Charles, wearing cargo khaki shorts and a fitted T-shirt with sports sunglasses pushed up into his hair. Honestly, I hardly recognized him outside of his usual monkey suit.

He glanced over my shoulder with his brows pinched together. "Didn't you tell her?"

"No," Nan answered. I hadn't even heard her creep up behind me. "You said you wanted it to be a surprise. I'll go grab her bag for you."

"What's going on?" I asked, turning to look from Charles to my grandmother, hoping that one might provide me with an explanation.

Nan walked away, raising a hand over her shoulder as she went.

I turned back toward my boyfriend, who stared at me with wide eyes and an even wider smile. "We're going on a surprise getaway," he announced, grabbing my hands and giving them a good squeeze.

"But I just got back from getting away," I said with a frown. I hated to be a downer; however, my last vacation was anything but relaxing. Between driving cross-country, winding up in a car accident, and finding out Nan had been blabbing my secrets to anyone who would listen, I was just plain exhausted.

"This time it will be just you and me going out for a long and quiet weekend," he explained, before leaning into whisper, "No pets."

This drew a happy sigh from me. I loved my animals dearly, but I could never fully relax in their presence knowing I had to work hard at not exposing my secret in front of the wrong person. Even though they knew very well that I couldn't talk to them in front of people who didn't already know about my ability, that didn't stop them from chattering on and filling my head with constant noise. The worst part was when I had to try to follow two separate lines of conversation. It made my brain tired.

A weekend away could be just the trick

Nan returned rolling a wheeled suitcase behind her. "All packed and ready to go. I just need another five minutes to finish packing the picnic." She left the luggage with us and hurried back to the kitchen.

"Where are we going?" I asked, starting to get a little excited.

Charles pressed his lips into a firm line and shook his head. "It's a surprise."

"But there will be a picnic?" I prompted, tilting my head as I studied his face for hints. "Does that mean we're going somewhere outside?"

He drew his thumb and forefinger across his mouth. "Not telling. You'll see when we get there."

I raised an eyebrow. "What about work?"

"The firm can keep things together for one day without me. I don't think I've ever used a full vacation day. It was time. And besides, I may have snuck into the office early to get a few things taken care of before coming here."

"Ah-ha. I knew it!"

Charles laughed. "Yeah, we both need this break."

Nan returned with a cute woven basket in hand and gave it to Charles.

"Thanks," he said with a big grin. "And you're sure you're okay to look after Jacques and Jillianne while we're away?"

Last year, Charles had taken in my former neighbor's two

Sphynx cats after her untimely demise. They had never much warmed up to me, and I doubted they liked Nan, either. Still, Charles had grown quite fond of his two hairless babies.

Nan nodded vigorously and pushed us toward the door. "I've got it all under control. Paisley and I will go pay them a visit later this afternoon. Now get out of here. Go have some fun. Goodness knows you two both need it!"

Well, she was right about that, I supposed.

I just hoped whatever Charles had planned for us would be every bit as relaxing as he'd promised.

And that Octo-Cat wouldn't be too mad at me for abandoning him this weekend.

4

Outside, a massive white vehicle sat waiting partway down our driveway.

"Surprise!" Charles shouted as he strode ahead of me with both the suitcase and picnic basket in tow.

I gasped and stopped in my tracks, blinking twice to make sure my eyes weren't misleading me. "You bought an RV?"

He turned back to smile at me before continuing on his way. "I didn't buy it. There's this new app that's kind of like Airbnb meets Uber. So I rented this baby from someone over in Cooper's Cove. It's ours through Monday. Your Nan's already agreed to return it for me, too."

I jogged to catch up. "There's no way you're letting Nan drive this. That woman is a terror on wheels, and you know it."

Charles just laughed and opened the passenger door for me.

"Climb on up. We've got about three hours to get to our destination, so not too bad."

"Climb on up?" I repeated. "I'm in my ratty bathrobe. I'm not going anywhere until I get changed."

"No, that's why I had Nan pack you a bag. You can get changed on the way."

"That's ridiculous. We're right here. I'm going to go inside and change and then we can get going."

Before he could drag me into the RV, I turned and climbed the porch and pulled on the door. Locked.

"Really, Nan?" I shouted at the locked door. "You're sending me off in just a bathrobe?"

"Don't worry, I packed you something nice," she shouted back through the door.

It was obvious that these plans were in motion and there was nothing I could do to stop this runaway camper. With a sigh, I wrapped my robe tighter around myself and walked back over to the RV.

I hoisted myself inside while Charles went around back to the living area where he stashed my suitcase and the picnic basket. Rather than buckling up, I spun in my seat to check out our hotel on wheels. It had a small kitchen area complete with linoleum floor and a sink, cute little stovetop, and a half-sized fridge. Across from that sat a comfy-looking booth and table flanked by a built-in couch. Further back, I could just glimpse a bedroom with dark drapes and what appeared to be a queen-sized bed—whatever the size, it definitely took up a good deal of space.

Charles swung himself up onto the driver's seat. "There's a bathroom back there if you need it, and I've stocked up on food for the weekend, too."

"Seems like you've thought of everything," I said as I settled into my seat and drew the safety belt across my lap.

"Nan and I planned the whole thing together last night while you dozed on the couch," he admitted with a sheepish grin.

"If you would have told me, I could have—"

"If I would have told you, you'd have found a reason not to go," Charles interrupted, which was fine. I hadn't really known where I was going with that statement, anyway.

"Fair, but you realize Nan could have packed my suitcase with nothing but evening gowns or pajama bottoms with silk blouses, or only old Halloween costumes."

A look of mock horror flashed across Charles's face, but then he shook his head and turned on the mega-watt smile again. "Nah, she knew where we were headed."

"Since when has that mattered to my nan?" I asked with an admittedly nervous laugh as Charles turned the key over in the ignition and slowly navigated the camper down the rest of the driveway.

"Not knowing what to expect is part of the fun. Right?" He stopped and shot me a quick glance before pulling carefully out onto the main road.

"Oh, I know exactly what to expect," I countered. "Complete and utter chaos. You know, you could have at least let me change out of my bathrobe before we left."

Charles tapped his bare wrist while keeping his eyes fixed on the road ahead. “We have a very tight schedule to keep.”

I tilted my head to the side and considered this. “But I thought this weekend was all about relaxing?”

“It is. Just within the parameters of our schedule. Besides, I have something special planned for later.”

“I don’t suppose you’re going to tell me what that is.”

“Oh, my sweet, sweet Angie, why won’t you let me surprise you every once in a while? It’s part of the fun in being your boyfriend, getting to spoil you when you least expect it.”

“I’ve dealt with too many murders, kidnappings, and thefts to ever fully let my guard down,” I admitted, then chewed on my lip as a fresh wave of anxiety washed over me.

Charles either didn’t notice my uncertainty or didn’t mind. “And that’s precisely why we need this weekend away,” he said. “Now sit back and relax. Here, this should help.”

He plugged his phone into the vehicle’s dash with a USB cable, then turned the radio on. Immediately upbeat percussion mixed with the cheerful tune of a whistle. I couldn’t help but roll my eyes.

“Bob Marley?” I asked with a laugh.

“It’s your Don’t Worry, Be Happy mix. Made sense to kick it off with the title jam. Now seriously, it’s time for you to chillax.” He was so cute when he tried to use slang. Not only was his vocab severely outdated, it was also from the wrong region. He’d grown up in California, which was just about as far from Maine as one could get.

"And I suppose Nan helped you with this, too?"

"Let's just say there's more Sinatra than I might have otherwise chosen."

"Not necessarily a bad thing," I said, then held my hand over my mouth in a weak attempt to hide the yawn that followed.

"See, your body wants to chillax. Let your mind follow," Charles said in a woo-woo voice like the people at the massage place in Dewdrop Springs liked to affect.

"Yeah, I'm wicked tired," I said, eliciting a groan from Charles. He'd once told me that no matter how long he lived in Blueberry Bay, he would never ever use the term "wicked" to refer to anything other than a warty green witch.

I smiled at the memory, then closed my eyes. I must have nodded off, because the next thing I knew, a sudden crash in the back of the RV startled me awake.

"What was that?" I shouted, jumping in my seat, only to be forced back down when the seatbelt jerked tight against my chest. It took me a moment to remember where I was and why.

"We're almost there, but I'll pull over at the next exit so we can investigate," Charles said from beside me.

I shook my head. "No, don't do that. I can go check it out."

Before he had the chance to argue, I unbuckled my seatbelt and stood on shaky feet, keeping my hands out to either side for balance. It took me a moment to locate the source of the crash, mostly because everything looked exactly the same as it had when I'd first taken stock of the living space.

I carefully made my way through the kitchen and dining

space and back to the bedroom, but it was completely undisturbed.

At last, I yanked open the door to the tiny bathroom and discovered exactly what I'd been searching for. Assorted toiletries covered the floor and the handheld shower head had come loose and was dangling toward the ground.

"Everything okay back there?" Charles called.

"Yeah. Just some stuff that fell over in the bathroom," I yelled back.

"Ouch, my ears," came a familiar voice, one I definitely hadn't expected to hear in that moment.

I followed the sound and spotted Pringle sitting on the floor beside the toilet. "Pringle, what are you doing here?" I shouted in disbelief. He was the very last creature I needed along for my relaxing weekend.

"We stowed away," the raccoon announced with a smile on his snout.

Horror knotted in my gut. "We?"

"Why didn't you let us out of here sooner? It's not at all comfortable in this cramped little bathroom," Octo-Cat whined, emerging from the narrow cabinet beneath the sink.

I balked. "Seriously, you're mad at me right now? You're not even supposed to be here!"

"We figured it was an oversight that you didn't invite us, so we invited ourselves," the irksome trash panda said matter-of-factly.

Blood flew through my veins and my heart whomped at an accelerated pace. "How?" I managed through gritted teeth.

Pringle pointed toward the ceiling, drawing my eyes to an air vent that sat propped open, providing more than enough space for two mischievous creatures to climb inside.

"Charles," I called, still staring at the open hatch above. "We have a bit of a problem back here!"

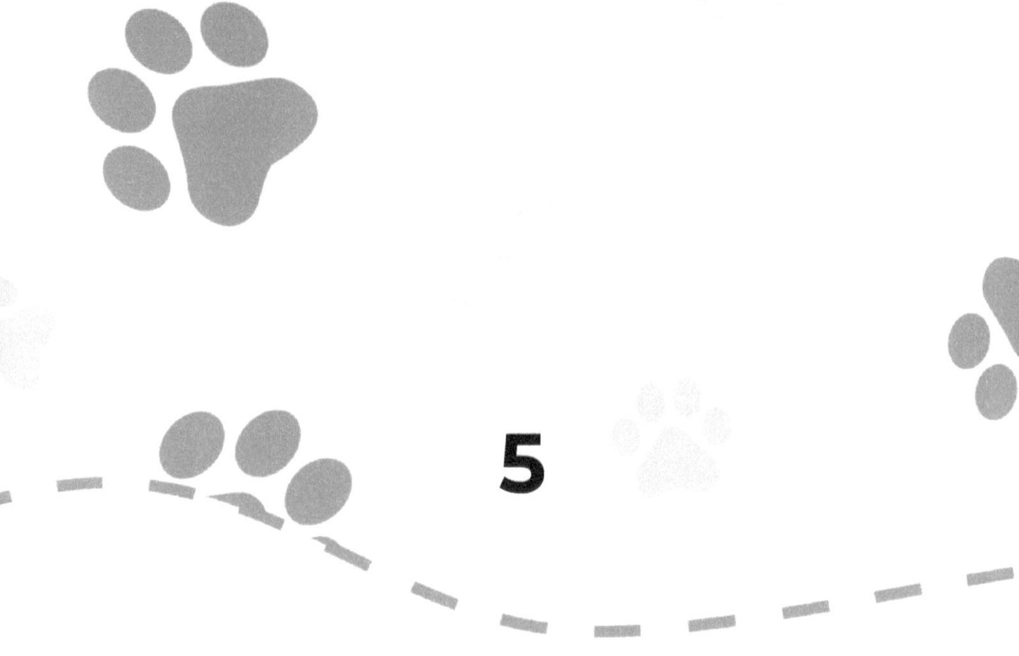

5

By the time Charles and I discovered our two furry stowaways we were less than a half hour from our destination, which put us in quite the pickle.

"Obviously we have to take them back," I tried to reason.

But he insisted that we stick to the schedule he'd already laid out, which meant we didn't have the time to add a five-hour delay by circling back home to drop off Pringle and Octo-Cat.

"It will be fine," he promised, even though I could tell that he, too, was unhappy about this particular turn of events. "They can hang back in the RV while we go do other things," he added, then turned up the volume on our no-worries playlist. Frankly, I had lots of worries, but there was no point in hashing them out over and over again. Like Charles, I would just have to sweep my troubles to the back corner of my mind and do my best to have a good time.

We only had time to listen to a few more songs before we pulled into a little campground near the base of Mount Katahdin.

"Surprise!" Charles cried as he navigated to an open lot. Of course, I'd already figured out our destination a long time back but hadn't let on.

"Mount Katahdin, the tallest mountain in the entire state. It's supposed to be really beautiful here," he continued. "The perfect place to kick back and relax, starting with a hike! After all, the name literally means, 'The Greatest.'"

Hiking up a mountain was definitely not what I considered R&R, but at least I could be certain our furry stowaways wouldn't try to follow us there.

Charles leaned over to give me a peck on the cheek. "You go get changed, and I'll check in with the owner of the campgrounds to let her know we're here." He clambered up from the driver's seat and almost skipped out the door, leaving me with the unenviable task of trying to find appropriate attire in a bag packed by my crazy nan.

I padded back to the bedroom where my suitcase sat waiting for me on a bed made with perfect, tight hospital corners. Octo-Cat and Pringle lay stretched out on either side of it, both dozing away as if they hadn't a care in the world.

I clapped my hands together as loud as I could, startling them both awake. "Out," I said when they turned their heads to me.

"You're disturbing our nap," Octo-Cat droned.

"And you're disturbing my vacation," I shot back.

"Do what you need to do," Pringle said while Octo-Cat stood and turned in slow circles, padding at the bed.

I'd changed in front of my cat hundreds of times, but I didn't feel comfortable getting undressed in front of the raccoon. Privacy was tricky business when it came to talking animals. Of course they didn't view things the same way humans did, but the ever-observant Pringle could easily spot a weird mole or birthmark and then find a way to bring it up in every single conversation we had from that point on. I, for one, refused to give him that kind of power over me.

"Out," I repeated, stamping my foot for good measure. When Pringle still didn't budge, I took off my bathrobe and threw it over him, then picked up the bundle and set it outside the door, which I shut firmly behind me.

"Your pajamas don't match," Octo-Cat said. And because nothing could ever be easy, he'd now settled himself on top of my suitcase.

I picked him up and sat him back on the bed. He wasn't happy about it, but at least I could trust him not to bite me.

Taking a deep breath in, I unzipped the suitcase, preparing for the worst assortment of clothes I'd long since relegated to the back of my closet. I hadn't, however, prepared myself to find a bag filled with outfits that weren't even mine.

I snapped a quick picture and fired off a text to Nan: Explain.

My phone rang a few seconds later. I picked up, and Nan's words rushed out. "I had to keep it a surprise, and you were in your room right up until go time. I had no other options, so I did the best I could."

"You do realize we don't wear the same size?" I said, eyeing the suitcase warily.

"That's why I picked stretchy things. Relax, you're going to look fabulous!"

I let out a long sigh. At this point, I was getting very sick of everyone telling me to relax. "Okay. By the way, Octo-Cat is with me. Long story. Tell ya later. Gotta go," I muttered before ending the call.

After rummaging through the bag, I found there were two choices here. I could choose from a couple different floor-length, form-fitting gowns, or I could wear Nan's hot pink sweats with the word "juicy" written across the tush.

"Kill me now," I moaned as I cycled through my options again and again, trying to pick the lesser evil.

"Ask me later after I've had my nap," my cat answered unhelpfully.

In the end, I chose the juicy track suit, opting to keep my pajama T-shirt on top so that I could tie the jacket around my waist and hide the branded booty.

I'd just finished pulling my hair into a high and tight ponytail when a knock sounded on the door. "Ready to hit the trail?" Charles called.

"Ready." I opened the door, and he grinned, handing me a bottle of water.

"Looking good." He winked and he motioned for me to lead the way out of the RV.

I exited into the bright sun, wishing I'd had the foresight to grab some sunglasses on my way out of the house. I hadn't been awake enough yet to think properly then. I wasn't even sure I was awake enough now.

Charles exited the RV after me with a picnic basket slung over his arm.

"Wouldn't a backpack be better?" I asked, pointing to the awkward cargo.

"We don't have that far to go. It's just a short walk to a nice clearing that overlooks the water." He locked the door and then shoved the keys in his pocket. "Don't you think I know better than to make you work out on your big day off?"

I smiled and leaned into his side, and he slung an arm over my shoulders.

Perhaps this wouldn't be such a terrible trip after all.

6

Charles and I walked hand in hand to the spot he'd pre-selected for our picnic, and it was every bit as lovely as promised.

It was still quite early in the season, but this was also the first nice weekend after a long and hard winter, which meant that campgrounds were packed. In fact, all of the tables that had been setup in the clearing were already filled with picnickers.

"C'mon," Charles said, tugging me along. "Let's find our own little spot off the beaten path.

Thankfully, the fresh air and beautiful scenery had already begun to do wonders for my sour mood. As we walked, I glanced back at the trail behind us a few times to make sure no uninvited animals had decided to join our trek, and each time I didn't spot them, my smile grew wider and wider.

And my fantastic boyfriend had planned an impromptu getaway because he knew that I needed it. How lucky was I?

We walked another five minutes until we came upon an enormous white ash tree. By the time we settled ourselves at its base, I was more than ready for the break—and the sustenance. I'd only managed half a mug of coffee that morning before our big adventure began and was looking forward to filling my stomach with the feast Nan had prepared. Yes, even though she was terrible at picking out clothes for me, Nan's cooking beat all.

"Let's see what we have here," Charles said, rubbing his hands together before lifting the lid on the basket. The scream that followed made us jump back in fight.

"What is it?" I asked with a gasp.

But Charles didn't answer. He simply pointed at the basket with a shaky finger.

Okay. I gulped and crawled forward on my hands and knees to see for myself.

I'm not proud to admit that I yelled out a string of curses at the top of my lungs when I discovered what was inside. Needless to say, there was no delicious picnic waiting for us. Instead I found one very fat and happy raccoon covered in sticky berry juice.

"Pringle!" I cried. "How could you?"

He flopped out of the basket and rolled right into me, splattering my borrowed hot pink sweats with deep red juice.

I groaned in frustration.

Pringle moaned in discomfort. "I was just going to nab a quick taste, but then I heard Charles coming, so I hid. I didn't know he'd take the basket with me in it. And then the two of you were walking and walking for what felt like forever, and I'm a nervous eater, so I decided to help myself to the rest of what you had in here."

"Why didn't you say anything?" I demanded, my brows pinched together in fury.

He rolled his eyes as if this whole thing was my fault and not his. "I just did."

"Before that, I mean."

The raccoon moaned again and clutched at his belly. "Everything was so good. I just couldn't stop." He rolled onto his side and studied me with dark, glistening eyes. "Say, do you think Nan will make me another of those strawberry cream cakes once we're back home? Because that was one of the best things I've ever tasted."

"I'll make sure she doesn't," I fumed. At least none of the other campers were around to see the crazy lady yelling at a raccoon.

"Now go wash yourself off in a creek or something. You look like you just walked out of a crime scene," I said with a scowl before relaying the whole thing to Charles.

As I talked, Pringle loped away. His entire coat was stained with berry juice, giving him a blood-soaked zombie roadkill appearance that made us both cringe.

"It's fine. Everything will be fine," Charles said with a smile that felt forced. "We'll relax here for a little bit before heading back. We can grab something for lunch once we're back at the RV."

"Yeah, if Octo-Cat hasn't already eaten it all." I crossed my arms over my chest and frowned. I didn't want to be a bummer, but I was just so, so disappointed, and I knew Charles was, too.

"We can still turn this weekend around," he promised as he leaned back against the thick tree trunk and pulled me to his chest. Then he repeated for the dozenth time, "I have it all planned out." It was quickly becoming his getaway mantra.

He then went on to tell me about his plans for campfires and swimming and simply lounging about in the RV, enjoying each other's company. "We're skipping fishing, though. I figured with your ability, that would be kind of a nightmare scenario. Ah, please don't eat me!" he cried in a silly, high-pitched voice.

Honestly, I was already this close to becoming a vegetarian. The only thing that stopped me was that all my animal friends also ate meat, even though they could talk to each other, too.

"Are you ready to head back?" Charles asked after we'd sat snuggled up against that tree for a good twenty minutes.

I stretched my arms overhead, then let out a groan. "We can't leave without Pringle. He might not be able to find his way back."

Charles arched one eyebrow. "And that's a problem because?"

I shoved him playfully. "I know he can be a pest, but for better or worse, he's our pest."

"You won't be calling me a pest when you see the present I've brought you," Pringle called, emerging tail-first from the nearby brush.

Uh-oh. There's no way a present from Pringle could be a good thing.

A glint of silver caught my attention—the sunlight reflecting off the scales of an enormous salmon that Pringle dragged behind him.

"How did you manage to get that?" I asked in surprise.

He paused to flash us a giant grin. "I felt bad about eating all your food, so I went and secured new food."

"And by secured you mean...?"

Pringle dragged the fish the rest of the way to us, then stood on his hind legs and admitted, "Okay, so I had a little help. Gloria, come on out!"

I followed his eyes as he turned back toward the brush, where a massive grizzly bear emerged.

Charles jumped to his feet and spread his arms to block me. "Angie, get down! Or run! I won't let him hurt you!"

I gulped hard, then rose to my feet and put a hand on my boyfriend's shoulder. "It's okay. I think the bear's friends with Pringle. Let me just talk to them before you freak out. Okay?"

I turned to Pringle so he could explain.

"Not a friend. A client," Pringle bit out the words, taking extra care to enunciate clearly. "Gloria's just brought us a new case, and she's already paid up front with this beauty." He motioned toward the fish. "Isn't that great?"

I could think of a lot of words to describe this situation, but not a single one of them was "great."

7

"What have you gotten us into?" I whispered to the raccoon, all the while hoping that bears had poor hearing. I'd never come across one face-to-face, so I honestly didn't know what to expect.

"Relax," Pringle said, holding his hands out in front of him. "She just needs a small favor. It's easy, I promise."

"We'll talk about this later," I said from the side of my mouth, then strode toward the bear with a tight-lipped smile. I didn't know enough about bears to determine whether showing my teeth would be construed as a threat, and with an animal as big and powerful as this one, I wasn't taking any chances.

"Hello," I called cheerfully, stopping several feet away. "Gloria, is it?"

The grizzly dipped her head in a nod. "Are you the Pet Whisperer P.I.?" she asked in a soft, feminine voice.

I hated the moniker that Nan and my mom had stuck me with. They thought it was a fun gimmick, but I thought it was way too close to revealing my secret. As it was, half the world thought I was crazy while the other fraction believed I really did have some kind of magical or psychic powers.

"I am," I answered, mimicking the bear's movement from before. "But I'm only here for the weekend. Can I help you with something before I go?"

Gloria padded forward on all fours, and it took everything I had not to flinch or back away from fright. "I won't hurt you," she said.

"I know. I'm sorry. It's just my first time meeting a bear."

She plopped into a sitting position and sighed. "That's the thing. Everyone assumes that bears are so scary, but really it's us that are afraid of you."

I raised a finger and pressed it into my chest. "Me? You're afraid of me?"

She nodded. "You seem like a nice enough human, but so many others..." Her words faded away, and a shiver wracked her enormous body.

We looked at each other without saying anything.

Pringle hung back with his fish, but Charles crept forward and stopped at my side, threading his fingers through mine and giving my hand a good squeeze.

"Is this your mate?" Gloria asked, studying him with wide eyes.

"He is," I answered decisively. Charles and I weren't married

—or even engaged—but animals tended to commit to each other very early on in their acquaintanceships. In the animal kingdom, Charles and I were basically like an old, married couple at this point.

"He protects you. That's good." Gloria gave an approving nod, then redirected her gaze toward the ground. "My mate was not so kind. He was at first, but as soon as the cubs were born, he tried to kill them—his own children—and so I ran away with the cubs and ended up here. It's close enough to the humans that he won't attempt to follow us here. But being close to the humans has created other problems for our little family."

My heart went out to her. Of course, I would help if I could. I wasn't even angry at Pringle anymore for bringing Gloria to meet me. Granted, I was still mad at him for half a dozen other things... but not this.

"How can I help?" I asked, suddenly viewing bears in a whole new light—or at least the female ones.

"We only woke up from hibernation a few days ago, but already we're having big problems. The people who come to this park wander too close to our den, and sometimes they bring loud, exploding lightning that makes the little ones quake with fear."

It took me a moment to realize she meant fireworks. No wonder she and the cubs were so afraid.

"I'm pretty sure people aren't allowed to bring those into the park."

"Well, they do."

"If it's already against the law, I'm not sure what I can do to make it stop."

Gloria glanced back over her shoulder as if searching for something. When she continued, her words came out much faster. "There's a woman who oversees the campgrounds. She's in charge of looking after the visitors. Maybe she doesn't realize what's going on or how distressing it is—not only to the bears, but to all wildlife that call this park home. Would you please talk with her on our behalf?"

"You want me to talk with her?" I asked, cocking my head to the side.

The she-bear nodded. "Be our voice."

"Okay, Gloria. I'd be happy to do that for you." I smiled, forgetting to keep my teeth concealed.

Gloria stumbled back, then caught herself. "Please promise me you'll do it soon. I'm not sure my cubs can take another sleepless night."

I bowed. "You have my word."

"When it's done, come back to this spot and call my name. I will bring you another salmon as thank you for your efforts on my family's behalf." She shifted back onto all fours, watching me closely.

I raised a hand in protest. "That's okay. You really don't—"

"I must. That way I'll also know when it is done. Thank you, kind human. You do the animals in this wood a great service." And with that, she turned and wandered back from whence she came.

Well, what was one more task before finally settling into our relaxing weekend? Ultimately, it wouldn't make much of a difference for me, but it could be a huge help to Gloria, her cubs, and the other animals who called the park home.

Charles squeezed my hand, and I turned into his chest. "Is everything okay?" he asked.

"Yes, we just have to make a quick pit stop before we can have lunch. C'mon."

8

Charles and I made quick work of the walk back to camp, mostly because my stomach was growling worse than a grizzly in distress. And now that I had an adequate frame of reference, I could totally make that comparison, thank you very much.

Pringle hitched a ride in the berry-stained picnic basket, which I carried while Charles handled the salmon. To prevent our little stowaway from getting dirty again, I padded the basket interior with Nan's track suit jacket. Of course, this meant that my juicy booty was now exposed to anyone who dared take a peek at my derriere.

And that wasn't the only thing I had to be embarrassed about in this campsite full of strangers. I also desperately clung to the hope that no one would ask us how we managed to catch this massive salmon without any fishing gear on us, because I had no idea what lie I could tell to get us out of that one.

That's how we returned to the RV park—a hidden raccoon, a berry-stained track suit, juicy booty, and big fish to boot. Understandably, a few people paused what they were doing to openly gawk at us. But mostly folks let us go about our business.

"That's her camper right there." Charles pointed with his chin as we approached an older model RV with an army of pink plastic flamingos forming a makeshift fence around the front.

He took the basket from me, struggling to hang on to both it and the fish.

Pringle chittered something as he got jostled around, but it was too muffled for me to make out his exact words. Also I didn't care. Frankly, the whole thing served him right.

"I'll see you back at ours," Charles said, dawdling off with a very awkward gait as he attempted to balance the salmon on top of the heavy raccoon basket. "Good luck. I know you'll do great!"

Well, at least one of us had confidence in me and my persuasive abilities.

I ran my hands over the front of my pants to wipe off the dark juice that had transferred from the basket onto my fingers, then walked past the tango line of flamingos and knocked on the door.

When no one answered, I knocked again.

"If she's not answering, feel free to go right in. Junetta has a door's always open policy for folks at the campground," someone called, then popped her head through the open window of an aqua-accented Airstream parked in the adjacent lot to the right. She brushed her also aqua-accented curls out of her face and studied me with casual interest before pulling her head back inside.

"Thank you!" I called after her, then pushed the door open and stepped inside the dimly lit interior.

This was not nearly as luxurious as the model that Charles had rented for our weekend away. For one, it looked like the darker side of my normal wardrobe. Not everything about the 80s was fun and brightly colored. Some parts were brown and orange with avocado-colored refrigerators. I even spied a bit of rust around the faucet of the sink in the kitchenette. It all sort of clashed with the happy kangaroo logo on the outside.

Never matter.

No judgment. That wasn't what I was here for. I was here to negotiate on behalf of the animals. I didn't know this person, so I had no idea what to expect. Still, the worse she could do was say "no" to what I asked. Part of me wondered what she'd say to Gloria if she could've asked for herself. I chuckled to myself a bit at the thought.

"Hello," I called as I tiptoed back toward the bedroom.

The door hung open just a crack—not enough for me to get a good look inside. Seeing as I didn't want to catch Junetta in a compromised position, I knocked gently.

The door creaked open a little more, and a familiar, rotten smell wafted out to assault my senses.

"Hello?" I asked again, begging my suspicions to be wrong.

When no one answered, I held my breath, covered my nose, and pushed the door open the rest of the way.

On the bed, an older woman with a wrinkled face and unnaturally curly, copper-colored hair lay splayed out. One hand clutched at her stomach while the other groped the comforter—or at least it had until all life had left it. The bed had been nicely made, but a portion of the blanket had since been pulled and twisted.

The scene showcased a jarring mix of chaos and slumber. Junetta had suffered, but now she lay still. The smell I'd detected came from a puddle of pink-tinged vomit that had seeped into the carpet in front of the bed.

I stepped back out, taking care to shut the door behind me and give the poor woman some semblance of privacy. Partly just to shut the smell out. My fingerprints were already on it, anyway.

As I carefully retraced my steps back through the main living space of the camper, I spotted a half-eaten slice of pie sitting on the table. The fork had fallen to the ground, while the remainder of the pie was nowhere to be seen. Provided it had even been in here at all.

I stepped toward the table and examined the dessert. Mixed berry. Judging from the scene in the bedroom, my best guess was that it was poisoned.

I had to tell somebody.

Tearing my eyes away from the murderous pie, I rushed back out the door and jogged right toward the Airstream where the woman had stuck her head through the window to urge me into Junetta's RV when she hadn't answered the door.

This time, I must have knocked with a bit too much vigor because when the woman pulled the door open, her eyes darted back and forth wildly, her large, cat-eyed glasses making her look more like an owl as she attempted to make sense of the scene.

"Sh-sh-she's dead," I sputtered, taking a step back and pointing toward the flamingo-adorned trailer.

"What?" The woman clambered down the steps and stood to face me outside. While she'd stood in the doorway, I hadn't realized just how tiny she was. If I had to guess, I'd say she barely cleared five feet.

I sucked in a deep breath and let it out again before I attempted to explain. "Junetta. She's dead. Someone poisoned her, I think."

She squinted her eyes at me as if gazing into the sun—and given the angle she had to tilt her face to meet my eyes, perhaps she was. "Who are you?"

"I'm Angie. My boyfriend and I just arrived today. I had to talk to her about some-thing, and you told me to go right in. When I did, I found her body in the bedroom."

She studied me for a good long moment without saying anything more. And even though I towered over her, and even with her resembling a lawn gnome from the 1950s, I still found her quite intimidating as she sized up me and my story.

Her eyes bore into mine as she announced, "I'm calling the

cops." Then she hurried back into her Airstream, slamming the door straight in my face.

Well, that had not gone as planned. Nope, not at all.

9

I returned to our RV to find Charles standing at the kitchenette with a spatula in hand.

"Hope you're in the mood for grilled cheese. It's the house, er rather, RV special today," he said, but then he caught the look on my face, set both the spatula and the fry pan aside, and came to meet me where I stood. "What's wrong? Did you talk to the camp manager? Was she not willing to help?"

I stared straight ahead, my head shaking and eyes unfocused, still recalling the horrible scene I had stumbled upon only moments before.

"Angie?" Charles prompted, placing a hand on my arm.

"She can't help," I whispered as I finally met his eyes. A shiver wracked through me. "She's dead."

"Who's dead?" Pringle chirruped from the front of the camper, bringing me back to the present moment. I craned my head and spotted him in the driver's seat where he stood gripping the steering wheel in his tiny hands, pretending to steer through traffic.

"Get back here," I demanded. "Those windows aren't tinted. Anyone could see you."

Thankfully, and rather uncharacteristically, he didn't argue. Which I was grateful for because I just didn't have the energy for it. It also told me I needed to be suspicious of the mischievous procyonid. But I also didn't have the energy to deal with the questions if another camper spotted him. Maine wasn't one of those crazy states where you could have a pet raccoon. We weren't like Delaware.

Pringle hopped down and then scampered over and hopped onto the couch. "Could, but didn't. Now what's your twenty, Mama Bear? I'm getting shutter trouble over here. Someone's dead? Who? Do we need to pull stakes and put the hammer down before this place is crawling with Smokies? Or do we have another case on our hands?"

I sank down into the booth seat, propped my elbows on the table, and cradled my head in my hands. Pringle was exhausting at the best of times. Right now, though, it was like he was speaking another language.

"Sorry," Charles said as he slid onto the seat beside me and whispered, "He's been listening to the CB radio. Are you sure she's dead?"

"Positive."

"Do you need me to call the police or did you do that already?"

I shook my head and sighed. "I didn't have to. One of the other campers already did."

"Hey, that's good, right?" Leave it to my lawyer boyfriend to remain calm and log-ical, no matter the circumstance. I appreciated that about him, but right now I needed him to understand.

"No, it's not good at all. She called the police on me." My voice cracked at that last part. "She thinks I'm the one who killed her."

"Well, that's ridiculous. You haven't been out of my sight long enough to murder someone. Besides, who's to say she was even murdered?"

I lifted my head and stared at Charles with wide eyes. "I say she was murdered, Charles. Most likely with a poison pie. At least that's where the evidence is pointing."

His face fell and voice softened. "Oh, no. I'm sorry you had to see that."

"You'd think I'd be used to it by now with all the bodies I've managed to stumble upon lately."

"Well, I love you because you haven't gotten used to it." He kissed me on the forehead. "But you do seem to have some kind of gift for stumbling across bodies."

"Yeah, too bad I can't return it," I quipped. I went to drop my head back into my hands, but a blur of movement caught my eye.

Octo-Cat appeared bleary-eyed in the doorway to the bedroom. "Why so much noise? Some of us are trying to keep up with our beauty sleep. And aren't you all sup-posed to be out on a picnic?"

Pringle at least had the good sense to look embarrassed about the part he'd played in ruining this day. "10-44, good buddy. Smoke those brakes, it's a long story. And it ends with a Windy City rollover on our shoulder." When he was met with a sea of blank looks, Pringle brushed his face and added, "We've got dead body next door."

Octo-Cat reared back and hissed. "Angela! This is supposed to be a vacation. Heaven knows I've needed it. You're a lot to put up with even on your best days, I'll have you know. You can't just go around uncovering dead bodies while I'm trying to enjoy a long-overdue nap."

I groaned. "I didn't uncover the body on purpose, and I also never invited you to tag along. So no more complaints. I'm having a hard enough time dealing as it is."

Charles rubbed my back in big, sweeping circles. "Are they giving you a hard time?" he asked.

"They always give me a hard time," I moaned. This time we didn't even have sweet Paisley around to help keep spirits high. No, I was stuck with sassy and sassier.

"We should probably head out," Charles murmured. "When the police get here, they'll want to talk to you." He got up and moved back toward the kitchen, grabbing for the pan with the grilled cheese. Even off the heat for the length of time we'd been talking, one side was practically charcoal. He shook his head, then opened up one of the cabinets and took out a box. “You must be starving by now. Take this.”

He handed me a Clif bar, and even though I had been famished not even ten minutes back, my appetite had now disappeared entirely.

“Thanks,” I muttered anyway as I forced myself to stand.

“There are some folding chairs stashed in the cargo hold. I’ll grab those and then meet you outside. And Angie?”

He waited for me to meet his eyes before continuing, “It’s going to be all right.”

All right, yeah. Everything would be fine.

It had to be, right?

I certainly hadn’t murdered the campground manager. In fact, I didn’t know a thing about her except that she could be a bit lax with the rules.

Still, I’d been under suspicion before. And for a lot less, too.

Now I couldn’t dismiss the nagging feeling that things would get a lot worse be-fore they got any better.

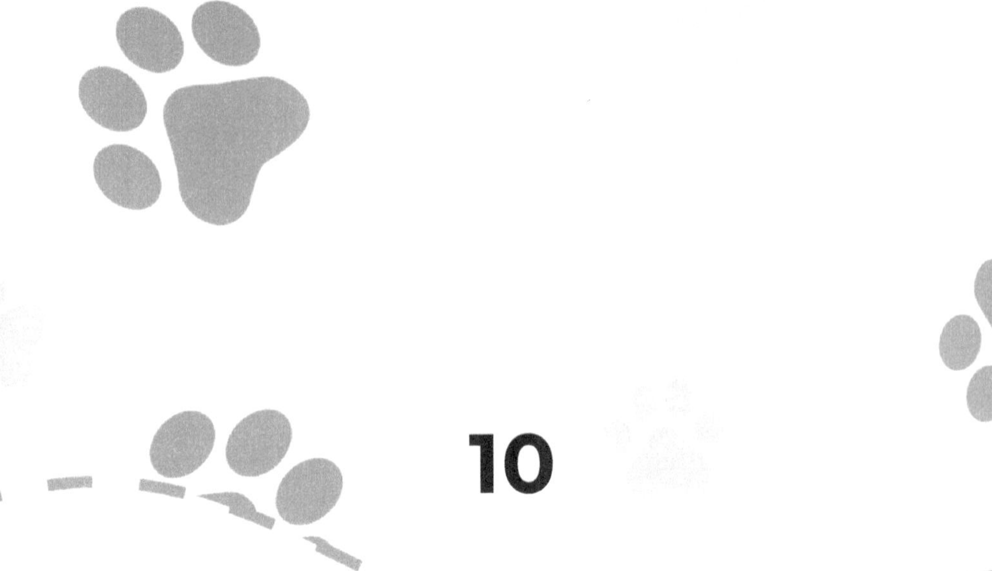

10

"Let's get this convoy moving! Wait for me," Pringle shouted right before I closed the door to the RV.

Of course, I had to go back in to explain why I would not be waiting for him. "You have to stay inside," I said, hoping that would be enough.

He squinted his eyes and spoke in a husky voice not at all befitting of him. "But what if I have to pay the water bill?"

I blinked down at him in utter bewilderment. "What are you even talking about?"

"You know." The raccoon dropped his voice to a whisper. "The bathroom?"

"You're smart enough to use the toilet, aren't you?" I challenged with a smirk. "Either that or you can wait for dark and then sneak out to do your business then."

His shoulders slumped and he dropped down onto all fours.

"Are you really going to make me hide out in this crummy camper the whole weekend?"

I glared down the bridge of my nose at him. "Yes, I really am. I would never have willingly brought you on this trip, but you took that choice away from me when you forced your way on board. The way I see it, you have no one to blame but yourself."

"Well, I am coming with you," Octo-Cat called from the kitchenette counter.

I glanced over and found him cleaning his face and paws after presumably licking all the butter off the unfinished side of the grilled cheese sandwiches.

"What? Why do you want to come?" I asked.

"Mostly because 'The Bandit' wants to but can't." The cat lifted his head and grinned at the raccoon. "But also because I'm your partner, and it sounds like we might have an investigation on our paws. I plan on claiming my share of our payment, so I might as well take on some of the work, too," he added, licking his chops with glee.

"Fair enough," I said, not bothering to tell him there wouldn't be any payment for this particular case.

"Not fair at all!" Pringle cried, throwing his body up against the door so we wouldn't exit without him.

Goodness gracious! Why did it feel like I was trying to deal with a couple of ornery toddlers here?

I shook my finger at him. "Listen up, good buddy. If I catch your big-rig raccoon butt outside of this camper even once, I'm demolishing your tree house, cancelling your cable TV, and throwing out the Nerf guns, too. Got it?"

He gulped hard. "N-n-not Carla. You wouldn't." Yes, the silly trash panda loved his Nerf gun so much, he'd named the darn thing.

I narrowed my gaze. "Care to try me? You know, I also think I heard Nan talking about a beagle at the shelter that needed a new home. Maybe you'd like a new play-mate?"

"You'll pay for this," the raccoon muttered as he stepped back from the door and disappeared into the bedroom.

"If I pay, you pay!" I shouted after him.

Octo-Cat chuckled as he leisurely made his way toward the door. "You sure told him."

"Don't think you're off the hook," I said, spinning toward the cat. "I'm still mad at you, too."

Octo-Cat gave his best approximation of a shrug. "You may be angry with me today, but I'm angry with you pretty much every day. As far as I see it, we're even for the time being," he said, sauntering over.

There was so much wrong with that statement, too much for me to even attempt to address. So instead of trying, I simply opened the door and motioned for my cat to walk out ahead of me.

Charles had grabbed a set of green fabric camping chairs and set them out in front of the RV.

The police had arrived as well. A cruiser sat parked at the edge of the campground, but the officers were nowhere to be seen. Probably already inside Junetta's home, taking stock of the scene.

A few other visitors to the campground had pulled out lawn chairs of their own and sat watching the scene unfold.

"Ugh, it smells bad," Octo-Cat said before unleashing a trio of mighty sneezes. "What is that strange yet alluring smell?"

"Charles..." I said, practically collapsing into the seat at his side. "Please let Octavius know that I'm not available to speak with him at the moment."

"Yeah, yeah, I get it," the tabby groaned. "Can't let these unimportant strangers know your big secret. Never mind that you'll probably never see any of them ever again. I'm sure they're all watching with rapt attention just in case they catch you talking to a magnificent specimen of the feline species rather than—I don't know—gawking at the police investigation happening right under their noses. No, better you play it extra safe rather than actually discuss the case with your partner. Yeah, no thank you. While you sit here twiddling your thumbs, I'm going to investigate."

"No, bad kitty!" I called as he trotted away with his tail raised high and haughty. "Come back here right now!"

He'd almost made it to Junetta's trailer when a middle-aged woman with a blonde pixie cut and enough scarves to qualify as a makeshift kite stepped out from between two campers and scooped him into her arms.

"Where are you going, Mr. Tabby? You look way too fat and happy to be a stray. Maybe I should call you Mr. Tubby?" She stopped to laugh at her own joke. "You don't want your mommy worrying about you, do you? What do you say we go find her together?"

"I've never been so insulted in all my life," Octo-Cat yowled and attempted to squirm out of her arms.

"Now, now, Mr. Tubby-Tabby," the woman said. "I'm just trying to help you."

"I don't need your help," he growled as his wide amber eyes scanned the area in a panic. When he spotted me standing at the RV and attempting not to laugh, he shouted, "Angela! Help me!"

"He does not look happy," Charles said. "Are you going to go claim him?"

"In a second," I said, watching Octo-Cat's pupils grow wide with terror.

The blonde woman caught me watching her and called out, "Does this chubby little guy belong to you?"

"Again with the insults!" Octo-Cat hissed. "Bah!"

"Yes, he's mine. Thanks for grabbing him," I said, then silently added, and for teaching him a bit of a lesson.

11

"I'll go grab another chair," Charles said as the woman carrying Octo-Cat made her way over.

"Is that your husband?" she asked, watching Charles with a little too much interest as he left. "Because, if so... Well done, sister."

"My boyfriend," I corrected with an awkward smile. "And that's my cat."

"Lucky lady on both counts." The woman said plopped down into Charles's vacated seat while keeping a firm grip on Octo-Cat.

"My name's Angie," I offered.

"Sharon. Ahh!" Suddenly, she pulled her hand toward her face, showing off a bright scarlet scratch that now marred her pale skin.

Octo-Cat shouted a string of kitty curses and ran off to hide somewhere.

Sharon popped out of her chair to follow him, but I called her off. "Don't worry about him. He always comes back."

She clucked her tongue and settled back in the chair. "My Chester could sure take a lesson or two from him. What's your little tubster's name?"

From a distance, Octo-Cat yowled and spat even more insults at the woman. De-spite my irritation, even I was starting to feel a little bad for him.

"His name is Octo-Cat, and the vet says he's in the healthy weight range for his size. He's actually part Maine Coon on his grandmother's side." At least he always said that about his lineage. I had doubts about its veracity, though. It also wasn't exactly what the vet had said during our last visit. Octo-Cat had, in fact, crept a little above the recommended weight range—thanks, lobster rolls—but I had chosen not to share that particular tidbit with him.

Sharon shrugged and leaned back in the chair, stretching her legs straight out in front of her. "My Chessy just loves the RV life, even though he never leaves our little home on wheels. Why, I imagine he's enjoying himself a little nap in a sunbeam right about now."

Hmm. A regular. Perhaps she knew a thing or two about who might want Junetta dead.

"Do you and Chester come here often?" I asked conversationally.

Sharon laughed so hard she began to cough, then formed a

fist and punched her chest several times. "Whoo! It's been a long time since I heard a pickup line."

My eyes widened. "I didn't mean—"

"Now don't you go taking it back. Just let me enjoy it." She let out a happy sigh, then sat silent for a few moments before speaking again. "Chester and I have a nice little rotation, and Katahdin is part of it. Each month we hit several of our favorite parks so that we can see all our friends across the state. Of course, most folks stay put during the winter months. But not Chester and me. We're always on the move. We're like sharks. If we stop swimming, we die." She laughed again, but not hard enough to send herself into another fit.

Throughout my life, I'd met few people who could talk as much as Sharon did—or with as little input from a conversational partner. So, yes, if I asked the right questions, I might be able to sneak a little of the local park gossip out of her.

"Did you notice the police car when it pulled up?" I asked, nodding toward the parked cruiser.

"Oh, yes. I most assuredly did. A couple of officers got out and marched right over to Junetta's. Between you and me, that woman is always in some kind of trouble. She had a nasty divorce last year. That's why she gave everything up and moved into the park permanently. Of course, that snake of an ex of hers shows up every so often begging her to take him back."

My features pinched in sympathy. "I had no idea."

"Well, why would you? You're a first-time visitor, right?" She bobbed her head and grinned. "I always recognize a first-timer."

I nodded, even though it seemed Sharon didn't need any confirmation from me.

At the same time, Charles returned with empty hands. "Couldn't find another chair, but I don't mind getting a little dirty," he announced before settling himself on the ground.

"Oh, I bet you don't." Sharon growled flirtatiously.

Charles's cheeks turned beet red.

"Well, I best get back to Chester. Say, why don't the two of you and Octo-Cat stop by mine later for coffee and gossip. What was your name again, dear?"

"Angie. And this is Charles." Of course, she remembered the cat's name, but not mine.

"Yes, definitely bring him along." Sharon puckered her lips and made a smooch-ing sound, then burst out laughing yet again.

"Well, as Tigger says, TTFN!" she sang, blowing us both kisses as she left.

"Wow," Charles said when the two of us were alone again. He got up from the grass and settled himself in the chair Sharon had just vacated.

"Yeah," I agreed, then hung my head back and watched the clouds as they idled by.

Finally, a moment of peace.

Of course, it didn't last anywhere near long enough.

"Over there! That's her!" a familiar voice shouted.

When I lowered my gaze, I saw the woman from the Airstream marching straight at us with a police officer following hot on her heels.

12

"She's the one who did it!" the woman cried in hysterics.

I rose from my chair, and Charles did the same. "I'm the one who discovered the body," I admitted.

"She's guilty!" the woman shouted again even though we were only standing a few feet apart.

"Ma'am," the officer said in a stern voice. "I'm going to have to ask you to give us some privacy."

He then turned toward me. "Mind if we talk inside?"

Unfortunately "inside" was something of a problem. That's where we had a rogue raccoon acting like a toddler while pretending to be a big-rig trucker.

I couldn't exactly refuse a request from the police, and the longer I hesitated, the more suspicious we would appear.

I shot a glance to Charles, who met my gaze with a subtle nod.

Charles strode up to the door and pushed it open.

I whispered a quick prayer under my breath as the policeman and I followed him inside.

"Is everything all right, miss?" the officer asked, catching me as I frantically searched the camper's living space.

No Pringle, which meant he was either hidden out of sight, or he'd snuck away despite my orders to remain put.

"I'm fine," I answered, perhaps a bit too tersely.

Charles motioned toward the table that was flanked with booth seats. "She's still in shock after that discovery. Please, won't you come sit?"

He studied Charles with fresh interest. "Were you with her when she discovered the body?"

"No, but I'm Miss Russo's attorney," he answered glibly.

Now the officer turned back to me. "You sure lawyered up quick for someone that—"

"She's also my girlfriend," Charles added before the officer could take that any further. "We came up here for a relaxing getaway."

The policeman slid into one side of the booth, and I took the other. Charles sat beside me and held my hand under the table. The officer eyed us both for moment before pulling out his notepad and beginning.

"Ms. Stevens out there seems pretty convinced you're the one who killed our victim," the policeman said slowly, keeping a careful watch on my reaction.

It took everything I had to remain calm. Yes, I'd been suspected of murder before, but that was on my home turf. Here, I knew no one, and no one knew me.

"She's wrong." I pressed my free hand flat on the table. "I'm just the one who had the bad luck of discovering—"

"And why is that?" the officer interrupted, clicking his pen. "Why were you in her trailer uninvited?"

"She was the one who—" I spat, but Charles raised a hand to stop me.

"Angie was urged to enter the premises when her knocks went unanswered. Ms. Stevens herself was the one who told her to proceed."

"She said Junetta had an open-door policy," I added in a whisper.

The policeman tapped his pen on his notebook for a few beats. "What did you need to see her about?"

"My client is not under suspicion. Is she?" Charles asked, flipping into full lawyer mode. He moved his eyes from the officer's face down to the shiny badge on his shirt. "Officer Hamil, is it?"

"Yes, that's my name. And we're just gathering information right now," he replied before getting up to wander the tight living space.

He stopped at the kitchenette. "Burnt grilled cheese sandwiches. Are you usually such a disaster in the kitchen, Ms. Russo? Perhaps you're better at baking? Like, say, a pie?"

I gritted my teeth. Officer Hamil was clearly trying to rile me up. I knew that, and yet I had a hard time letting his rude and sexist remarks slide.

Charles squeezed my hand as a reminder that he was there for me, that he would make sure I came through this all right. "I was the one cooking lunch. Understandably, I stopped when Angie returned to the trailer and told me what she'd found."

"Boyfriend, lawyer, and personal chef," Hamil said to me with a wink. "Is there any-thing this guy doesn't do?"

"He doesn't accuse innocent people of murder," I shot back before Charles could remind me to keep mum.

The policeman tilted his head to the side and opened his mouth without speak-ing. Was it really so hard to believe that someone would talk back to him in the same manner in which he spoke to others? "Now you wait just a min—"

A knock on the door cut him off.

"Mind if I answer?" he asked me, choosing to ignore Charles completely. Apparently he thought he had a better chance of getting a confession if he dealt directly with me. Too bad I wouldn't be confessing to a crime I'd had zero involvement in.

"Go right ahead," I said without missing a beat.

Officer Hamil kept his eyes on us for another few moments before sighing and heading toward the door.

"Yeah, what have you got?" he mumbled to whoever was there.

I strained to see, but his wide body blocked my view.

After a couple minutes of hushed conversation, he stepped back into the trailer and walked up to the table, standing close to

Charles and blocking him in as some kind of intimidation technique.

"Not just a lawyer, chef, boyfriend, but also a convicted felon, eh?" He paused and sucked air through his teeth. "Sir, I'm going to ask you to come with me."

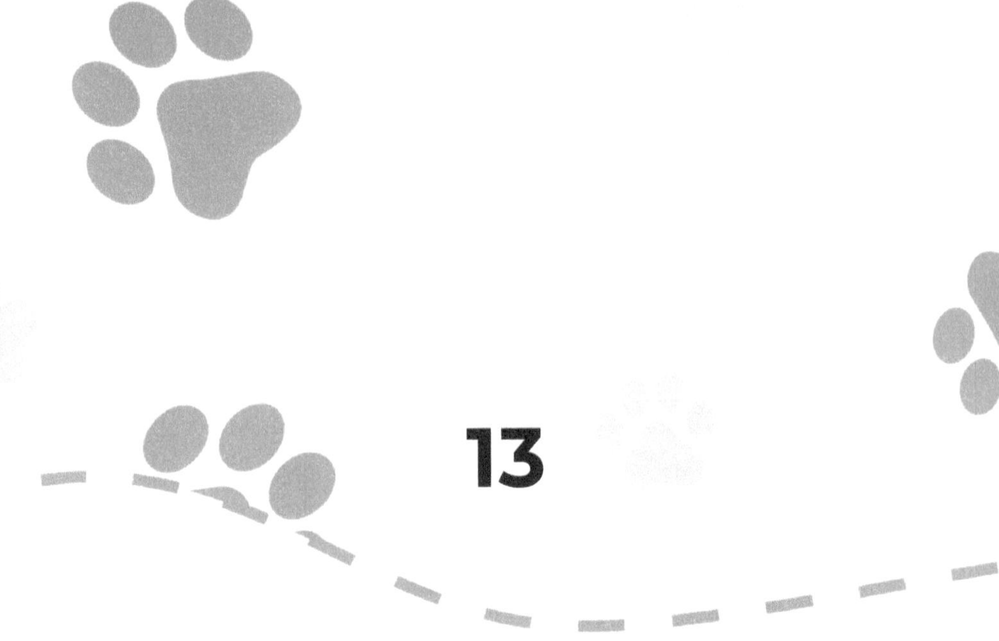

13

I tried to follow, but Officer Hamil wouldn't allow me to exit the vehicle.

"We'll just be a moment," he said before shutting the door firmly behind them.

Shoot. As much as I hated being the one under suspicion, I liked it even less when Charles came under fire. But the investigation wasn't my only problem.

"Pringle?" I whispered, still unsure where the nosy critter had gone.

When he didn't answer, I moved to the front of the RV and lowered the window a crack. Thankfully, it was just enough to listen to the conversation outside if I strained.

Officer Hamil was now joined by a female speaker. I didn't recognize her voice as belonging to the Airstream lady—Ms.

Stevens—who was so completely and totally convinced that I had offed a woman I'd never even met.

This left me to assume that the woman in question was the other police officer who had arrived on the scene.

"This isn't my RV," Charles explained calmly.

"Stole it, did you?" Hamil asked, but the other officer shushed him.

"If it's not yours, then why is it in your possession?" she pressed. Already I liked her a lot better than her partner.

"Do you mind if I reach into my right front pocket to get my phone?" Bless him, Charles always knew exactly how to act in these situations.

"Go ahead," the woman said. I imagined her nodding, even though I hadn't the slightest idea what she even looked like.

"I'm watching you, lover boy," Hamil growled.

His partner shushed him again, then everyone fell silent as they waited for Charles to bring up what he wanted to show them.

"See," Charles said a short bit later. "This app lets you borrow campers and camp equipment short-term. It's a bit like Airbnb. If you click here, you'll see the booking I made with the owner."

"That's the name that comes up for the plates," the lady cop said.

"That doesn't mean you're in the clear, though. Hand over your ID." Hamil was quick to take back control. It must have been awful having that blowhard as a partner.

"I'm going to reach into my back pocket now," Charles enunciated clearly.

"Hamil, why don't you run a scan while I take over here?" the woman officer suggested in a way that said compliance was non-optional.

Nobody said anything for a moment, and then the back door to our RV swung open.

I stayed where I was in that big bucket seat, mostly because I didn't want to get caught eavesdropping.

"Thanks, Officer Lenard," Charles said, his deep voice filling the space.

"You don't look like the aggravated assault type," she said kindly. "But just because I don't believe you committed this murder doesn't mean I don't want to talk to you."

"Understood. How can I help?"

The squeaking of leather signaled that they had slid into the booth.

"Walk me through your day," Lenard instructed after taking a moment to get settled. "Take extra care to mention any contact you had with the deceased."

"Well, this morning I woke up early to get some work in before picking up the camper, picking up my girlfriend, and hitting the road."

"Fast-forward to your arrival, please." Lenard would have made a good lawyer if she hadn't chosen to pursue law enforcement instead. She and Charles had the exact same way of being assertive while also remaining kind and professional.

"It was about a three-hour drive," he explained. "We arrived a little before two. I went to check in with the camp manager before taking my girlfriend to a picnic area a short walk away."

"You checked in with the camp manager? Tell me more about that."

"There's not much to tell. She came to the door when I knocked, but didn't invite me in. When I told her who I was so she could confirm my appointment, she asked me to wait and went back inside. She emerged a couple minutes later with a big logbook in hand and marked off my name. She said to stop on by if I needed anything during my stay, and that was it."

"Did you notice anything unusual during your interaction with her?" Officer Lenard pressed, her voice smooth and practiced. She'd likely questioned witnesses hundreds of times before. I imagined her as an older lady. Maybe a few years off from retirement, if she played her cards right.

"Just that she seemed distracted," Charles said. "But since I'd never met her before, I couldn't speak to whether or not that was normal behavior on her part."

"Understood, understood." They sat in silence for a few beats before Lenard spoke again. "So just to confirm, it was about two o'clock when you went to check in?"

"Yes."

"And your girlfriend discovered the body. What time was that?"

"Well, we left a few minutes after I checked in and walked about fifteen minutes to the picnic area. All the tables there were filled so we walked another five. We sat and relaxed for close to half an hour and then walked back. As soon as we arrived back at the campground, my girlfriend went to speak with the manager. I'd say that puts us at about three thirty this afternoon."

"Which gives us an hour and a half window for the death," Officer Lenard supplied. "What made your girlfriend so eager to check in, if you'd already done so?"

Oh, no. That question would have totally made me freeze up. If Charles explained what we'd really been doing—making business deals with bears—he'd instantly move up the suspect list.

"We thought we heard fireworks while we were out there," he explained, then stopped and sighed. "As an animal lover, she was quite distressed to think that something like that could be happening in a protected nature park."

Charles's reply came out so smooth and convincing that even I believed it. Well, the best lies were based on truth, and this was as close as we could come to sharing the conversation I'd had with Gloria at Pringle's behest.

"Are you certain you...?" I didn't hear the rest of the officer's response because something else caught my focus.

Pringle.

Straight ahead on the roof of the camper parked in front of us. But before I could say or do anything, he dropped through the vent and disappeared from view.

Oh, he'd be in big trouble once I caught up to him!

14

I opened the passenger side door just as quietly as I could and slipped outside while Charles and Officer Lenard continued to converse inside.

I crept over to the RV where I'd seen Pringle sneaking about on the roof, all the while trying to figure out what I would say to explain myself to whoever was inside.

But when I knocked, nobody answered—an unfortunate theme of the day.

"Pringle!" I whisper-yelled. "Pringle! I know you're in there!"

"I think I have some Pringles back at mine if you've got a craving," Sharon yelled from somewhere behind me.

I jumped and did an about-face. "Oh, Sharon. Hi, again!" I cried, wiggling my fingers in her direction. "I was just searching for my cat."

She squinted at me in confusion. "I thought his name was Octo-Cat?"

"Oh, yes. Yes, it is. Pringle is his middle name. Well, one of them, anyway. His full name is Octavius Pringle Maxwell Ricardo Edmund Frederick Fulton Russo, Esq, P.I. See, that's why I had to shorten it. He comes to all the names, though, and since I haven't seen him for a while, I'm running through the list." I let out a nervous laugh. She was going to see right through me on this one.

But I got lucky.

"Tubby Tabby is missing?" Sharon shrieked, fanning herself with one hand. "Well, why didn't you come and get me straight away? Of course, I'll help you look for him. Tell you what, you just come with me."

When I hesitated, she motioned me forward, saying "C'mon now. C'mon."

I shot one last look at the camper containing Pringle, then dawdled after her like a lost baby duckling.

"Now, normally I wouldn't offer up anything on my Chessy's behalf, but I like you and I have a feeling he will, too." She stopped outside her RV and waited for me to catch up. "Yes, that's right. C'mon inside."

Somewhat reluctantly, I followed Sharon into her camper, which stood parked somewhere between the camp manager's and the one that Charles and I had rented for the weekend.

And if Junetta's RV had been straight out of a 1980's fever dream, Sharon's was a futuristic space-scape. Everything inside was pristine and white and adorned with polished chrome accents. None of it had sharp edges. Instead, everything flowed seamlessly from one piece into the next. On the sleek leather sofa sat an all-white cat with extra-long hair and stunning blue eyes.

Sharon waddled right over to him and tugged him into her arms. "Oh my sweet, sweet Chessy baby," she cooed.

"This place is amazing," I said on the wings of an exhale, still taking stock of the luxury camper and all its amenities. One of the walls sported an enormous TV, which was tuned in to the nature channel.

"Oh, this? It's Chester's world. I'm just lucky to live in it," Sharon prattled on.

I reached out to let the cat sniff my hand, and he instantly began to purr. Wow, she even had the luxury cat model. Octo-Cat never treated me with such kindness, not even when he was at his happiest.

"I do mean that literally by the way," Sharon confided. When she shook her head, her pink cheeks jiggled. "Chester has all kinds of fe-fans on the social media. That's feline fans for the uninitiated. Now, when I started posting photos of our camping ad-ventures, one of those Hollywood types reached out to us via private message. One thing led to another, and now Chessy and I are going to be on reality TV. Filming starts this summer. They sent us this new house on wheels so we had time to get used to it before the show starts."

Wow, there was a lot to unpack there.

First off, why hadn't she led with this information? I'd have found her a lot more interesting if she had. After all, she was the first person I'd met—other than me—whose cat paid all the bills.

"Chester is such a talented kitty boy. Aren't you?" she continued to coo as she fawned over her feline life partner.

Pringle was going to die when he found out he'd been this close to a future reality TV star without ever actually meeting her. I couldn't wait to tell him.

"Angie?" Sharon stared at me with wide eyes and a concerned expression. I must have missed something.

"Have the police talked to you yet?" she said for what I guessed wasn't the first time.

"Yeah," I admitted, casting my eyes to the floor and discovering a luxe white marble with little glints of silver.

"Such a shame what happened to Junetta." She clucked her tongue and set the cat back on the sofa. "Why, she'd seemed entirely normal when I stopped off this morning to bring her my fresh-made and famous lingonberry pie."

My mind zoomed back to the scene I'd discovered earlier that afternoon. The pink-tinged vomit, the half-eaten pie. Mixed berry, I'd thought. But since I had no idea what a lingonberry was supposed to look like, that could very well have been what I'd seen.

Had Sharon just inadvertently confessed to the camp manager's murder? Yes, she liked to talk, but enough to accidentally slip up in such a major way?

I didn't know, and I was terrified of finding out.

Yes, suddenly I was very uncomfortable being alone with her in the RV...

15

"I have to go," I blurted out, but Sharon's wide body filled the passageway that led toward the door.

Her face turned down in a pout. "But you've only just gotten here."

"I have to find my cat. Remember?" I tried to push past her, but either she didn't get the hint or she didn't want to let me get away.

"Oh, look at me, so carried away with introductions that I plum forgot." She pressed her palm into her forehead and sighed. "Before you go, I have something for you."

The moment she turned to get whatever it was, I raced through the door and back out into the open where presumably no one would try to kill me while I was in plain sight of the others.

"I'm watching you!" the Airstream lady screamed from several lots away and shook her fist in the air.

I glanced at her briefly, then went running back toward Charles's and my camper.

At this point, I just wanted to go home and forget this whole day had ever happened, but I doubted the police would allow that while Charles and I were still under suspicion in an open investigation.

"There you are," Charles said from where he'd taken up in one of the chairs out-side our RV. "Angie, you're bright red. What's the matter?"

"Angie! Why'd you run off like that?" Sharon called, jogging to catch up.

A few other campers watched us and whispered to themselves.

A little girl with curly pigtails turned and hid her face against her father's leg. He stared daggers at me. This more than the interaction with the police made me feel very exposed and misunderstood.

Charles stood and wrapped an arm around me while Sharon finished her approach.

"Here," she said between gasps for air. It wasn't a long walk from her RV to ours, but I wasn't one to judge. Before Nan had forced me into morning runs with her and Cujo, I, too, would have been out of breath from the short jaunt.

When I tore my eyes away from Sharon, I looked down and saw a short, flat metal can resting on my palm.

"For your cat. I sure hope you find him." Sharon bent forward and took another deep breath, then left us to return to her own camper.

Charles took the can from me and read the label. "Albacore tuna. Huh."

"Tuna?" Pringle repeated from somewhere nearby.

"Pringle, where are you?" I whispered, scanning the area.

"Under here," the raccoon called quietly.

I got down on my hands and knees and peered into the darkness beneath the camper.

Two little hands reached out in supplication. "Tuna me, baby!"

"I'm going inside. If you want this, then maybe you should come inside, too." I huffed, then climbed back onto my feet and into the RV.

A moment later a thunk sounded from the bathroom.

"I'll get it," Charles announced as he paced across the living space.

As soon as the door clicked open, Pringle tore out of the bathroom in a manic fury. "Tuna, tuna, tuna," he chanted, jumping up beside me.

"You've been a very naughty raccoon."

He folded his hands in front of him and blinked up at me with large eyes. "What? Me?"

I scowled at him, ripping the can away when he tried to make a grab for it. "Yes, you. I told you to stay put."

"I did!" he squeaked. "See, I'm right here?"

"Then why did I spot you creeping into that other camper?"

Pringle took a step back. "Wh—?"

"Don't play stupid with me. I saw you."

"Okay, fine." When he sighed, his little shoulders rose and fell in defeat. "Okay, so maybe I was trying to solve the murder for you. Thing is, I want in on Pet Whisperer P.I., and I figured if I cracked this case single-handedly, you'd have no choice but to invite me to partner."

"Keep dreaming, ringworm," Octo-Cat snarled before appearing as if out of no-where. He padded over to us, stretching each leg as he walked, making him look like some kind of bizarre circus act.

"And where were you?" I demanded, folding my arms over my chest, tuna still in hand.

A shudder wracked his striped body. "Hiding from that awful Sharon person."

"Ah, too bad you think she's so awful," I teased with a half-grin. "She brought a can of tuna for you, but seeing as you don't like her, I'm sure you don't want anything to do with—"

"Mine!" Octo-Cat cried, then batted the can from my hands and sent it crashing to the floor.

Both animals fell upon it at once, embroiled in a bitter fight for dominance.

"Do I even want to ask?" Charles pulled two bottles of soda from the mini fridge and handed one to me.

"Probably best that you didn't." I scooted over to make space for him on the sofa. "Did the police say anything more to you?"

"Not really. Although I was thinking you might want to change."

"Why?" I asked, a fresh wave of embarrassment washing over me as I remembered about my "juicy" booty.

He glanced down at my lap. "Well, the campground manager was murdered with a poisonous pie, and you're covered in berry juice. Looks a little suspicious."

"Oh, I haven't told you yet. I know who made the pie." I loved sharing what I'd learned with him. Even though I'd been terrified at the time, now I was quite pleased with myself for gathering this little piece of intel.

He took a swig from his soda and then lowered the bottle. "Who?"

"Sharon," I revealed, pressing my lips in a tight line to keep from saying more.

He snorted and took another drink of soda. "But you don't think she's the one who did it, do you? I mean that's circumstantial evidence at best."

"Are you kidding? She totally did it," I said even though I still wasn't entirely convinced myself. I felt better having a primary suspect in mind rather than keeping the entire thing open-ended.

"I guess we'll see." Charles leaned forward and plucked the can of tuna away from the bickering animals, then went to stash it in the glove compartment where neither of them would be able to get it.

"No fair! No fair!" Pringle cried, jumping up and down in protest.

"Upchuck strikes again," Octo-Cat declared using his preferred nickname for whenever he was feeling irritated with my boyfriend.

"Where's that salmon?" I asked whoever was willing and able to answer.

"I left it outside, Charles replied, returning from the front and settling beside me on the sofa once again. "Couldn't very well bring it in here and stink up the rental."

"Look, how about this?" I attempted to reason with our furry stowaways. "If you two can be good for the rest of this weekend, I'll let you share that salmon."

"I don't want to share with him," they each cried in unison, sticking their tongue out at the other.

I shrugged as if none of it mattered to me. "That's my offer. Take it or go hungry. Frankly, I don't care what you do."

"Are you going to change?" Charles prompted, staring pointedly at my messy lap once more.

I sighed, knowing I didn't have any good options waiting for me in that suitcase. But he was right. Even if not for the incriminating berry stains, the outfit was decidedly filthy, thanks to our brief adventure in the woods.

Back in my room, I found a floor-length dress made of black crushed velvet. It had no back, which meant I couldn't wear a bra with it, but seeing as it was far less ostentatious than the other option—something that looked like a cast-off from the old film adaptation of Gone with the Wind—I pulled the garment over my head without giving it a second thought.

Of course, floor-length on Nan equated to mid-calf on me, but if anything, that just made it easier to move around in.

"You look amazing," Charles said, taking me in his arms when I exited the bed-room. He sang an old love song we both liked, and together we swayed between the kitchenette and the dining area.

"Ugh, get a room!" Octo-Cat cried when Charles bent down to kiss me.

"Get a life!" I shot back.

"I already have one. And she's currently right in my arms," Charles said, flashing me a debonair smile.

I giggled and rolled my eyes. But that was Charles for you. He made everything better, even an open murder investigation.

"Be right back," he said, letting go of me.

"Where are you going?" I pouted. I loved our impromptu dances and didn't want this one to end.

"If you're wearing this, then I've gotta change. I can't be camping while you're over here glamping it up," he said, then closed the door behind him.

16

"This is the best I could do on such short notice," Charles said when he emerged from the bedroom, spinning to show off his form-fitting black polo shirt and smooth khaki short combo.

"Not exactly black tie, but I suppose black shirt will do." I giggled as he pulled me in for a hug. "Oh hey, I rummaged through our supplies a bit while you were changing and found a bottle of champagne. That gave me an idea."

Charles crossed to the mini fridge and grabbed the bottle by its neck, then reached into the cupboard and pulled out a box with two glass drinking flutes inside. "I was saving this for our last night out, but I guess we could have it now," he said with a shrug.

"No, don't open it yet!" I cried as he began to work at the foil top.

He paused, his shoulders tensing as he waited for me to reveal my big idea.

"We need to take it to Sharon's," I said.

Of course, he didn't get it. "What? Why?"

I put a hand on his waist and leaned in close. "As a means of entry. I'll apologize for being weird earlier, thank her for the tuna, and present the champagne."

He smiled now, coming around. "Yeah, and then what?"

"Well, we'll have Octo-Cat with us, too, and I'll ask her if her offer from earlier still stands. The one that involved coffee and gossip. She won't be able to resist. Once we're inside, you distract her while Octo-Cat and I talk to Chessy."

His brows pinched. "Chessy?"

"Her cat. If she really comes here as often as she says, then I bet Chessy has picked up on some gossip as well. He can also tell us if he noticed anything funny with Sharon earlier today."

"Like putting poison in a pie?" he suggested with a mischievous smile.

"Exactly." It might not be that easy, but given Sharon's penchant for gossip, it might not be that much harder, either.

"My girlfriend is so smart," Charles said, giving me a quick peck. "Do you think it matters that we only have two glasses?"

I pulled away from him. "I'll abstain. I need my wits about me anyway."

"There's one problem with your plan," Octo-Cat said from where he lay splayed across the sofa. "I'm not going."

I sat down beside him and attempted to stroke his fur, but he batted my hand away. "Please? You're kind of our ticket inside."

"I don't want to go, and you can't make me," he pouted, his expression sour.

But I knew how to get kitty to come out and play. "I still have that can of tuna, you know."

He turned his face away from me and mumbled, "If you're trying to bribe me, it won't work."

"Charles?" I said, holding my hand out.

Catching on immediately this time, he retrieve the can from the glove box and placed it on my hand, then went to the kitchenette and retrieved a crank-style can opener. He handed that to me, too.

As soon as the seal popped on the can, Octo-Cat's tongue poked out of his mouth and his eyes grew wide. No cat could resist the sound—or the smell—of a freshly opened can, and that's exactly what I was counting on now.

"Just a small taste now, but you can go nuts once we're back," I said, waving the can around to entice him. "I promise we'll be as quick as possible."

"I'm not sharing with the raccoon," the tabby responded, unable to look away.

I glanced around the camper. Usually, the promise of food would send Pringle into a tailspin as well, but he was nowhere to be seen. Had probably snuck out to do some snooping again. The scamp.

"It's all yours, promise." I plucked the lid from the top of the can and grabbed a chunk of fish from inside. "In fact, here's your down payment."

Octo-Cat gobbled down the flaky morsel in a single breath. "Very well," he said after licking off his chops and tending to some light grooming ministrations.

"Can you put this somewhere Pringle can't get into it?" I asked Charles and went to wash my hands.

And then we were off.

Refusing to be carried in my arms, Octo-Cat trotted at my side.

Charles walked on my other side, hanging onto the wine and both glasses. I was also counting on the fact that Sharon wouldn't be able to resist him, given her flirtatious overtures earlier.

Sure enough, all the various pieces of my plan came together. It took almost no convincing at all for Sharon to welcome us into her home on wheels.

Inside, her best feline friend Chester lay curled up on the sofa, napping peacefully.

Octo-Cat took one look at him and turned his nose up. "Ugh, what a house pet."

Since we were in mixed company, I couldn't exactly point out that he was a house pet, too. Instead I kept quiet as Charles deftly maneuvered the conversation, seeking out a way to buy me some alone time with the cats.

After about five minutes of fawning over her luxury camper, Charles said, "I bet this baby has a massive cargo hold."

Sharon was quick to take the bait. “Oh, yes. It really does! C’mon. Let me show you.”

My boyfriend turned to me with raised eyebrows.

I laughed and waved both him and Sharon off. “Go, go. You know that stuff isn’t very interesting to me, anyway. Nope. Octo-Cat and I will just hang out in here and get to know Chester a bit better.”

As soon as the door shut behind them, I nudged the white cat awake. “Chester, Chester. Sorry to bother you, but we need to talk.”

His blue eyes blinked open slowly. “I must still be dreaming,” he muttered to himself. “Otherwise I could have sworn there’s a human here talking to me. Strange.” He chuckled and then curled back up into a sleeping position.

“You better believe this is real and not a dream,” Octo-Cat shouted, jumping up and getting right in the other cat’s face. “This is my human, Angela, and she’s special. She *can* talk to us.”

Chester lifted his head slightly but appeared unimpressed.

Seeing as I didn’t know how long Charles would be able to keep Sharon occupied outside, I cut right to the chase. “Chester, there’s been a murder, and I was wondering if you know anything about it.”

“No, I don’t watch those channels,” he said, craning his neck to look past me and stare at the TV on the far wall, which was still tuned in to the nature channel. “Sharon says they’re a bad influence.”

“She’s not talking about TV. This is real life,” Octo-Cat spat.

Never mind that he also loved filling his days with TV and film. That is, when he wasn't napping, eating, or demanding ridiculous things of me.

"Who's been murdered, then? Not Sharon." Chester yawned and licked at his paw.

I sighed. "Sharon is fine. She was just here a second ago, remember? Anyway, the person who was murdered is named Junetta. She's the manager at this campground."

Chester watched a bird feed its young on the TV. "Which campground?" he asked absent-mindedly.

"This one," Octo-Cat hissed. "Yeesh, it's like you don't listen at all."

"I am listening," the white cat drawled. "But where are we? That's what I don't understand. Sharon and I travel back and forth so much, it's hard for me to keep track of where we are at any given time."

"Katahdin," I supplied.

"No, I don't know anyone by that name. I'm not allowed to leave the RV," Chester explained, although clearly misunderstanding. "So the only people I meet are the ones who come inside. Like you."

I decided to try a different tactic. "Sharon made a pie earlier today. Did you see her put anything into it?"

He shrugged. "The usual. Butter, eggs, flour, berries. Why are you so interested in the pie? It's not very good. Most humans don't even like it all that much."

"Did you—?" I began, but then the door swung open and Sharon's boisterous voice filled the space.

"If you decide to buy one of these beauties, give them my name. It just may get you a special deal."

"I'll do that," Charles promised, accepting a business card and gingerly placing it inside his wallet.

"Everything okay in here?" Charles asked when he spotted me on the couch with the two cats.

"Everything's just peachy keen," I said with a syrupy smile, even though it was the exact opposite of how I felt. We still didn't know whether Sharon was to blame, and even if I talked to Chester all night, I doubted I'd make any progress with him.

Well, Chester would be in for a rude awakening once his reality show began filming. Something told me the producers wouldn't be content to film a lazy cat napping all day.

And here I'd always thought Octo-Cat was spoiled!

17

"Well, that got us exactly nowhere," I confided in Charles as we strolled back to our camper.

He grabbed my hand and pulled me into his side. "The police are here. Sooner or later, they'll figure this out. Why don't we just try to enjoy a relaxing night in?"

I chuffed at this notion. "Relaxing went out the window several hours ago. Besides, if the police are still here, then they may come back to ask us more questions."

"Let's try not to worry about that until it happens," Charles said softly. "Hey, we're all dressed up with only one place to go. Let's have some dinner and just enjoy each other's company. We can still enjoy what's left of this vacation. It's not too late."

I blinked up at the darkening sky. It had already been such a long and exhausting day. "Can we finish watching the movie from last night?" I asked, thinking back to the happy little cartoon characters.

Charles sucked air in through his teeth. "Oooh. Again? We already finished that."

I jabbed a finger at this chest. "You finished it. I fell asleep."

He laughed at my bluster. "And what makes you think you won't fall asleep again?" he asked, but as soon as we returned to the trailer, he started up the show for me.

And, yes, Charles was correct.

I fell asleep fairly early in.

He woke me up to eat a dinner that he'd prepared while I dozed. We watched some more.

And then I fell asleep again.

Charles must have carried me to bed, because that's where I was when I woke up with a chittering raccoon on my chest.

"Pringle," I whispered in irritation. "Go away!"

"Hey, lady. I solved the murder," he ground out, wiggling his fingers in a silly jazz hands maneuver. "Come with me. I'll tell you everything, then you can go back to sleep. Cross my heart."

I glanced over to Charles who was still sleeping peacefully tucked in tight beneath the comforter. Gosh, I loved him so much. He didn't deserve the level of crazy I regularly brought to our lives. Yet what would I do without him? He was my rock in a world of sand.

"Make it quick," I grumbled, grabbing my robe and tying it tight around me, then shoving my bare feet into sneakers before following the raccoon out of the camper.

Other than a few scattered interior lights and the stars above, the campground lay obscured in complete darkness. Luckily, I always had my phone on me—a force of habit—so I clicked into the flashlight app and used it to illuminate my steps.

"Where are you taking me?" I called after Pringle as he scampered ahead.

"Almost there," he called back, moving faster and faster. We walked for a long time.

But despite my questions, Pringle didn't explain, and he didn't stop. Not until we reached a large clearing in the woods where half a dozen wooden tables had been set out for picnickers.

"It's okay. You can come out now!" Pringle called into the night.

I shone my light toward the tree line just in time to see the massive grizzly crawl out to join us in the clearing.

Oh my!

I'd been so caught up in Junetta's murder that I'd completely forgotten about poor Gloria and her plea for help. I was just about to tell her that—and to apologize for not being able to help—when a bullet whizzed past me and lodged itself in a thick tree trunk a few feet behind and to the side of Gloria.

I spun and saw a man, probably about sixty years of age, holding a smoking hunting rifle. "Get back!" he cried. "There's a wild grizzly on the loose!"

"It's okay. I'm okay!" I said, raising my arms to show him I meant no harm. "And she's not on the loose. This is her home."

Oh, how I prayed that both Gloria and Pringle had the good sense to remain hidden while I dealt with this gun-toting lunatic.

"Why do you have a gun? This is a protected nature park," I reminded him rather pedantically.

"For safety and maybe for revenge," he growled back. "Who are you?"

Uh-oh. I did not like the sound of this one bit.

Still, I tried my best to keep my voice calm. "I'm Angie. My boyfriend and I are staying at the campground. We only just got here today. Who are you?"

"Carl. I came as soon as I heard about Junetta's passing. I loved her, you know? And whoever killed her is going to pay big time."

Carl must be the ex-husband Sharon had mentioned, the crazy one who still came around from time to time to try to win her back.

"Well, Carl." I paused and licked my lips. Suddenly they felt so very dry. "I want justice for Junetta, too," I continued. "I'm the one who discovered her body."

I expected him to yell and snarl at me, to demand answers I didn't have to give, but instead the old man let out a strangled cry and sank to the ground.

The gun clattered at his feet but didn't go off.

I swooped in and grabbed it, then stood by idly as Carl cried his heart out. I had a million and one questions in that moment. Like why Pringle had brought me here and what Gloria had to do with it. But I had no doubts as to whether the weeping man in front of me was innocent. The man was simply too torn up about his ex's passing to be the culprit.

As Carl's sobs grew more and more muted, I heard Pringle and Gloria's voices rise into the night.

"He brought the exploding lightning," Gloria whispered in anguish. "He tried to aim it at me. If I die, my cubs won't make it on their own. Please, Pringle, you have to help us. It's getting so dangerous here, but where else can we go?"

"Relax, lady," the raccoon said with his signature lack of empathy. "My human sidekick and I nearly have this figured out. You and the tikes will be fine. Raccoon's honor."

I glanced over to Carl, trying to determine if he'd heard the animals calling out. But he was so lost in his own sorrow that he didn't even notice me look his way.

And so I took a chance, keeping the rifle gripped tightly in my hands, and crept deeper into the woods. I'd switched off my phone's light, which meant I had to rely on my other senses to guide me.

"Pringle? Gloria?" I whispered as I treaded over dry leaves and loose twigs.

"Over here," the raccoon called from somewhere nearby.

"I can't see anything," I whispered back. "Can you come to me?"

"I'm here," Pringle said from much closer now. "But the bear went back to be with her babies."

"What's going on? You said you figured out the murder?"

He let out a huff. "Well, I thought I had, but something tells me I got it all wrong."

"What was your theory?" I begged.

"So when we first met Gloria, she mentioned how her mate had tried to kill their cubs and that she was on the lam. Then I figured any guy who would kill his own kids could easily off a human," he said. I couldn't see him, but I imagined him making big sweeping gestures to emphasize his assumed brilliance.

Unfortunately, I had to burst his bubble. "But that makes no sense," I said in exasperation.

"Of course it makes sense." Hurt echoed in his voice. I loved that he was trying to help, but one of us could have been shot back there. This was serious business, and I needed him to take it as such.

"The murder weapon was a poison pie," I reminded him with a sigh. "Do you know any bears who can bake?"

"Hey, I could bake if I wanted to."

"Well, you never have, and also you're not a bear. Is that why you brought me out here?"

"I wanted to tell you and Gloria at the same time. That way I could get my second salmon and make partner in the P.I. firm in one nice combo move." He sounded completely chastised now, which meant it would be the wrong time to point out that he wouldn't be joining Octo-Cat's and my business any time in the near future.

"So you told Gloria to meet us here?" I prompted.

"Yeah. Yeah, I did. I just had to go and get you first."

Now that the shock of meeting Carl had worn off, something important clicked together in my mind. "I overheard the two of you talking about exploding lightning. Gloria wasn't talking about fireworks like I thought before. She was talking about guns. There are illegal hunters in the area. If Junetta figured that out, she could have put a stop to it. Someone didn't want that to happen, though."

"Yeah, I guess that makes sense," Pringle agreed.

Yes, yes, we were on to something here. We could still solve this thing.

"Pringle, I need your expert snooping skills," I said, hoping I wouldn't later come to regret it. "Do you think you can help me close this case?"

He pumped his arm and made a terrible honking noise, then shouted, "Okay! Let's hit the road, sweetheart!"

Of course, he happily agreed.

18

By the time I got back to the picnic area, Carl had already gotten up and left.

Shoot. I still had some questions I wanted to ask him, but I'd have to worry about that later.

Pringle went to find Gloria so that he could explain our plan and to promise we'd do something about the illegal hunting as soon as we found some answers. Much to his chagrin, I also made him tell the grizzly that a second payment would not be needed, that we were happy to help simply out of the kindness of our hearts.

While he took care of that, I sat at one of the picnic tables with the rifle laid out on its surface and called Charles to tell him what had happened and what Pringle and I were planning next.

Luckily, Pringle liked guns—although his primary experience was in handling the Nerf variety. Still, he was excited to implement the plan exactly as I'd laid it out. And if there was one thing I'd learned about working with animals in all my time as a pet whisperer, it was that the best results came when you got them to act on their natural behavior. Pringle loved collecting secrets via his snooping endeavors, and I'd already caught him slipping into RVs undetected earlier that day. In fact, that's how this whole adventure started in the first place.

So now when I asked him to keep doing it, he readily agreed. The plan involved him sneaking into the campers parked at the grounds and searching for rifles or any other hunting paraphernalia. Once we found out who all might be engaged in illegal hunting, we could narrow down our suspect list.

First, though, I needed him to pay a quick visit to Junetta's camper and find the logbook Charles had mentioned to the police. She'd recorded our arrival, which meant she had likely recorded everyone else's, too.

Pringle made quick work of this first task and delivered the logbook to me and Charles, even taking care to set it down nicely and turn to the page we needed so that neither of us would get our fingerprints on it.

"Charles," I said after studying the logbook for a few minutes. "Do you remember the name of the woman who accused me of killing Junetta?"

He thought for a moment. "We never got her first name, but the police officers referred to her as Ms. Stevens."

I nodded. That's what I had thought, too. "She's not in here," I said, chewing on my lip.

Charles read through each line, then swore under his breath. "You're right. What do you think it means?"

"Octo-Cat," I called. "Come here. We need your help for a second."

He groaned but got up and hopped onto the table. "What do you need, your majesty?"

"Can you turn the page for us?" I asked, letting his insult slide. "Go back to the older entries."

"Smart," Charles said bumping his shoulder into mine. "No prints."

Octo-Cat struggled with the task but eventually got the page turned.

I read through that page but still found no mention of Ms. Stevens's check-in.

"Again, please," I asked my cat.

It took three more turns of the page before we finally found an entry for a Miss Sara Stevens. The entry was made so long ago that it was in a different handwriting. She'd been here even longer than Junetta had. *Hmmm.*

Charles pulled out his phone and opened the Notes app. "I'm making a list," he said as he typed furiously on the tiny keyboard. "Every lot number and the date of the most recent check-in."

While he did that, I jotted down any names that occurred multiple times—identifying the grounds' frequent visitors, people like Sharon.

Octo-Cat helped us turn the pages as needed, but not without the promise of many, many lobster rolls, shrimp kebabs, and cans of tuna in his future.

When Pringle returned, he looked absolutely exhausted. I poured him a dish of water and waited for him to catch his breath before asking for a recap.

"Well?" I prompted when he still hadn't shared his findings with the group.

"Twenty-two RVs," he said, sucking in a deep, dramatic breath, even though he'd had more than enough time to recover. "I was able to break into seventeen of them. Of those, four had rifles and two had handguns."

"Do you remember which ones?" I prompted, after relaying this info to Charles.

"Do I remember?" he spat. "Of course, I remember."

"Then show me."

Pringle scampered around telling me what he'd found in each RV as well as identifying which ones he couldn't open. I jotted it all down in a series of text messages to Charles so he could check the occupancy periods for each of our gun owners on the premises.

As Pringle approached the end of the line, I pointed to Sara Stevens's aqua-accented Airstream. "What about this one? Did it have a gun?"

"No gun, but lots and lots of ammo. I found trail maps, too, with paths marked in red," he said, unwittingly revealing our smoking gun.

Just then the door to the Airstream flew open, and Sara

Stevens stepped out in a robe not entirely dissimilar to my own. "What are you doing out here?" she shouted, then pointed at Pringle. "And what is that thing?"

Another camper door opened and a man and woman wearing matching flannel pajama bottoms exited from it.

"Go get Charles," I muttered to Pringle from the side of my mouth.

He saluted, then scampered off.

"Not going to answer me?" Her face was red, her eyes wild. "Then I'm calling the cops. I'm sure they'll just love coming back out after spending half the day with us."

She grabbed her phone and punched in the number.

"That's enough, Sara," a man said. "This is a public campground, not your private property."

Sara stood on tiptoe trying to see past me in search of the voice. Even with that added bit of height, she wasn't tall enough, though.

"Is that you, Carl?" she called out. "Don't be fooled by her pretty face. This woman murdered Junetta today, murdered her in cold blood!"

Aww, she thought I was pretty. Not that that made me despise her any less.

Sara lifted up her phone and shouted, "Do you hear that? I have a murderer sneaking around outside my camper. Come and get her, boys."

"Funny, from what I understand Angie only just arrived here today," Carl pointed out.

Sara ended the call with humph and thrust her phone back into her robe pocket. “Yes, and an hour later Junetta was dead. Coincidence? I think not.”

“I didn’t kill her,” I insisted for what felt like the hundredth time. This time my confession of innocence was more for the benefit of the other campers who had come out to gawk at our confrontation. “Someone poisoned her with a pie, and I don’t know the first thing about baking.”

A gasp sounded across the way. “With my pie?” Sharon cried, waddling over in a hurry. “The secret ingredient is love, not poison. Never poison.”

Behind Sharon, I spotted Charles striding over. This gave me all the courage I needed to trot my theory out for all to hear.

“The pie wasn’t poisoned when you gave it to her,” I called to Sharon, then fixed my gaze directly on Sara Stevens. “Someone added it in after the fact. Someone who’s been around for a bit and knows all about Junetta’s open door policy.”

I paused to gauge everyone’s reaction, but no one said a thing. Charles was at my side now, standing in a silent show of support.

And so I continued. “And Junetta wasn’t murdered in cold blood. Her death was planned. Somebody was very unhappy with her. From what I can gather, she might not have been the best campground manager, but she was learning on the job. And recently she’d learned all about an illegal hunting ring operating right here under her nose. She planned to put an end to it, to make sure the guilty parties were held accountable. But they silenced her before she could say a thing.”

"She knew." Carl's voice cracked and he hung his head. "This whole time, she knew. Oh! This is all my fault!"

"So you confess!" Sara shouted and pointed. "Filthy scum, no wonder Junetta left you."

"No, no, it wasn't me. I would have never..." His words fell away as he stumbled backward.

Catching him in a weak moment, Sara pounced. "You killed her. It makes perfect sense. You couldn't have her, so you decided no one could."

"When Junetta found out I'd been coming out here to hunt illegally, she was so upset. That was the beginning of the end for us."

"You came here?" I prompted, even though I was already pretty sure I knew what he would say next.

Carl pumped his head. "Yes, I came here many times over the past couple years. The animals aren't expecting it, so they're easy shots. I'd bring Junetta with me on my trips sometimes, but never tell her where I was going after dark. I guess that's why she came after the divorce, why she decided to take a job here. She thought it was just me hunting out here. She didn't know there were more of us. Didn't know who made it so that local law enforcement didn't catch on."

"Who was in charge, Carl?" I asked. "Who made it all possible?"

"She was your friend!" he shouted at Sara. "Why would you do this?"

The accused took a giant step back and pressed herself against her Airstream. "I… I don't know what you're talking about."

"It's easy to blame others when you're trying to cover your own back," I said, taking a step toward the cornered killer.

"You! You can't prove anything," she spat at me.

"Oh, but I can," Carl said, taking out his phone and jiggling it at her. "I kept a record of every hunt. Won't be difficult to match you up to the timeline."

"Go away! This is my home, and you're not welcome here!" Sara shouted, completely losing it now.

"You're going to jail. For Junetta's sake, I hope you rot in there," Carl hissed.

More and more campers overheard the yelling and came outside to investigate. The police arrived a short while later to take things over. And the hysterical killer was the one who had called them herself.

19

With Junetta's killer behind bars, Charles and I headed back to our little home on wheels for the weekend. Pringle and Octo-Cat had made themselves scarce, allowing us to cash in on some much-needed relaxation.

We slept in late the next morning, then ate our way through a massive stack of messy, syrupy pancakes in bed. It was bliss.

"If we don't go anywhere, we can't be forced out of relaxation mode," I reasoned, and Charles agreed enthusiastically.

"I still feel bad about dragging you all the way out here only to have the worst weekend ever," he said with a slight frown pulling down the corner of his mouth.

I pushed my last bite of pancakes around the edges of my plate to collect the remaining drips of syrup, then shoved the whole thing in my mouth and sighed with delight. "Well, it was a pretty bad Friday," I said once I'd managed to swallow down that heavenly bite. "But the weekend as a whole has yet to be determined."

Octo-Cat, who lay cuddled at our feet, popped his head up and said, "Life with Angela is often irritating, but it's never boring."

I decided not to translate that for Charles.

"Hey, should we grill up that salmon for lunch?" he asked with a laugh.

"Are you kidding me? It's been sitting out since yesterday. The thing is probably covered in flies by now."

"Actually, I already took care of that," Pringle announced, standing in the doorway with one paw to the wall. "Sorry. I know I was supposed to let you have it as a way of saying sorry for ruining your picnic, but I was just so hungry after all that sneaking around I did on your behalf. You know how it goes."

I nodded and set my polished-off plate at the end of the bed. "I do, and it's okay. We weren't going to eat it, anyway."

Pringle cast his eyes toward the floor, then grabbed the tip of his tail and began grooming it nervously with his fingers. "Sure, but I still feel really... I don't know... sick to my stomach. It's weird."

"That feeling is guilt," I supplied with a lazy grin. "You feel bad about ruining our picnic, but really, it's okay. I'm not mad."

"If you're not mad, then why do I still feel this way? How can I make it stop?" He pouted and began to twist his tail in his hands.

"Really, it's—"

"Oh, I've got it!" Pringle shouted, then turned and ran off. When he returned, he jumped up onto the bed and climbed onto my lap. His little black fist was closed tight around something, but I couldn't see what.

"I've been feeling sick like this for a while now, and I think it all started after Chucky and I helped those seagulls," he said, pointing toward Charles with his free hand. I was definitely not okay with him nicknaming my boyfriend after a demonic horror doll, but seeing as Pringle was attempting a genuine, heartfelt moment here, I let it slide.

Instead I asked, "What's wrong with the seagulls?"

"Nothing's wrong exactly. But Charles helped with that case, and I didn't share the payment. I thought it's what I wanted, but I hate feeling this way. So..." He opened his palm to reveal a sparkling diamond solitaire.

I gasped, completely taken by surprise. "What? Where did you get that?"

"The seagulls gave it to us, remember? I always keep it nearby, since it's one of my greatest treasures."

"It's been here all weekend? Where?" I glanced around the room. This RV was packed so tight I had no idea where Pringle may have made his secret stash.

"Don't worry about that. If I give up all my good hiding spots, I'll feel sick for a different reason." He attempted a smile, but it looked wrong, thanks to all those sharp little teeth. "So do you forgive me?"

"Of course, I forgive you, Pringle." I reached out and patted his head. Pringle wasn't a domesticated animal and didn't like it when I touched him, but I felt like I had to do something to connect with him in that moment.

He winced at my touch, then straightened his posture and pressed the ring into my hand. "Then here. Do with it what you will."

"I have a feeling this is going to get real gross, real fast," Octo-Cat droned as he jumped off the bed. "Come find me when you want to feed me."

Pringle disappeared after him, leaving my boyfriend and I on our own. We both stared at the ring, neither saying anything. Talk about opening a giant can of worms.

When at last I couldn't take the awkward silence any longer, I giggled and joked, "So you wanna get married or something?"

But Charles didn't laugh. Not even a little. Instead he cleared his throat and got out of bed.

"No, no, come back. I'm sorry!" I called after him. Me and my big mouth. *Stupid, stupid, stupid.*

He rooted around in his luggage, then climbed into bed beside me, holding out both hands in fists. "Pick one," he said.

I tapped on his right fist, and he opened it up to reveal a little satin box.

My breathing hitched as I looked from the ring in my hand to the box in his. "Charles, I…"

"Open it," he said with a soft smile, watching me so closely I doubt he blinked at all.

Delicately, I lifted the lid to reveal a princess-cut diamond surrounded by a tight outcropping of amethysts.

"I planned to ask you this weekend. On our picnic actually, but then..." He sighed and watched me with wide eyes. "Well... you know the rest."

"Are you really asking me—?"

"To marry me? Yes." He sat up higher in bed and grabbed both of my hands in his. "This isn't how I'd planned it, but I love you, Angie Russo. For better or worse. No matter what. Do you love me like that, too?"

"Yes, I do," I said as he took the ring out of the box and slipped it onto my finger. "And yes, I will marry you."

I wiggled my fingers, delighting in the heft of my new prized accessory, at the way it sparkled in the light. Then I reached for Charles's hand and slipped the seagull's ring onto his pinky finger.

"A perfect fit," I said. "Just like us."

"Just like us," he agreed.

We shared our first kiss as a betrothed couple, and then I pulled away and asked, "What would you have done if I picked the other hand?"

My fiancé's eyes flashed with mischief. "Hmm, I guess we'll never know," he teased, and then kissed me again.

20

When we returned home Sunday evening, my entire family stood waiting on the porch.

"Congratulations, Mr. and Mrs. Charles Longfellow the Third!" Nan cried, setting off a party popper.

"I have a new daddy!" her Chihuahua Paisley barked happily.

My mother and father rushed down the steps to greet us, exchanging hugs and congratulations.

Octo-Cat hopped out of the camper and groaned. "Remind me again why you thought it would be a good idea to bring a cat on a camping trip?"

"It wasn't our idea," I muttered and rolled my eyes. Knowing my luck, the tabby would punish me for this sleight for many months to come—and it hadn't even been my fault.

"I missed you, Octavius!" Paisley squeaked, then slathered him in kisses.

"Get off me, you demented creature," he growled.

Paisley pinned him down and took great care cleaning out each of his ears.

"Okay, okay. I've missed you too, you little scalawag," Octo-Cat acquiesced. He even stopped struggling as Paisley continued to pepper him with sloppy puppy kisses.

While everyone's attention was on the cat and dog, the raccoon exited the RV the same way he'd initially entered, through the bathroom vent up top. "If anyone needs me, I'll be in my tree house, starting my third watch-through of the cult reality classic *Survivor.*"

I turned away from my parents and called out to him. "Pringle, wait. Come inside and join us for dinner. I'm sure Nan has something wonderful prepared."

Nan's face lit up. "I sure do. We're having blackened salmon and risotto."

My stomach turned at the mention of salmon, but I worked hard to keep my face light and happy.

"Sounds delicious." Charles threaded his fingers through mine and then raised our joined hands and pressed a kiss to them.

"Everything's ready. Just step inside." Nan guided us back into the house. "I even brought out the good china. Why, it's not every day my favorite granddaughter gets engaged."

"And it's not today, either," I pointed out with a chuckle. "We got engaged yesterday."

"Oh, hush, you." But Nan laughed, too.

Pringle scampered in after us and climbed up onto the table.

"Manners," Nan said, fixing him with a stern look.

He hesitated before climbing down onto one of the chairs. His face barely cleared the surface of the table, the cutie.

"I'll go get you a booster," I said, heading toward the entry closet where Nan kept all kinds of strange knickknacks. I wouldn't be surprised if I found a booster chair there, too.

A light tapping at the door drew my attention away.

I opened it up and found Bravo and Abigull standing on the porch together. "Hi, guys. What's up?"

"Angie, Angie," the young bird cawed. "We found her!"

I was almost afraid to ask. Mostly because I already knew the answer. "Found who?"

"Your long-lost grandmother," Bravo confirmed. "She hasn't left the state. Just moved. We found her somewhere in the middle."

"Near Mount Katahdin?" I ventured.

"Affirmative," Bravo squawked.

"How did you know?" Abigull asked, tilting her head to the side.

I let out a tired sigh. "Because with the way my life has gone lately, it just makes sense."

"We can take you to her. Are you ready?" the elder seagull asked.

"I'd like that very much, but first I have a dinner engagement. Can you come back tomorrow?"

When both birds agreed, I said goodbye and rejoined my family in the dining room. There would be time to tell them all about the seagulls' discovery later.

Tonight, we would celebrate.

Tomorrow, we could chase after our next big mystery.

PERSIAN PENALTY

PET WHISPERER P.I.

We've finally found my long-lost grandmother, and I refuse to wait another day to meet her in person. Unfortunately, she's proving rather difficult to pin down.

So Charles and I decide to finish our search on the ground and book a quirky lakeside B&B to serve as our HQ while we're in the area.

But because nothing is ever easy, we stumble across mystery after mystery while simply trying to get a good night's sleep. Precious items from our luggage keep going missing, the door to our room won't close properly, and bad reviews online hint at even worse things to come. Of course, the ill-tempered proprietress and her even crazier Persian cat refuse to help—or even to apologize.

All of which makes me wonder, will I finally get to meet my missing grandma face-to-face, or could the trouble at the inn have us packing our bags long before then?

1

I'm Angie Russo, and my life has never been normal. My family is full of superstars, most notably my nan, who once stole the stage on Broadway and is to this day the most memorable character you'll ever meet. For the longest time, I searched for what would make me special, too. I guess that's why I racked up seven associate degrees before finally settling into a career.

My calling was actually a cat call—no, not the sleazy, random-guy-on-the-street kind. An actual *meow.* A meow that I heard loud and clear, and in English of all things.

Yes, I can talk to animals. Just call me Miss Dolittle.

I was working as a paralegal when a will meeting went awry. One thing led to another, and I got zapped by a faulty coffee maker, lost consciousness, and then eventually woke up with a talking cat on my chest.

And, boy, did he have a lot of demands!

Fast-forward a couple years, and now he's my partner in the P.I. business. Thanks in large part to his former owner, his name is Octavius Maxwell Ricardo Edmund Frederick Fulton Russo, Esq, P.I. Since that's way longer than any honest name should be, I've taken to calling him Octo-Cat.

Together, we live in a beautiful manor home not too far from Blueberry Bay in Maine. Nan lives with us, too, as does her syrupy sweet rescue Chihuahua, Paisley. Our backyard neighbor is a sticky-fingered raccoon named Pringle; he helps us occasionally and bribes us regularly.

Never a dull moment with this colorful cast of sidekicks.

Of course, I'd be remiss if I failed to mention Charles Longfellow, III. He's the senior partner at a local law firm, the same one I used to work at back in the day. He's my boyfri—I mean, *fiancé!*

He's my fiancé!

Wow, I still haven't gotten used to saying that.

He proposed to me on a surprise weekend getaway that came with a rented RV and a crazy murder mystery. It was supposed to help me relax, but I'm honestly more wound up than ever.

Not just because of the proposal, but also because of what happened after we returned home.

A few months ago I made a deal to help some seagulls with an inter-flock dispute. In exchange, they promised to find my long-lost grandmother, whom I only knew about thanks to a hidden letter Pringle filched from the attic.

Nan—my best friend and the woman who raised me while my

parents were busy focusing on their careers and each other—well, it turns out she's not actually blood related.

I'm still getting over the shock from that particular revelation!

Needless to say, Nan has had a rough time accepting that I want to connect to the grandmother I never knew. I've taken every opportunity I can to reassure her, but it's still hard. She didn't choose for her best friend—my blood grandfather—to hand her his baby and ask her to run. Nan never asked why, and he died before I could suss out any answers. That leaves my long-lost grandmother as the only one who can explain why things happened the way they did.

I've got to find her and learn more about my family's secret past. Yes, I've considered that she might be dangerous, especially considering the great lengths old grandpa went to get my mother away from her.

But I'm pretty sure I can handle a confrontation with an octogenarian, no matter how intimidating she may be.

Anyway, I tell you all this now because the seagulls have finally located my secret grandmother just outside of Katahdin.

And I'm preparing to go meet her for the first time ever. I'm so excited, I can hardly—

Deep breaths.

Okay, I'm scared out of my mind, but that doesn't mean I'm going to pass up this opportunity. I mean, it's like pulling off a bandage, right? I just have to do it if I ever expect the wound beneath to heal.

. . .

I stumbled into the kitchen, practically tripping over my oversized slippers as I moved from the hardwood of the dining room to the tile in the kitchen.

"Good morning," Nan sang, floating over and pushing a banana-nut muffin into my hand. "I'll put the coffee on now."

"Thanks," I murmured, shoving the muffin in the general direction of my mouth, and hoping it would end up in the right place. I'd never been a morning person. Even less so since developing my fear of electric coffee makers.

Don't judge. I'm sure if you ever got electrocuted, you'd fear the appliance that attacked you, too.

I'd tried a million different caffeine solutions from canned coffee to instant powder, and most recently a French press. Nothing beat the freshly brewed stuff, though. It was the whole experience, really. The smell, the sound, all of it.

Thankfully, Nan was only too happy to aid in my addiction.

And so I munched on my baked good while she tidied up the kitchen and the coffee brewed. When it finished, Nan poured me a cup and mixed a bit of pumpkin spice flavored creamer in. It was one of her greatest joys to discover PSL off season, which meant it was always in season for me.

She allowed me to take a few life-giving sips before attempting a conversation. Smart woman.

"What have you got planned for today, dear?" she asked, pouring a cup for herself, and then drifting toward the living room.

I dutifully followed, shuffling my feet so that the little kitty heads on my slippers shook with each motion. Nan had purchased them for me as a Valentine's gift, remarking how much the plush felines looked like Octo-Cat. I now wore them most days, partially because it made Nan happy and partially because it bugged my cat to no end.

"I should get slippers with little human heads attached. See how you like it," the tabby muttered from atop the sofa, his tail flicking in tell-tale irritation.

I took a seat in my favorite armchair while Nan settled herself on the couch. Paisley hopped up beside her and shoved her wet little puppy nose into Octo-Cat's rear end.

"Ick!" he shouted as the hair on his back went up. "Why must you always sniff me there? Surely, the scent hasn't changed from yesterday!"

"Good morning, big brother!" the little dog squealed. She wagged her tail so hard, her whole body shook from the effort.

Octo-Cat growled and ran away to hide.

And so went our morning routine.

"Dear?" Nan prompted, casting a quizzical glance my way. "Your plans for today?"

Oh! Oh, right.

"Sorry. The pets were distracting me," I mumbled to buy myself some time. Now that I had enough caffeine in my system to form a few coherent thoughts, I realized what I needed to do, and it was the very thing I'd been dreading all night. No wonder I was so tired this morning.

"Nan?" I asked, fixing my eyes on the mug in my hands as I

continued. “Bravo visited last night. He’s found my bio grandmother.”

“Oh,” she said simply.

When I glanced up again, she had her gaze fixed on an indeterminable point in the distance and sat stroking Paisley without really seeing her—or me.

“Nan?” I prompted again. I hated that she felt this way, but I also couldn’t live with myself if I didn’t at least try to meet the woman who had birthed my mother. Whether she’d been part of our lives or not, she was still an important part of who my mother and I had become.

Nan sighed gently. “I suppose you’ll want to go meet her, then.”

“Yes,” I answered firmly. That was not up for debate, no matter how much Nan disliked the idea. But I had a plan to soften the blow…

I waited for her eyes to meet mine, and then I flashed her a reassuring smile. “I want you to come with me.”

2

Nan traced her finger along the rim of her mug, then winced. "Oh, shoot. I can't. I already have something planned for that day."

I cleared my throat. "Um, I haven't said what day I'm planning to go yet."

She hit herself in the forehead with her palm, and a few drops of coffee sloshed out onto her neon pink yoga pants. "Silly me!" she cried. "I better go treat this stain before it sets." She rushed into the kitchen far faster than she normally moved around the house.

When I joined her there, she was manically dabbing at her lap with a wet paper towel.

"Nan, we need to talk about this," I said gently.

"It's not coming out. I'm going to throw these in the wash," she muttered, then rushed past me, heading straight for the stairs.

I sighed and trudged up the stairs after her. "Come with me to meet her," I called through her closed bedroom door. "Please. I want you there."

She didn't say anything for several moments. Just as I decided she wasn't going to answer me at all, the door creaked open, and Nan's fingers wrapped around the edge.

One wide eye looked out at me through the tiny opening. "You don't understand, dear. That other woman—your true grandmother—she must hate me for what I did."

"You didn't do anything," I insisted, trying and failing to pull the door open wider. "My grandfather was the one who took Mom away. He forced your hand."

"And I chose to keep you both hidden, even when she came looking all those years later." She let out a shaky breath and cast her eyes to the floor. "If I were her, I'd hate me."

"Don't talk like that. Mom and I have both had great lives, thanks in large part to you." I smiled wide, meaning each word with everything I had. "Plus, doesn't time heal all wounds?"

She shook her head slowly on the other side of the door. I could just barely discern the motion. "Live long enough, and you'll learn that's not true," she muttered eerily.

"But Nan," I whined, not knowing what else I could say to make this better. I'd waited for months after finding out I had a secret grandmother—months for any clues to turn up and even more for the seagulls to locate her. I couldn't just *not* meet her. But I also hated to see Nan hurting like this.

"Please don't ask me again," she whispered. "You know I have a hard time saying no to you."

"But I can't do this on my own," I insisted, not trying to burden her but rather to show how important she was to me—to this.

We both sighed.

"Then take Charles with you, or your mother for that matter," Nan said before pressing the door shut between us.

The sound of overgrown claws scrabbled across the hardwood floor, then stopped.

"Mommy," a small voice rose from beside me.

I glanced down to find Paisley staring up at me with a slowly wagging tail.

"I'll go with you," she volunteered before tucking her tail over her privates and dipping her head. "But I don't think you should ask Nan again. She doesn't like it."

I sighed. Leave it to a dog to be more perceptive than me. "You're right." I bent down to scoop Paisley into my arms.

She immediately began to lick my face and make happy high-pitched noises. "I love you, Mommy."

"I love you, too."

Technically, Paisley was Nan's dog, but that didn't stop her from calling me *Mommy*. It worked, considering everyone in town called my grandmother Nan, even those who weren't related. Also, I was the only human who could understand her, and Paisley loved shouting the maternal moniker whenever she got a chance.

Her first family had abandoned her to the animal shelter, so I think she needed the added reassurance that when she called out for her family, someone answered back in kind.

I carried Paisley with me as I headed back downstairs. Nan clearly needed some time to herself to process everything, but I needed someone to talk it over with.

Mom was out of the question. Yes, it was *her* birth mother I was planning to go meet, but I wanted to make sure our missing family member was receptive to us before involving Mom. It would be a much bigger blow to her—should this other woman reject us—than it would be to me. Although that would be a sting I'd have a hard time recovering from as well. Still, I loved my mom, and I wanted to protect her if I could.

Yes, my missing grandmother had tried to approach Nan years ago, but who was to say that time hadn't hardened her heart to us?

There were so many unknowns in this situation, and no one I could turn to for advice, either. Because nobody else had gone through a situation like this before—at least not anyone I knew. And the last thing I wanted to do was entrust such a doozy of a family drama to strangers on an Internet message board or social media site.

I didn't want to bother Charles at work, especially since he'd just taken the long weekend off and this was his first day back at the office. I decided to shoot him a quick text: *Call me when you get a break at work. No rush.*

Much to my surprise, my phone began ringing almost immediately after I hit send.

"What's up?" Charles asked when I picked up the call.

"Oh, hey. I didn't mean that you needed to call right away," I chided him. "You need to focus on your work. At least that's what you're always telling me."

He chuckled at my attempt to scold him. I normally never gave him guff like this, but I'd also been hoping for some more time to sort my thoughts out for myself before attempting to share them with him.

"Yeah, but it will be good to have a quick break before switching client files," he said. "Long day ahead. Probably a long night, too."

"I'm sorry," I apologized without knowing why.

"Nothing to be sorry for. This is what I signed up for when I became a lawyer. And you know I love it. Also, I love you..." He paused dramatically, and I could just picture the big goofy grin that accompanied this silence. *"Fiancée."*

A tiny thrill rushed through me. "I love you, too, *fiancé."*

His smile came through in his words, and I was pretty sure it matched mine. "Now this time really tell me. What's up?"

"Bravo found my grandmother," I revealed, then pressed my lips into a tight line.

Charles sucked air in through his teeth. "Never a dull moment, huh?"

I smiled and shook my head even though he couldn't see the gesture. Talking to him was just natural like that. It never felt like there was any distance between us when we chatted about our days. "Nope."

"So when are we going to meet her? I am invited, right?"

I let out a giant sigh of relief. "Yes, please come with me," I said so fast all my words ran into each other.

"Darling, you couldn't keep me away. I want to be there for my fiancée whenever and however I can. By the way, you're my fiancée."

I smiled to myself. Oh, how I wished I could give him a giant hug of gratitude just then. "I love you, fiancé," I said, twirling my hair like a giggling schoolgirl.

"Uh-oh," Charles said and then let out a rolling groan. "Just got an urgent email. Gotta go, but I'll call you when I take lunch. I can't wait to hear all the sordid details. Bye. Love you."

Well, there was a pretty major thing decided at least. I probably should have asked Charles first, considering I'd just agreed to be his partner in life. It was hard to break nearly thirty years of seeing Nan as my main partner and confidant, but I guess that was part of growing up. Growing. Changing.

I just hoped things wouldn't change too much.

3

I spent the rest of that week trying on various outfits and attempting a cool new style with my hair. I'd only get one chance to make a first impression on my grandmother, and I really wanted her to like me.

It was silly, but a small part of me thought that if I nailed my outward appearance, I could tip the scales in my favor. After all, I knew next to nothing about this woman. Only that the grandpa I hadn't known deemed her an unfit mother decades ago, and that the seagulls had hinted she might have strange abilities like mine. But how would I even be able to determine that? It's not like I could come right out and ask her such a bizarre question. All that hard work I was doing to look good would go—*whoosh*—right down the drain.

As it turned out, Charles had a busy week at work but was putting in early mornings and long nights at the office so he could leave a couple hours early on Friday. Together, we would head to Katahdin and this cute little bed-and-breakfast we had decided to book based on the online reviews.

Nan made a full-time job of avoiding me. Rather than joining me for morning coffee, she'd brew a pot and leave it on the counter so that I could heat it up in the microwave myself. Each day she had a different reason for being gone, but I knew they were all excuses.

I couldn't wait to punctuate this chapter of our lives with a big, fat period. We both needed to meet my missing grandmother and be done with it. The unknown that would come from this relationship had lingered over our heads for far too long.

With no new P.I. cases coming my way and every possible combination of clothing exhausted, I was quickly running out of ways to keep my hands and mind occupied. I attempted to lose myself in my favorite book series. But my brain was too busy with all its myriad questions to focus on the words before me.

I checked social media, even my long since defunct MySpace account. Yes, I was that desperate for ways to keep myself busy.

I just wanted to get this whole thing over with, but I also knew I wasn't strong enough to go on this crazy adventure by myself.

It was at that point a most excellent thought occurred to me. I could enlist the help of someone else to research my grandmother while I waited for my chance to go meet her in person. I had this thought on Wednesday—two days before Charles and I were scheduled to leave and three days before we'd actually get the chance to meet my grandmother, provided everything went well.

I had to do something to pass the long, anguish-filled hours, or I'd have found my grandmother but lost my mind.

Which brought me back to my would-be helper. She traveled a lot, but she was also the only person I knew with ties to the Katahdin area. And so I gave Sharon a call.

Sharon and her cat Chessy traveled up and down the coast in a luxury RV funded by their upcoming reality show. The cat was the real apple of the producer's eye, but he and his human came as a package deal.

When I first met Sharon at the RV park just last weekend, I'd mistakenly assumed she was a killer. Hey, sometimes that happened in my line of work.

Once I figured out that she was just a busybody without a single mean bone in said body, I actually grew to like her a lot. She'd been kind and welcoming to Charles, Octo-Cat, and me when no one else at the campsite had taken any efforts to get to know us. That made her good people in my book.

Also, busybodies and private investigators were pretty much a match made in heaven. True, I needed her insights on a personal matter, but that just made me all the more eager to recruit her to my cause.

Sharon picked up on the fourth ring. "Hello? Hello! Are you still there?" she shouted into the phone. "Oh, please don't tell me I'm too late! I just had to finish up in the bathroom, and— "

"Sharon," I interrupted, having to shout so she could hear me. "It's me, Angie. Do you remember meeting me last weekend?"

"Angie Russo, mother to one Octo-Cat and girlfriend to one of the most handsome fellas I've ever seen in all my life. Yes, hello, Angie. What can I do for you?"

"Actually, Charles and I are engaged now," I said as a delicious smile spread across my face.

Sharon crooned happily at this news and then started recounting every wedding she'd ever attended.

I had to interrupt her again. "Yes, yes, we're both very excited, and you'll definitely receive an invite, but that's not why I called."

She sucked in a deep breath and then let out a long, belabored "Ohhh?"

"Well, it's a long story," I admitted.

"Do go on." I could practically see her grabbing a snack and settling in at her RV's booth seat. "Long stories are my favorite kind."

And so I told her everything, leaving out any part that included talking animals, which was no small feat, let me tell you.

"So that's why I'm calling," I said after pausing only briefly so as not to invite any wild conversational tangents from her end. "To see if you can help me find out some info about my grandmother before I come out to meet her this weekend."

"Now who's this Bravo fella again? And why isn't he helping to fill in these details, seeing as he's the one who found her for you?"

"Just an old friend from... uh, Charles's time in the service." Well, that was almost true, except Charles's service was to a militarized flock of seagulls rather than an actual government body. "He had to fly out of town for a bit, but I'm wondering if you're still in Katahdin, maybe you could—?"

This time Sharon was the one to interrupt. "Darling, you just leave it to me. Tell me her name and whatever info you have, and I'll fill in the rest."

"Oh, so you are still there? Good!"

"No, but I'm turning this RV around and heading that way right now."

I loved this woman. Seriously, how had I ever seen her as anything but a friend? "Her name is Marilyn Jones," I said, picturing the old birth certificate Pringle had unearthed from the attic. "She's in her eighties and lived in Larkhaven, Georgia, at one point, but I don't know much more than that."

"You will," Sharon promised. "Just give me forty-eight hours."

"Perfect, because that's just about as much time as we have."

"You'll let me pay you a visit once you've checked in at Katahdin, won't you?"

"Sharon, thank you. Thank you so, so much."

"Don't fret it, honey. That's what friends are for. Plus, Chessy and I always did love a good mystery."

It was at this point I realized Sharon was basically me minus the boyfriend and plus a decade or two.

Honestly, I kind of loved that.

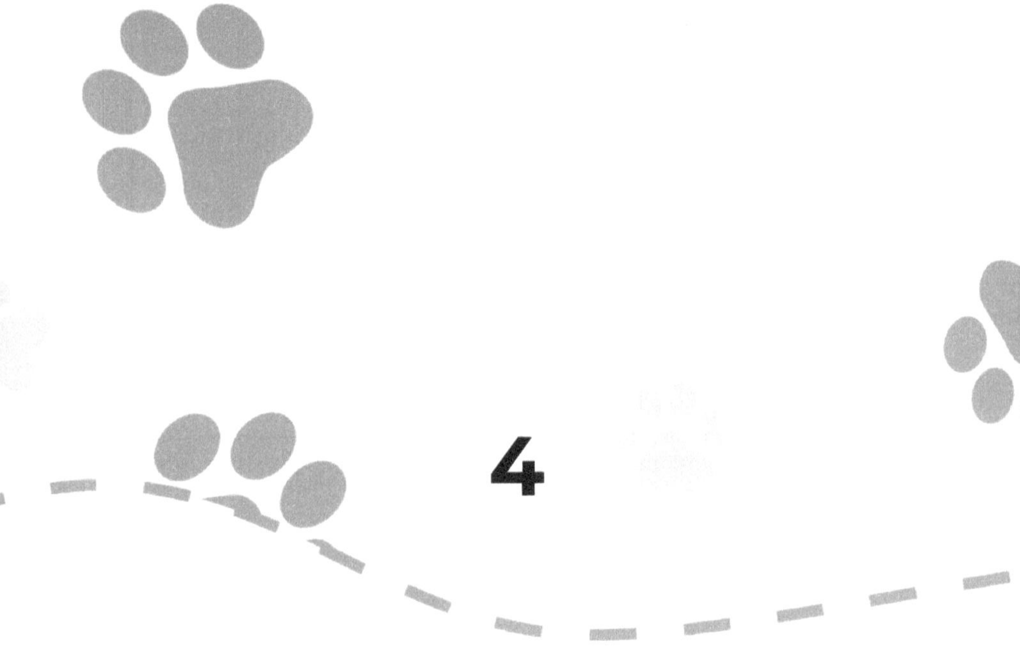

4

That Friday, I was like a kid at Christmas waiting for Santa. I couldn't eat. I couldn't sleep. I just sat on the living room couch, watching for Charles.

I knew he would pick me up between two and three so we could make it to the Katahdin area before rush-hour traffic hit, but I still planted myself on that couch as soon as I cracked an eye open after one very restless night of failed sleep.

Sharon and I played phone tag most of that morning. I was always it, trying to catch her. Even though she wasn't that old, she hated texting—said it took away that human connection society so desperately craved. Yeah, it's not what I would have expected to hear from an up-and-coming reality star, either.

She'd managed to unearth some info about my long-lost grandmother Marilyn Jones but was being coy about it. If conversations were meant for the phone, she reasoned, important ones should be had face-to-face. And no matter how hard I tried, I couldn't get her to reveal her findings otherwise. This meant our calls were solely about finalizing our plans for meeting up.

Once that was taken care of at last, I was left waiting for Charles with only Paisley at my side to stick it out. Nan, of course, had disappeared, as was becoming normal for her these days. Octo-Cat complained that he had not enjoyed his nightly feline excursions because of how restless I'd been. Apparently, whatever he did at night was completely ruined by the very thought of me blearily stumbling upon his antics. I didn't want to touch that one with a ten-foot cat toy, quite frankly.

"Is it time yet?" Paisley ruffed, hopping off my lap and pressing her paws into the back of the loveseat to peer out the window; her little tail beat furiously.

"Not yet," I said with a moan. This was at least the hundredth time she'd asked me that day, and every time I had to tell her 'not yet,' her ears fell back against her head and she let out a sad whine.

"Oh," she squeaked before sinking back onto the couch and curling into a tiny, shivering ball. As much as I hated to wait, I hated seeing her like this even more.

"I've got an idea," I said, putting on the happiest voice I could manage, given the current circumstances.

Her deer-shaped Chihuahua head popped up, over-sized triangle ears erect once again as she tilted her muzzle to the side.

"Let's play fetch," I said as I slapped my palms against my lap to make this declaration even more irresistible and exciting.

Paisley flew off the couch in an impressive display of athleticism, then slid across the hardwood floor until she found the small stash of toys she liked to keep tucked away. She pranced back over with a tiny stuffed lamb clenched proudly between her teeth.

"Good girl," I enthused. Octo-Cat hated being talked to like a baby or a pet, but Paisley lapped it right up.

She dropped the toy at my feet and began to kick her legs back in excitement, my sweet little chicken.

I picked up the toy, faked throwing it once or twice, and then launched it across the room.

Paisley scampered after it, barking the whole way.

I waited.

And waited.

When she didn't return after a full minute had passed, I got up to check on her...

And found Octo-Cat nestled on top of her hoard of toys with the little lamb clutched between his paws, claws extended and pressed right into the soft fleece.

"Why?" I demanded, thrusting a hand on my hip.

"You're anxious, which makes her anxious, which makes me anxious. It's a whole vicious cycle," the tabby said around a yawn. He let out a low growl as he so often liked to do when he was feeling testy, which was almost all the time. "I'm ending it here."

"No, you're only making things worse," I countered, reaching down to snag Paisley's toy from him.

Octo-Cat growled again and batted my hand away. He didn't even bother to retract his claws first.

Paisley began to bark and kick back her feet again. Unlike Octo-Cat, who always had something to say, Paisley sometimes stuck to the pure guttural sounds of barking, whining, and woofing—no added context necessary.

"Ouch," I cried, ripping my hand away. "Why do you have to be so mean?"

"It's for your own good," he answered, eyes narrowed and tail flicking. That thing was like a metronome, steadily counting the beats until his next tantrum.

I narrowed my eyes right back at him and crossed my arms over my chest. "No, it's not."

"Fine, whatever." He sighed mightily, as if this very conversation were miles beneath him. "It just makes life more interesting, you know?"

I rolled my eyes. Why could he never give me a day off from his signature snark? And it was even worse when he admitted that he bugged me simply for entertainment's sake.

"Well, I don't exactly need your help with that," I muttered through clenched teeth.

"Because waiting by the window for Prince Charming to ride up on that white horse and rescue you from your boredom is oh-so riveting?" Octo-Cat shook his head then sneezed.

"I knew I shouldn't have let you subscribe to Disney+," I shouted in a huff.

He let out a laugh worthy of a classic animated villain but refused to relent.

"Sorry, Paize," I said at last, drifting away from the bad kitty and taking up my seat by the window once more.

Did my cat have a point? *Yes.*

Would I ever admit that to him? *Oh, heck no!*

Doing so would only make his sizable head even bigger. That cat was already vain enough without any added assistance from me.

"I'm coming, by the way," the feline bully informed me once Paisley had finally stopped barking at him and come to settle on my lap. He walked over, placing one foot carefully in front of the other, tail and nose both held high. I imagined him on a tight rope in the jungle with angry crocs snapping underneath, but that only made me feel marginally better.

"Who says you're coming?" I demanded, blinking hard to clear my eyes of the imaginary crocs.

"I do, and as you know, I'm the highest authority on this and all other matters." He jumped up onto the coffee table and sat before me, padding at the polished wood as if it were a warm blanket.

"Why do you even want to come? Remember how you used to hate the car? What happened to that?"

"What can I say? I'm evolving. It's possible for some, though not for others." He shot a sideways glance at Paisley and sneered.

Sometimes I really questioned his love for her, but he liked the little pound puppy as much as he could like anyone, I guessed.

I waited for him to go on rather than pointing out the slight to Paisley. It would only hurt her feelings.

He sighed when I didn't take the bait. "Okay, maybe Pringle got me somewhat invested in his reality TV programming."

"So you're going because you want to see Sharon and Chessy again?" He'd hated meeting them both last weekend, so this made zero sense to me.

Octo-Cat made a terrible noise like he was about to barf on the carpet.

And then he actually did it.

"Eww, gross!" I cried. "What is wrong with you?"

He chuckled. "Oh, it's not about what's wrong with me. This time it's about that whole messed up family dynamic you have going on, and I refuse to miss out on the big reveal."

"So glad I have your support," I mumbled, then went to get a roll of paper towels to take care of his mess.

If there was one thing my cat excelled at, it was adding the occasional injury to the steady stream of insults that worked their way off that sandpaper tongue.

Sometimes I really wished he would find a hobby.

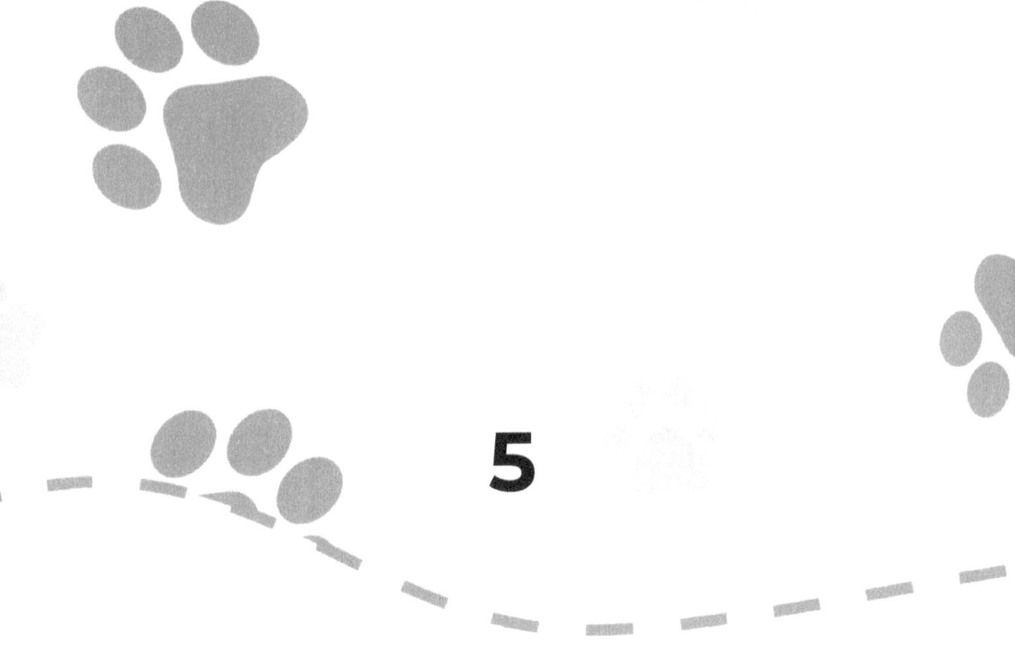

5

"So how did you find this place again?" I asked Charles as we rolled up to a small bed-and-breakfast that sat near the shores of a beautiful lake. We'd elected to stay a short way out of Katahdin proper because Charles and I both liked it best when we were near the water—him being a California boy, me a Maine girl.

"One of the associates at work told me about this site that only lists hotels and rentals where pets are allowed," he explained as he pulled to a stop in the small gravel parking lot out front. "I filtered by waterfront properties, and this was the closest property with a vacancy. It also had decent reviews, so I figured why not?"

"Decent, huh?" I asked, raising one eyebrow in extreme suspicion.

"Yeah, but don't read too much into that. You know how

online reviews can be." He paused for a moment, regarding me carefully. "Not everything is a mystery just waiting to be solved."

"Says you," I shot back as I unbuckled my seatbelt and clambered out of the car. I held the door open so that Paisley and Octo-Cat could hop out, too.

"I love it here!" Paisley cried and then took off running in wide, looping circles. "Wheeeee!"

"Why did we bring her again?" Octo-Cat demanded of me with a sneer.

I didn't get a chance to answer, though, because Paisley zipped and zoomed out of view. I was just about to call her back when a sharp yelp rent the air. We all took off running in pursuit of the sound.

Octo-Cat moved the fastest out of the three of us, which meant he was first on the scene. I couldn't see anything, but I heard a mighty hiss followed by a low, ominous growl. When I finally rounded the corner, I found my tabby in a beach stand-off with an enormous orange Persian.

Paisley cowered behind Octo-Cat, shaking violently as the two cats stared each other down.

"Nobody hurts my kid sister," Octo-Cat hissed at the strange feline.

The orange Persian extended his claws and took a swipe at Octo's face.

"You s-st-struck me?" he sputtered in shock. "You actually struck me?"

The Persian wore a satisfied expression on his flat face.

"Maybe next time you'll remember who lives here and who's simply an unwelcome intruder," he said, then raised his tail high and sauntered off down the sandy beach.

"That does it! I'll end him! I'll— "

I grabbed Octo-Cat in my arms before the fight could escalate any further. The last thing we needed was to get kicked out of our accommodation before I even had a chance to meet my grandma.

"Be the bigger person," I said through gritted teeth.

"There's so much wrong with that statement I don't even know where to begin," my cat shot back. "Just keep that giant, fluffy wad of mouse breath away from me."

Funny how much he hated this cat with its long hair and flat face, when his true love Grizabella was a former show Himalayan and looked quite similar if you ignored the coloration. I guessed that meant my cat wasn't a breedist, and that was a good thing for sure.

"I'm sorry, Mommy," Paisley ground out, coming to stand at my feet. "I was just so happy to be out of the car."

"It's fine. It's not either of your faults. Just calm down and try to put it out of your mind," I cooed.

Charles grabbed Paisley and clutched her against his chest. "Everything okay?" he said, expression askance.

"It will be," I assured them all. "It's just been a long week for all of us."

"So we're staying?" Charles wanted to confirm.

"We're staying," I said with a tight nod, then motioned for everyone to head back the way we'd come. "Let's go check in to our room. Sharon will be here soon, and I want some time to get ourselves set up first."

Charles and I entered the sprawling ranch, each carrying an agitated pet in our arms. Just past the door, we found an elderly woman with dyed orange hair that matched the mean Persian cat's to the exact shade.

"I've been expecting you," she said, uncrossing her legs and placing the paperback novel she'd been reading face-down on the arm of her chair. "Mr. and Mrs. Longfellow, I presume?"

I smiled at that. It was the first time I'd ever heard it aloud, and I rather liked the sound.

"Almost," Charles said with a huge grin to match mine. "For now, it's Mr. Longfellow and Ms. Russo."

"I see," the woman said, tightening her expression. She drifted over to a desk at the corner of the room. "I'll just update your reservation from a king to two doubles then. That's an easy enough fix."

Charles looked like he wanted to say something, but I nudged him in the side and shook my head. Separate beds would make the sleeping situation with the pets much easier anyway, since Octo-Cat threw a right proper fit whenever Paisley tried to snuggle up to him.

"My name is Millicent Strobel," the woman droned, handing us the keys to our room. "I can normally be found here in the front room if you need anything. We don't have room service, but I do serve breakfast from five thirty until eight o'clock."

Wow, that was early, but I doubted I'd be able to sleep well tonight, anyway.

My guess was that the B and B lady gave this same spiel to all her guests, considering the dry, bored way she addressed us.

"Thank you, Millie," I said when it became clear Millicent expected us to say something in response.

"No," she corrected harshly, taking the opportunity to look us both up and down and shaking her head in apparent disappointment. "Don't do that. It's Millicent to you. Or better yet, Mrs. Strobel. Now if you don't mind."

I said nothing as she resettled herself in the chair and returned to her book.

With that dismissal, we left her behind as quickly as possible —for one, because she obviously was done with us, but also because Octo-Cat had begun to weigh heavily in my arms.

"Well, I think we solved the mystery of the reviews." Charles set Paisley on the floor so he could wrestle the doorknob with both hands. "I think it's stu—Oh, there it goes," he said when the door finally popped out.

"Jeez. For a minute there, I thought this was her way of getting rid of us."

Octo-Cat sniffed hesitantly around the room, his tail almost a bristle brush of aggravation. "I wish she would've," he snarked. "This place smells awful."

"Hush, you," I admonished with a scowl.

"Whatever," my spoiled kitty shot back. "This one will be my bed." He hopped up on the bed farthest the door and promptly laid out, stretching so as to take up as much of the mattress as possible.

I rolled my eyes, but he was too busy enjoying the soft bed to notice.

"Can I go out?" Paisley asked, scratching at the doorframe.

"Stay close," I warned before sliding open the glass door that led out to the beautifully manicured property. "You don't want to run into that mean kitty again."

"Yes, Mommy! I will, Mommy!" she called before taking off at full speed once more.

Charles took me in his arms. "Alone at last," he said, giving me a slow, lingering kiss.

"Kill me now!" Octo-Cat yelled.

Yup, this would definitely not be a romantic weekend. Not unless we got our cat his own room, and I just didn't have that in the budget, unfortunately.

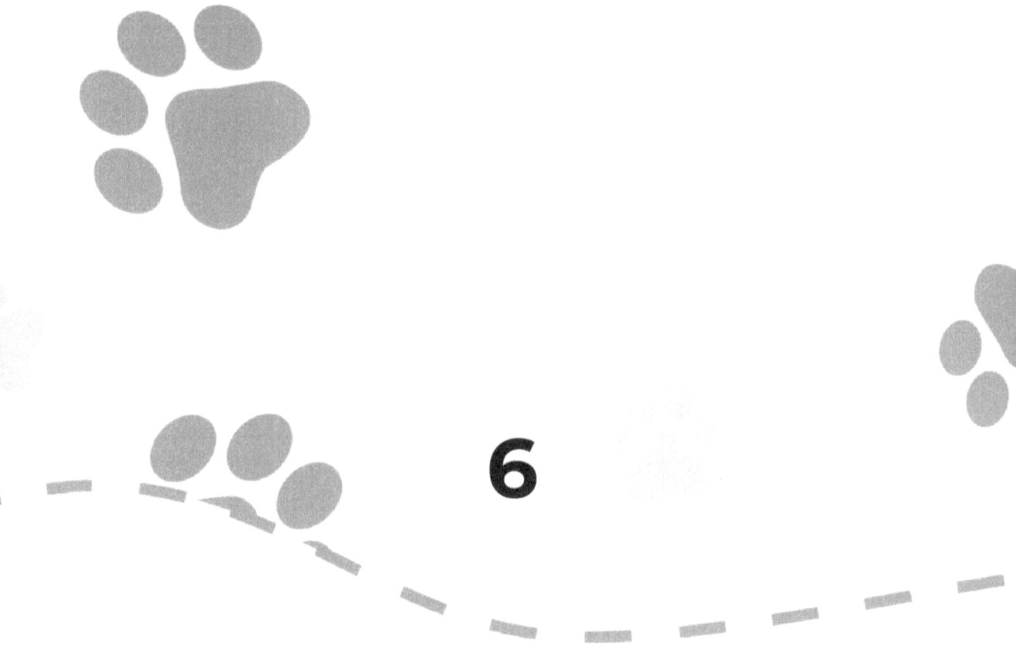

6

"Knock, knock." Sharon's singsong voice floated into our room a short while later. I turned and saw her standing outside the glass sliding door that separated our bedroom from a short walk down to the lake and its sandy beaches.

Charles yanked on the handle to open the door, and I rushed out to give her a big, fat hug. Once we'd given each other a good squeeze, I pulled back and studied her face for any hints as to what she'd learned about my missing grandmother.

She simply raised a finger and shook it at me. "First let's get this picnic situated, and then we can dish."

I followed her eyes toward a nearby pair of Adirondack chairs with a small wooden plank table nestled between them. On the table sat a beautiful wicker picnic basket. When Sharon said she'd be bringing dinner, I had assumed she'd pick up a pizza or something easy. I hoped she hadn't gone to too much trouble, considering I'd already called in a huge favor from her, and our acquaintanceship was hardly even a week old.

"Oh, don't you worry," she said as if reading my mind. "It's just my newly famous lobster rolls and bisque. I'm staying away from desserts of all sorts after what happened to our poor Junetta."

I nodded stoically. It wasn't Sharon's fault that someone else had placed poison in her pie, but clearly the affront had taken a toll on her all the same.

"Lobster rolls!" Octo-Cat cried before zipping through the door. "No way I'm missing this!"

Paisley came surging forward from places unknown to chase after him.

"So just a light meal then," Charles quipped as he closed up our room and then plucked the basket from the table.

"Oh, you!" Sharon trilled and hit him playfully on the chest. She wasn't kidding about her attraction to him. Thankfully, I didn't feel even the slightest bit jealous. I knew Charles's heart—and his future—were all mine.

The three of us walked down to the beach, both animals circling back to follow close at our heels.

"Where's Chessy?" I asked, remembering how inseparable Sharon had been from her fluffy white cat when last we met.

"He's staying back in the RV. I just could not get him to agree to the harness today, and he's not well-behaved like your Octavius. He'd run away in a heartbeat if he could. That little man of mine has an adventurer's heart, let me tell you." When Sharon chuckled, her billowing duster cardigan and loosely wrapped pashmina twirled around her hips and thighs.

"Well, at least one cat around here has some sense," Octo-Cat muttered, presumably referring to that Persian from earlier.

"Mommy, that mean cat won't bother us again, will he?" Paisley barked.

I shook my head, unable to answer in mixed company. I really liked Sharon, but she was a gossip *and* a future reality star. If she got word of my special abilities, they'd no doubt become front-page news at some national rag before even a full day could pass.

We reached the beach, and Sharon slipped out of her sandals, sighing happily as her painted toes sunk into the sand. "Still a bit early in the season, but, oh, it's nice."

Charles and I followed suit and padded after her with our bare feet as Paisley splashed around in the ebbing surf and Octo-Cat trotted after us from several yards up shore, refusing to get anywhere near the water.

"It's like one giant litter box out here," he mused. "It would be perfect if not for all the water."

We stopped at an old wooden dock with a paddle boat tethered to either side. Sharon traipsed to the very end and then sat with her legs dangling toward the water.

"I hope you don't mind, I made some supper for the critters, too." She opened up the basket and handed me a lobster roll wrapped snugly in wax paper.

"Oh, yeah." Octo-Cat quivered, his eyes growing comically wide. "Come to papa, you delicious little thing."

I opened the savory-smelling package and set it on the dock in front of him, but Sharon reached over me and scooped it away before my gluttonous cat could manage so much as a single sniff.

"Almost lost your sandwich there!" she said breathlessly, then dipped her hand into the basket and pulled out a much smaller parcel. "*This* is for Octavius."

I popped the lid off the small Tupperware container and set it down beside me, trying to keep my expression neutral.

"What fresh torment is this?" he snarled and stared daggers at both me and Sharon.

Paisley skipped over and stuck her snout in the mush Sharon had prepared for Octo-Cat. It appeared to be canned cat food slathered on a special type of cracker.

"Seafood medley on my own special snack biscuit recipe. Chessy loves it."

"Chessy doesn't have a choice, but I do." Octo-Cat lunged at Sharon, causing her to drop the lobster roll she'd just narrowly saved from him before.

He grabbed it between those sharp, greedy teeth of his and took off running. Paisley used that opportunity to gulp down the specialty cat sandwich. Charles laughed, while Sharon looked like she was going to cry.

"It's okay," I said softly. "I'm much more of a bisque girl myself. I can't wait to try yours."

And with that, her eyes grew bright again. She talked me and

Charles through the process of developing her new recipe as she ladled out a serving for each of us.

I listened to every single word, taking slow, contemplative spoonfuls into my mouth. The soup was rich and creamy, filling my stomach perfectly without the help of an added course.

I was grateful for the hot meal but had a hard time following the conversation when there was only one topic I wanted to discuss with Sharon.

When she finally paused to take a bite of her own meal, I saw my chance to get us back to the reason we'd all gathered there that night.

"So about my grandmother..." I started, then bit my lip and waited.

7

Sharon cleared her throat as she wrapped up her uneaten lobster roll and placed it back into the picnic basket. "Oh, sorry. Did you want this?" she offered with an uncharacteristic flush on her cheeks.

"Is it really that bad?" I choked out. Suddenly my chest felt heavy with the weight of an unknown shame. I'd asked for Sharon's help because I was bursting with curiosity—not because I actually expected her to find something terrible about my missing family member.

Charles scooted along the dock until our hips were touching and then wrapped an arm around my shoulders. "I'm sure it's nothing too big," he reassured me.

Sharon cleared her throat again. "Welllllll." She twisted her hands in her lap and refused to meet my eye, instead gazing out across the lake as the gentle ripples reflected the sunlight.

"Please just tell me," I begged. My stomach threatened to give up the bisque that I'd just filled it with. "I need to know," I added softly. "Please don't make me wait any longer."

Sharon nodded; a tuft of her short blonde hair caught the breeze and flickered distractingly. "It took me a while to find out much of anything. She's changed her name, you see."

"Oh, so she remarried?" Charles asked brightly, drumming his fingers against my upper arm. "I mean, that's probably to be expected seeing as it's been about sixty years."

"Her first name," Sharon corrected.

At the same time, I said, "She and my grand-dad were never married. He was a McAllister. She was a Jones."

"She still is a Jones," Sharon murmured. "She was born Marilyn. Then went by Mary for a spell, and now she's Lyn."

"So she switched up her nickname? A lot of people do that, right?" Charles reasoned, always so optimistic. I honestly didn't know how he did it.

"Actually, she switched up her legal name. It took some digging to find all those iterations belonged to the same person." She paused and drew in several deep breaths.

What was coming next? I almost couldn't stand the anticipation, no matter how brief my wait.

"Luckily—or perhaps unluckily," Sharon continued with a sigh, "she was in the papers a lot, your grandmother."

Charles tensed at my side, tightening his grip on my shoulder. "Why?"

"She's lived a troubled life," Sharon said with a grimace.

"She's done a few rounds in prison. A few in the psychiatric ward. Seems to be a bit of a bad egg."

I stumbled to my feet. Perhaps Sharon wasn't the friend I'd thought she was. That was my fault for trusting a near stranger with something so important.

"What? Why? Why would you say that?" I demanded, feeling outraged on behalf of a woman I'd never even met. Sharon was saying my grandmother was a bad egg, and well, we were from the same nest.

"I don't know. The records are sealed, but I could see she got picked up once every few years. Did small amounts of time in prison, until suddenly they started sending her to the asylum instead."

"Not guilty by way of insanity," Charles murmured.

"Also, it's not called that anymore," I added spitefully.

"Sorry, I guess I'm a bit old-fashioned, and I know that's not always a good thing. I don't mean to make you feel bad, hunny bunny," Sharon said, softening my reaction to her harsh choice of words. But then she said, "I don't think you're crazy, even if your grandmother is."

I turned toward Charles with wide eyes. "Do you think she's dangerous? Is that why my grandfather kidnapped his own child? To keep my mom safe?"

He shook his head slowly but didn't glance up to meet my gaze. "I wish I had the answers for you, but there's only one person we can really ask."

"I found her number," Sharon said, pulling out a business

card that she'd kept tucked in her jeans pocket. It had Sharon's info on one side and another number scrawled with a failing ink pen on the back. She handed the card to me, and I read the string of numbers over again and again. I didn't recognize the area code, suggesting she probably moved around a fair bit, too—or had at least moved somewhat recently, even before she'd arrived in Maine.

That checked out, since the seagulls had eyes on her in the Blueberry Bay area but then lost her temporarily when she moved to Katahdin.

Just where had she lived before? And how many different places had she ended up over the years? I knew she'd lived in Larkhaven, Georgia, when my mom was born and caught up with Nan in New York when Mom was a pre-teen. But where else had she journeyed these long years apart?

"It's a California area code," Charles informed us. "A couple counties over from where I grew up."

"I wonder when she lived there," I said, turning the card over in my hand with a frown. There was so much I didn't know about this person—this stranger. Even though we shared some DNA, I knew absolutely nothing about her. Was I crazy for pursuing this?

"Are you going to call her?" Sharon prompted, nodding toward my hands.

I took a deep breath, then nodded slowly. Yes, maybe I was a little nuts, but I'd never considered that a bad thing before. "I've come this far. No sense in giving up now."

I misdialed twice before I finally got it right, and then the phone rang twice, three times... seven, eight. Nobody answered, not even the voicemail service.

"Now what?" I asked Charles as tears threatened to spill. I kept pumping myself up, only to be let down. All that adrenaline coursing through my veins didn't just go away. I stayed keyed up for hours after each near encounter with my grandmother. I had to meet her—and soon—for my own sanity.

"Don't worry. We'll find her," he promised.

"I'm sorry I couldn't be of more help," Sharon said gently as she struggled to her feet and opened her arms to invite a hug. "I really wanted to have good news to give you."

"It's okay," I said, hugging her once more. I couldn't be mad at her. Not about this. Not about anything, really. It was just so hard to keep my emotions straight given how many highs and lows I'd experienced lately. I needed...

I wasn't sure what I needed, but I had to figure that one out for myself.

"I appreciate the help," I told Sharon, then turned to look at Charles as well, "but if it's all right with you, I think I need some time to sit alone with my thoughts."

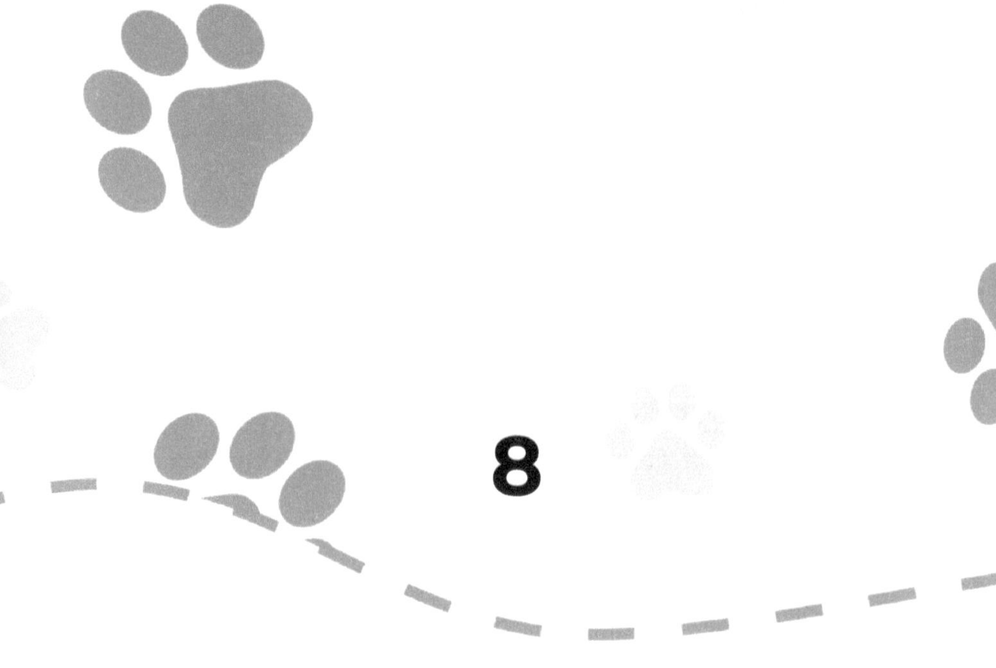

8

Charles and I escorted Sharon to her car before returning to the B and B via the main reception area.

Millicent still sat in that same chair, eyes glued to the pages of her book. I don't even think she noticed us come through—something I was grateful for.

"I know I shouldn't say this, but I can't wait for this whole thing to be over," I murmured to Charles as he fiddled with the lock and key.

"You can say and feel however you want, Ang. It's all perfectly understandable," he assured me with a sad smile, continuing to struggle with the doorknob.

Octo-Cat moaned. "I could open that thing ten times as fast, and I don't even have opposable thumbs." He and Paisley had rejoined us on the walk to the parking lot, and neither seemed any worse for the wear—which probably meant that mean old Persian was off troubling somebody else for the moment.

“Be nice,” the little dog yipped. “He’s doing the best he can. Right, Mommy?”

“Well, clearly UpChuck’s best isn’t quite good enough, is it?” came the cat’s snide reply.

I pressed my fingers into my temples and rubbed. “Ugh. I thought we’d moved past that horrible nickname.”

“What?” Charles asked with a furrowed brow.

“Here. Let me help,” I said rather than answering his actual question.

I took over and struggled for a couple moments before finally wresting the lock open. Another couple—old and married from what I could tell—came down the hallway and entered their room with no problem.

“I bet that was the room we were supposed to have,” I whispered to Charles. We both rolled our eyes.

The door eased open, catching me by surprise when it finally gave way.

“Took you long enough!” Octo-Cat said, heaving a dramatic sigh as he entered the room. “Seriously, humans. What are they even good for?”

I walked in behind him and was surprised to feel a chilly wind rush past.

“Charles, I thought you closed that.” I said, flopping over on the bed nearest the door, since Octo-Cat had made it clear none of us were to mess with *his* bed.

"I thought I had," he said, going over to secure the sliding door once again.

I could hear a soft swish as he flipped the lock latch back and forth. He opened and closed the glass door a few more times before turning back to face me.

"That's odd," he muttered.

"What is?" I asked, sitting up and petting Paisley as she climbed into my lap.

"This latch system doesn't work."

"So the door just slid open on its own?"

He nodded before coming over to join me on the bed. "Seems like it. I guess we can jam something in there to hold it before we go back out again."

"Isn't it kind of weird that one lock works too well and the other not at all?" I asked, quirking my head to the side.

Charles sunk onto the bed next to me and pulled me into his side. "Not weird. Just a simple coincidence. Now you said you needed some time alone with your thoughts. Did you mean alone together or *alone* alone?"

"Would it be all right if I had just a little bit of time to myself?" I asked with an apologetic grimace. It was strange how I'd been craving his company all week, and now that we were finally together, I needed to ask for space. It was nothing against Charles, of course. But Sharon had dropped a doozy on me. No wonder she hadn't wanted to tell me over the phone.

My fiancé pressed a firm kiss into my hairline. "Tell you what, you get some rest, and I'll head out to see if I can make some sense of Bravo's directions. Can you text those to me again?"

I breathed a happy sigh of relief. "That would be wonderful. Thank you for understanding. I grabbed my phone from the nightstand and brought up the notes app. I'd recorded the seagull's guidance there, and now I copy-pasted it into a fresh text for Charles.

Initially, Bravo had said he would take me to my grandmother, which I thought meant he'd be joining us for the trip.

Nope.

He actually meant he would take us there with his words. One thing I'd learned in all my conversations with animals is that every single species had a different way of viewing the world. I had the least experience with birds, given their flighty nature, but I figured between me, Charles, and the pets, we'd be able to find our way.

I pushed the button to send my text, and Charles's phone pinged a couple of seconds later.

He cleared his throat, then read aloud. "'Follow the water until the air begins to chill. Stop at the green dumpster with the good fries.' The good fries? What's good to a seagull? Oh, here we go. 'Follow the scent of fish several leagues until you reach a tan building with loose trash can lids. The dogs to the south have been restrained, so eat all you want. Short hops from here through the human encampment. Approach in a zigzag to avoid floodlights and bad air. Cross the dead river and find the target amongst the stick-colored domiciles with pink sentinels standing guard…' Seriously?" he asked with a chuff once he'd gotten to the end. "None of this makes any sense."

"He worked hard on those directions. If I had asked for clarification I would have offended him," I said with a tight-lipped smile. "Anyway, they're from a bird's-eye view. They don't think of things the way we do, so of course they don't describe them that way, either."

"I can't wait to eat the good fries!" Paisley chimed in, making me giggle.

But Charles still appeared quite frazzled. "Is she even in Katahdin at all? Do we know for sure?"

"Bravo said she was, but this isn't anywhere near his flock's territories, so I doubt he knows the actual boundaries."

"Right, so it's a wild goose chase—er, a wild seagull chase—for me. But it'll be fine. I can figure this out. I just have to think like the witness, put myself in his… wings, I guess. I've got this, babe. Enjoy your downtime. Call if you need me, and I'll come straight back."

"Thank you. I love you," I called after him. I really needed this. Of course, I wasn't properly on my own, thanks to the pets.

Octo-Cat had already fallen asleep on the pillow at the head of his bed while Paisley wagged her tail and licked between my fingers. "What now, Mommy?" she asked.

I had to think fast to come up with a valid excuse to be on my own, otherwise her feelings would be deeply hurt. I glanced around the room, landing on the door to the en suite bathroom. "Um, I'm just going to take a nice bubble bath."

"Okay, Mommy! What will I do?" she asked, cocking her head to the side.

"Why don't you curl up and take a nap with Octo-Cat?" I said, picking her up as I stood and then setting her onto the other bed beside the crabby tabby. When he woke up, he was going to be livid. Luckily, I'd already be locked safely away in the next room —provided that lock worked at all. Just to be safe, I crept back into the main room and grabbed my cell phone and bathrobe. That way I'd be prepared if I got stuck and needed to get someone to help me out.

Back in the bedroom, dear, sweet Paisley had wrapped herself around Octo-Cat so that he was the little spoon and she was the big spoon. Never mind that he was more than twice her size. It made for a comical picture, and I snapped a quick photo on my phone before leaving the pets to themselves and retreating to the bathroom to draw my bath.

What an adventure this was shaping up to be already. And no matter how things turned out with my long-lost grandmother, I doubted I'd ever be able to forget even the slightest bit of our journey to find her.

But oh, how I hoped this would end with a happily ever after.

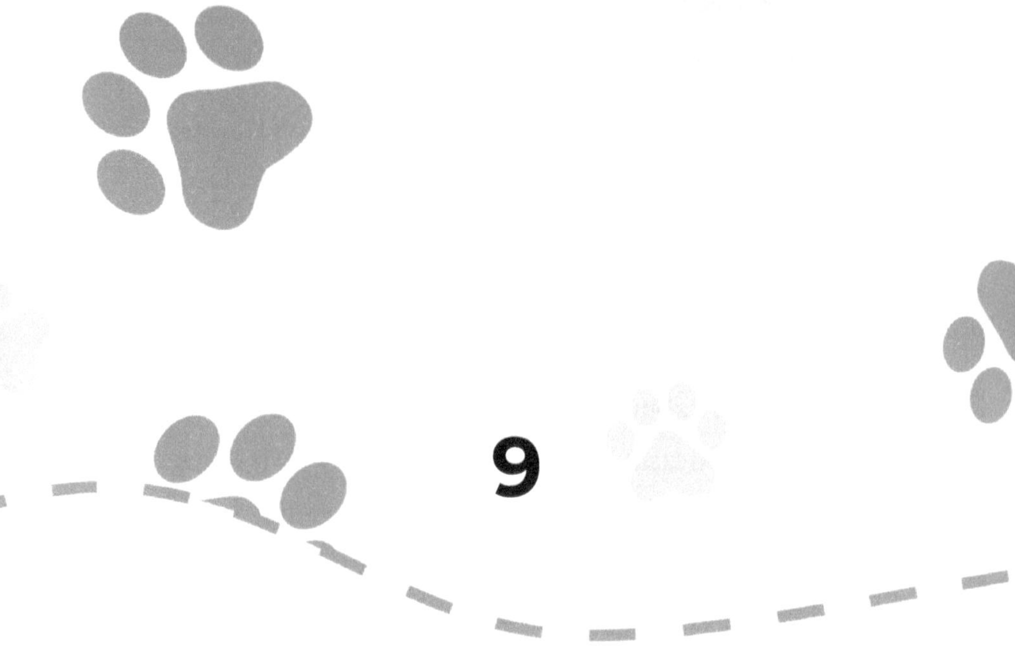

9

Evening gave way to night.

I trusted Sharon and the info she had located on my behalf, but there had to be more to the story. Deep down, I knew my grandmother couldn't be bad. At least that's what I told myself over and over again as I soaked in that claw-foot tub filled past the brim with bubbles.

Eventually, I gave up on relaxing in the bath and tiptoed into the bedroom to try to catch a nap. Cat and dog were both still curled together and snoozing softly, which meant I might actually stand a chance of grabbing some shut-eye. Heavens knew I needed it after the terrible sleep I'd gotten the night before.

I slid off my diamond engagement ring and placed it on the nightstand beside my phone, then pulled the quilt to my chin and shut my eyes. It didn't take long at all for me to nod off.

I awoke later when Charles returned via the sliding glass door. The room now lay in complete darkness other than the faint glow from his cell phone.

"Sorry, didn't mean to wake you," he whispered as he made his way over to the bed and began to grope for the lamp. "We forgot to jam up the door like we said, and I was having trouble with the lock and key again. Go back to sleep."

"It's okay. I'm up now," I mumbled, helping him with the lamp. Our hands collided, and something went skittering to the hardwood floor below.

"Oops," I said.

Charles dove to the floor so I didn't have to.

I glanced at the empty nightstand just as he popped up with my phone in hand.

"Can you grab my ring, too?" I asked, accepting the cell phone from him.

He returned to his hands and knees and searched under both beds. "Ang, I don't see it down here."

"But it's gotta be there. I took it off before my nap and put it right by my cell phone," I argued, getting out of bed to help.

We searched for a good five minutes but both came up short. So I decided to ask the cat for help—a decision I did not take lightly, but this was my engagement ring, after all.

"Octo-Cat, have you seen my ring?" I said, right after I picked up Paisley and removed any evidence of their shared nap. He'd never tell me a thing if he discovered what I'd let happen. He had a huge soft spot for the tiny rescue dog, but rarely was it enough to overcome the selfishness that came standard issue with his being an upper-middle-class cat.

"I've seen it," he answered around a yawn. "Nothing special, if you ask me, but then again, neither is UpChuck."

I pulled the pillow out from under him, and he rolled onto the mattress.

"Give that back," he moaned.

"Take what you said back," I demanded.

"No."

"Where's my ring?"

"I don't know."

"Yes, you do. You clearly have it out for Charles, so it makes sense you'd try to sabotage our wedding by—"

"I've had enough," he spat, popping to his feet. "Call me when you come to your senses. C'mon, Mutt."

Paisley looked at me with wide, shimmering eyes.

"Go," I said. "Keep him out of trouble."

She wasted no time scampering after him as Charles crossed the room and opened the sliding door, allowing both animals to disappear into the night.

"It's really not here, is it?" I said, staring hatefully at my bare ring finger. How had I lived with it like this for so long? Darn it, I never should have taken that ring off.

"Let's go check in with reception," Charles suggested, moving toward the wooden door on the other side of our room. At least it was easy to open from the inside. "I saw Millicent was still up when I came through that way."

Sure enough, Millicent sat in her chair with her book. At this point, I had to question whether our proprietress was, indeed, an art installation and not a businesswoman.

"Excuse me?" I said, stopping in front of her.

She held up a finger and continued reading for at least a minute before she finally raised her eyes to meet mine. "Yes?" Her eyes were wide, her expression mostly blank.

"Has anyone turned in a ring for the lost and found?"

"We don't have a lost and found," she replied with no follow-up questions and no hint of apology.

The fluffy orange cat hopped up onto a nearby windowsill to glare at me and Charles. Maybe all my time with Octo-Cat had made me cynical, or maybe I was still miffed about him bullying little Paisley, but something seemed off about him.

"Oh. Well, I have a lost item. A pretty important one at that."

"I'll let you know if anything turns up," Millicent said, tucking an orange curl behind her ear and revealing an earring I hadn't noticed her wearing before—a big dangly one with a little gemmed tassel.

The Persian's eyes zoomed toward the gaudy piece of costume jewelry, and he wiggled his behind as if to attack.

"Not now, Louis," the lady told him. He growled and ran across the room to hide. Poor cat must've been starved for stimulation if he got so worked up over earrings.

"Yeah, well, thanks for your help," I mumbled, wondering if Millicent would even remember having our conversation.

"Oh, while we have you," Charles interjected, waving his hand in front of her.

Millicent groaned and tore her eyes from the book a second time. "What is it now?"

"There seems to be a problem with the door to our room."

She bobbed her head and shifted her jaw. "Uh-huh. Which one?"

"Both, actually," he said with a chuckle. "One doesn't open, and the other doesn't close."

"Oh, right. I put you in the Shoreline suite. The locksmith should be here early next week to fix both of them. I wasn't going to book anyone in until that was taken care of, but then you two showed up with your little problem, and well, I had to do something to set it right."

Charles's brow furrowed. I could see he was about to go into full-on lawyer mode if I didn't do something fast. "But—"

"Yup! Okay, thanks," I said, grabbing him by the hand and leading him back around outside.

"I don't think she likes us very much," he said once we were both outdoors and out of earshot.

"Who would?" a nasty voice spat.

I looked around and found the big, orange Persian from earlier slinking by. Louis, that was the little scamp's name.

I tamped down my urge to scold him like I would whenever

Octo-Cat took up an attitude with me and refocused my attention on Charles.

"Care for a moonlight walk on the beach?" he said, waggling his brows.

"I thought you'd never ask," I said, falling into step beside him as we strolled outside and headed for the water.

"This would have probably been a better proposal than the RV, huh?"

"I liked your proposal," I said, stretching up to give him a quick kiss.

"If you liked that, you'll really like this. I'm pretty sure I found your grandmother."

I gasped. "Really? Where?" It's not that this news surprised me. It just made me so, so happy.

"Oh, no no no," he tsked playfully. "You don't get to jump to the end of the journey after sending me on that seagull chase."

He moved to regale me with tales of his heroic exploits as he tooled all around the Katahdin area, trying to make heads and tails of Bravo's directions. "I may have had to sample a few different fries to help me determine which were the good ones. Well, according to a seagull, anyway."

"Eww, you ate out of the dumpster?"

He fixed me with a wounded expression. "Drive-thru, but thanks for assuming that."

We both laughed for a good long while as we slowly moved along the beach, hand in hand beneath the night sky.

Everything would be okay. I knew it then. I'm pretty sure I'd known it this whole time, but it was easy to forget when my nerves got the best of me.

With Charles at my side, I could conquer anything. We'd meet my grandmother and find my ring.

We just had to take one thing at a time.

One foot in front of the other.

Yes, everything would be just fine.

10

I had another rough night of sleep. Coming here had only added to my worries. It's not like I expected to find instant relief just knowing I was near to my grandmother, but every time I was left alone to my thoughts, dread prevailed.

The walk with Charles on the beach had put my mind at ease, but as soon as he drifted to sleep, the swirling cyclone of anxiety wreaked havoc once more.

Sharon's news had set me on edge, and now every new inconvenience—whether big or small—pushed me closer and close to my falling point.

Quarreling animals.

A rude proprietress.

My missing ring.

The unlatchable door.

That last one really irked me. Generally, Maine was a safe

place to be, but I didn't like the thought that just anyone could walk off the street and accost us while we were sleeping.

Since I couldn't sleep anyway, I decided to research the bed-and-breakfast online. First I checked the site Charles had used to book our stay, where our host had a 3.5-star average. Some of the less favorable reviews mentioned how rude and off-putting Millicent had been toward them during their stay, but most of the negative remarks centered around far more mundane things—an uncleaned room, cat barf in the hallway, not enough gluten-free breakfast options.

Feeling somewhat justified in my disdain for Mrs. Strobel, I decided to dig deeper, moving on to the more well-known travel sites to see what I could find in the much larger sampling of guest feedback there. One of the more recent reviews actually mentioned the faulty door we'd gotten stuck with. I read on with interest. That was two weeks ago, and still Millicent hadn't bothered to fix the issue. I wondered if she even planned to fix it at all.

How far back did this issue go?

I did a search for "door" within the reviews and found three others that mentioned it. One was written several months ago. It also mentioned an antique brooch that had gone missing. I searched for "missing," "stolen," and other synonyms and found four more reviewers who had lost something valuable while staying in this bed-and-breakfast.

Was Millicent a thief? Were those gaudy earrings I'd noticed earlier taken from an unwitting guest?

And had Millicent moved Charles and me to this room with

two double beds not out of judgment but rather to gain access to my engagement ring?

These were the questions on my mind when I finally drifted off.

I didn't stay asleep for long, though. A cold breeze tickled at my cheeks, drawing my eyes to the glass door.

Open again.

Paisley lay curled at my hip, nestled between me and Charles under the blankets, but Octo-Cat's bed sat empty.

I pulled on my robe and worked my feet into my shoes sans socks, then headed out using my phone as a flashlight.

"Octo-Cat," I whisper-yelled after sliding the door shut after me. It would probably be open again by the time I got back to the room, but that didn't mean I couldn't at least try to close it properly. Had Octavius opened it on his way out, or did someone else enter our room?

I shuddered at the possibility of just that as I moved closer to the lake. An owl hooted in the distance, and a host of crickets sang a song about the night. It was catchy, that ditty of theirs. Perhaps one day I would learn the words for myself.

Right now, I was too worried about my cat to bother with anything else.

A dark shape shifted on the dock, and I increased my pace.

I pulled up short as I spotted Octo-Cat leaping and flipping into the air, almost dancing in the moonlight. This must've been what he was talking about when he mentioned his nighttime activities.

Standing there in the moonlight, I felt a little guilty for intruding on his joy.

"Angela, I can feel you standing there," he said suddenly, falling to all four feet and then pausing on the pier.

"Sorry," I muttered, going over to sit next to him. "I was just having trouble sleeping and you were missing. I got worried."

"I woke up because that stupid door was open again," he said, meticulously grooming himself. "I got up to see what was going on and I spotted that ugly, flat-faced, sorry excuse for a cat wandering around. I was going to give him a piece of my mind, but, of course, he disappeared before I could. You'd figure with a smell like that he'd be easier to follow."

"Don't get into any fights," I warned him.

"Relax, Angela. I know what I'm doing," he purred. "So why couldn't you sleep?"

"The door," I admitted with a sigh.

"Just the door? I figured you'd be nervous about meeting your grandmother," he said, smoothing out his tail. "But you know you don't need to be, right?"

I sat there shocked. Was Octo-Cat actually being... nice? To me? Now?

I stared at him, mouth agape.

"Don't look so surprised. Sometimes your human ways actually make sense," he continued, blinking slowly in my direction. "When we talked about finding my family, I was a bit nervous about the possibility. I mean, how could they possibly be as amazing as I am?"

He chuckled, and I found myself absently petting him behind the ears.

"But I realized something, Angela. If they aren't amazing or awesome, that doesn't change me. Because I'm still a superb specimen of feline perfection, even if they don't quite measure up. I mean, so few could ever hope to hold a candle to this." He postured himself with his chest puffed out and his nose held high, which made me burst out in laughter.

He nodded his approval. "The worst thing that can happen from meeting your grandmother is... well, nothing. Your life doesn't change, and you just go back and live like you always have. And if we're being totally honest here, you have a pretty great life for a human."

I didn't reply. I didn't need to.

If I drew this out, Octo-Cat would just return to his usual snark, and I wanted to savor this moment while I could. And so we sat there in the moonlight for a while longer before heading back to our room.

Yes, I needed the people and animals in my life to help me through this, which at first blush might make me seem weak and incapable of handling my own challenges.

But then again, that's why we have loved ones to begin with. To get us through the bad and to share in the good.

Hopefully tomorrow would bring the latter for Charles, Octo-Cat, Paisley, me...

And my grandmother.

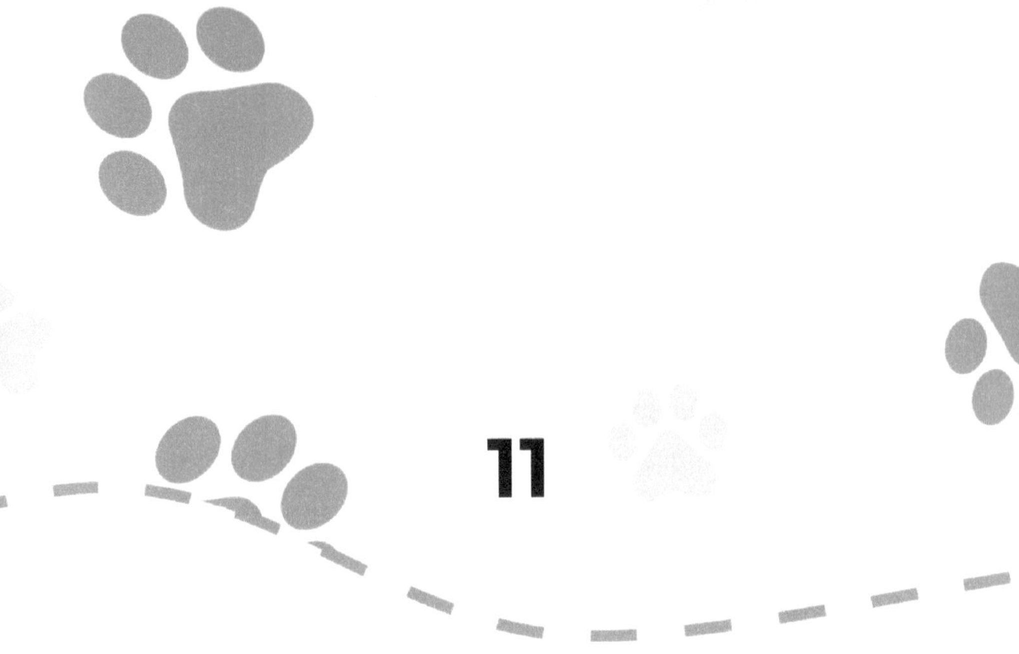

11

The next morning I was already showered, dressed, and ready by the time Charles woke up. I'd spent all week planning my outfit, and now that I was actually wearing it, an odd sense of reverence washed over me.

This was one of the most important things I'd ever done. And whatever happened—good, bad, or somewhere in between—this would be a defining moment of my life.

We fed the pets, then grabbed some coffee from the continental breakfast set-up Millicent had waiting for her guests.

Charles took a pre-packaged Danish, but I was too nervous to even attempt eating anything. Besides, I'd been spoiled by Nan's expert baking all my life and had become something of a muffin snob. The blueberry to cake ratio of the ones sitting before me was all wrong. I didn't have to try them to know that. The baked "goods" also looked more than a few days old. No wonder there had been complaints. The longer we stayed, the more and more reasons I was finding to justify the bad reviews.

"Let me just say it one more time," Charles said as he jabbed his key in the ignition, and I pulled my seatbelt over my lap. "I think I've found the right place, but we won't know for sure until we meet her."

I nodded once. "Right. And I'm going in without any expectations. *Que será será* and all that."

Charles reached for my hand and twined his fingers through mine. "No, you're not. And that's okay. It's okay to want things to go well, so stop giving yourself such a hard time about that. Whatever happens, I'll be right here."

"Holding my hand?" I suggested with a grin.

He returned my smile and gave my hand another squeeze. "If you want me to."

We held hands the entire drive, except for the few parts where Charles had a left turn to make or we ran into a bit of traffic.

Octo-Cat made occasional retching sounds from the back seat.

Good to see he'd recovered from the strange bout of compassion he'd shown me last night. I wondered if he was always like that at night. If he was only crabby during the day because he was sleepy.

"I can't believe you signed on to be Mrs. UpChuck," my cat ground out, "but then again, the role is perfect for you."

"Thank you," I said with a satisfied grin as the heated leather seat warmed my posterior.

"Huh?" Charles asked, briefly glancing my way.

"Thank you," I repeated, this time to him. "For being here, for being you, for all of this."

"Barf, barf!" Octo-Cat shouted at us.

I ignored him and leaned over to plant a kiss on my fiancé's cheek.

"We're here," Charles announced a short time later, pulling into a condominium complex. "I think."

Every single unit was a dull tan color, both the siding and the roof. It looked like we were stepping into a strange suburban desert right in the middle of Maine.

A group of high schoolers ambled past, their hands pushed down into the pockets of overly baggy jeans. One of them leered at me suggestively, sending a fresh wave of heat to my cheeks.

"Which one is hers?" I asked as Paisley barked furiously at the passers-by.

"Well, this was the one step of the journey I felt confident about. It's the one with all the pink plastic flamingos."

"Oh, right, the pink sentinels," I said, remembering the directions I myself had transcribed. "Do you think she's home?"

Charles turned off the engine and turned his full gaze toward me. "Only one way to find out. You ready?"

I swallowed down the lump that had formed in my throat. It was so thick, it felt as if it were stuck. Suddenly my eyes burned, and my skin tingled. My heartbeat sped to an upbeat tempo, and my chest grew heavy.

I let go of Charles's hand and used mine to steady myself, splaying my hands out and grasping at whatever my fingers came into contact with. It felt like the car was spinning wildly out of control, but that was ridiculous. We were simply sitting here, side by side, with the engine shut off. I knew that and yet...

Charles said something, but I couldn't make sense of the words. What was happening to me?

A million thoughts rushed through my mind, but I couldn't grab onto any of them long enough for it to stick.

Paisley barked wildly. Charles continued talking to me in a steady, soothing voice. But I kept spiraling into an idle chaos, unmoored in a storm only I could sense.

It wasn't until Octo-Cat climbed out of the back seat and settled himself on my chest that my breathing, heart rate, and everything else began to slow back to a reasonable pace.

I listened to him purr as I closed my eyes and rested my cheek on his fur and felt the vibrations warm my skin. "What happened?" I asked when I finally felt like myself again.

"I'm pretty sure you just had a panic attack," Charles said carefully. He didn't reach for me like he normally would but rather gave me some space to recover. "Are you okay?"

"I think so," I told him and then lifted my face to look at the cat sitting on my chest.

This was so much like the first time I'd met Octavius that I almost felt *déjà vu*. I'd had a medical issue, come to with him on my chest. The only thing missing was...

"I'm hungry," he said, emitting a noxious cloud of day-old lobster roll breath. "How long has it been since you last fed me?"

"Yup, there it is," I said aloud, nodding once even though I was only confirming it to myself.

"What?" Charles asked, reaching forward slowly before rubbing my arm in a steady, soothing motion.

"Cats will be cats," I said with a small smile. For all his faults, Octo-Cat was someone I could always count on to be himself. And that made marching into the unknown easier, knowing that stability was never more than a furry companion away.

"How did he know to do that?" Charles asked, assessing the tabby.

"Who, me?" the cat asked, then stood and moved onto my lap to look out the window.

"Happened to Ethel from time to time," he said while staring off into the distance. "Whenever she started breathing funny, she'd grab me and hold on tight. Eventually she would feel better. Figured it would work on you, too. You know, since all humans are pretty much the same."

Funny how even after all our time together, Octo-Cat could still surprise me. I liked that. And I appreciated him now more than ever. For all his bluster, he still cared about me and was always there for me whenever it really counted.

He was here now, which meant I could do this.

I could meet my grandmother.

Learn the truth.

And keep on living my life.

It didn't have to change me.

And I had a feeling my merry crew of tagalong companions wouldn't let that happen, anyway.

12

Charles held my hand while I clutched Paisley to my chest with my free arm. Octo-Cat nosed around the shrubs in pursuit of a fat robin.

"Okay," I said on the wings of an exhale.

Charles raised his finger and poked at the doorbell.

I focused on his fingers laced through mine, on Paisley shaking with excitement, on Octo-Cat making that ridiculous cat call that was meant to sound like a bird and lure them into his deadly clutches.

I listened for footsteps hurrying toward the door, but none came.

"Maybe it's broken," Charles said with a shrug before tapping his knuckles against the door three times in rapid succession.

"Aww, you scared it away," Octo-Cat whined, pulling himself onto the cement stoop to stand beside us.

I didn't bother to translate, but I did set Paisley down and tried pounding on the door myself.

"I want to help!" Paisley said before letting out a string of high-pitched barks.

"Make it stop. Make it stop," Octo-Cat groaned and rolled onto his back, wiggling his spine against the pavement.

Still, my grandma didn't come to the door.

"Okay, so she's not home right now," Charles said, turning back toward the street. "Let's take a walk around the complex. See if we can learn anything from the neighbors."

I nodded as he tugged me after him.

Paisley scampered after us, and Octo-Cat returned to the shrubs.

"I'm going to wait for that robin to come back. Let me know when it's time to go," he said before pouncing out of sight.

"You don't think she's avoiding me, do you?" I asked Charles as we rounded the block.

He shook his head emphatically. "Why would she do that? She doesn't even know you're coming, for starters, but also I'm sure she's dying to meet you. Why else would she have moved so close?"

She had moved close. For some reason, I hadn't considered that fact before. Hope filled my chest. "Do you think she might be looking for me and my mom, too?"

"Anything's possible." Charles picked up the pace. "Oh, look. There's someone out watering the grass."

A middle-aged man wearing cargo shorts and a sports T-shirt

stood in brightly colored crocs with a hose in one hand and a cigarette in the other.

“Excuse me, sir!” Charles called, raising his free hand.

“If Susie sent you, you can forget about serving me with any more papers,” the man snarled. I guess Charles gave off that attorney vibe even when he wasn’t anywhere near the office.

“No, I don’t work for Susie or anyone else. We’re just here to see one of your neighbors. Could you tell me about—?”

The man raised his hand. “That’s enough right there. If it’s about a neighbor, it doesn’t concern me, and I have enough trouble of my own without sticking my nose into anyone else’s business. So just go on. Keep walking. Find some other poor sap, but you won’t get a peep out of me.”

I pulled Charles ahead. “Sorry to bother you!” I called to the man.

“Hey, you! Get that overgrown rat of yours off my lawn!” the man raged from somewhere behind us.

Charles and I turned back just in time to see Paisley lift her leg and let out a mighty stream of pee right beside the spot the angry guy had been watering.

He turned his hose on her and she ran away yipping.

“Good dog,” I whispered when she caught up to us.

“I thought only male dogs lifted their legs to pee,” Charles said rather than remarking on the man’s defensiveness.

“Little dogs do it, too. You know, to put some space between themselves and the ground,” I explained.

“Ah,” was all he said to that.

We walked in silence for a while until we came upon a couple jogging.

Charles tried to flag them down, but they both pointed to their headphones and made to run past us. Surprising me and the joggers, Charles threw himself in their way, forcing them to stop.

"What's your problem, buddy?" The man loomed over us, ready for a fight.

"I'm just trying to get some information," Charles said, taking a step back. "We're looking—"

"Mitch. Yeah, he's just over there watering his grass," the man growled, pointing a meaty finger back in the direction from where we'd just come. "That's who you're looking for."

"That's who you guys are always looking for," the woman parroted with poorly concealed disgust. "Sue ought to just let up on the poor guy, but you vultures are all the same. As long as your invoices are paid, you keep on keeping on. How does it feel to ruin people's lives just to cut a paycheck?"

"We're not lawyers," I shouted in exasperation. "Well, Charles is, but that's not why we're here. We're looking for the woman that lives in the apartment with all the flamingos. Her name is Lyn Jones."

Both of them made faces like they'd just smelled something horrible.

"Her?" the guy asked.

"We don't know her and don't care to."

The woman scowled. "Yeah. Why would we? All those lawn ornaments? Yuck. As if this neighborhood wasn't bad enough."

They continued to bicker between themselves about new people coming into the neighborhood and messing up the good dynamic they had going.

"Thank you," I said with a sigh.

If they heard me, they didn't show it. The couple took off jogging again, leaving Charles and me standing there dumbfounded.

"Care to keep trying?" Charles asked, shaking his head. "Three strikes before we're out of here?"

"I don't think I can take another strike right now," I answered. The last thing I wanted was another panic attack.

He didn't even question my decision.

Together, we returned to the unit with the pink flamingos to collect Octo-Cat and the car. I tried the door one last time since we were there already.

When my knocks went unanswered, I chewed my lip, then said, "I'm going to try calling her again."

The phone rang and rang, but only on the other end of the call, not inside the house.

Charles frowned. "Like I said, it's possible I got the location wrong. After all, Bravo's instructions were pretty hard to follow."

"No, this is it." I wasn't sure how I knew this was the place, but something deep inside me refused to be deterred. Besides, just how many stick-colored houses were there with pink sentinels standing guard around this place?

"Why don't we head back to the bed-and-breakfast and get

some lunch?" Charles suggested as he opened the car door for me and the animals.

"Finally, UpChuck is good for something," Octo-Cat meowed as he settled himself into the back seat. "What are the chances we can find some lobst—?"

"No," I cut him off. "Hey, Charles. Which place had the good fries?" I said, suddenly craving something salty.

"My darling, I thought you'd never ask," he quipped, and we were off.

13

We parked outside the bed-and-breakfast, planning to go around back and enter our room through the sliding glass door. Charles carried the overstuffed bag of greasy fast food while I held an extra-large soda in each hand.

I'd planned on feeding the pets food we'd brought from home, but Octo-Cat had argued with me unrelentingly until I acquiesced, agreeing to purchase him a fish filet. We grabbed a plain burger for Paisley, too, since it would have been unfair not to treat her as well.

It wasn't a total defeat on my part, though. I made them both swear up and down they'd eat their pet food the rest of the time we were here.

"C'mon, let's get to the room before these babies get cold." Charles preferred that no one eat in his car, so we'd kept the bag sealed tight for the entire drive back, the delicious scents tormenting me the whole way.

A flash of orange caught my eye. At first I thought it was Louis the cat, but then I realized it was Millicent who had been watching us.

"And just where have you two been all morning?" she demanded, wrapping her long, red fingernails around a can of Diet Coke.

"Oh, here and there," I said with a shrug, then turned away.

But Millicent followed us, her flip-flops slapping against the gravel. "You weren't up to anything illegal, were you? Why, just last night I had a guest tell me her diamond ring had gone missing."

I gaped at her. "That was me. My ring went missing."

She balked, then sputtered as she searched for words. "Well, what did you do with it? Come out with it, then."

"I tried to tell you all of this last night. Weren't you listening? I took it off to get some sleep, then when I woke up it was gone."

She considered this before narrowing her eyes and demanding, "How do I know you're not trying to frame my establishment just so you can collect the insurance money and get something better?"

"Are you actually serious right now?" I exploded. She was lucky my hands were full, or I'd—Okay, I wouldn't actually do anything untoward, but sometimes it was nice to pretend that I might.

"C'mon, Angie," Charles urged, tugging at my elbow and motioning with his chin. "Our lunch is getting cold."

"But she can't talk to us like that," I insisted, returning the cruel woman's glare. "See, this is why I'm guessing you don't get many return guests. Personal items go missing, the doors don't work, and you're one of the rudest people I've ever met!"

"I can't believe *you* would talk to *me* like that," Millicent snarled. "I don't have to let you stay here. In fact, pack your bags and—"

"No," I said firmly. "I'm not going anywhere until my ring is returned. So if you want to get rid of me, I suggest you find it first. Now good day, Millicent."

I stormed off with Charles and the animals in silent pursuit.

"Meee-yeow," Octo-Cat said, then let out a low whistle. "I've never been more proud of you, Angela. It seems I have taught you something, after all."

"Yeah, well. Don't get used to it," I said, kicking off my shoes and slumping down onto the bed. My heart was beating like crazy again. I needed to stop getting so keyed up before it sent me to an early grave.

The toilet flushed in our connected bathroom, and I tensed up even more. "Who's there?" I shouted, still teetering on the edge.

The door burst open, and Sharon stepped out with her hands raised in the air. "Sorry, sorry. That glass door was open, so I let myself in. I wanted to apologize for how we left things yesterday and check to see how you're feeling today. Did you meet your grandmother? How did it go?"

Charles motioned for Sharon to join us and handed her a large container of fries.

"Oh, no. I didn't mean to intrude," Sharon began to argue, batting her eyelashes.

Charles pushed the fries at her again. "It's okay. I had at least five servings yesterday as part of my search. I'm all fried out."

She studied him with a furrowed brow. "That's a bit... odd. What do you mean you—?"

"Thanks for coming by," I blurted out, drawing her attention back to me. "We went to her house, but nobody was home."

She frowned. "Oh."

"Yeah, and she's still not picking up her phone, so we're kind of stuck."

"Oh, boo." Her features crumpled into an even deeper frown. It was totally at odds with her usual free-spirited style. And so was her current outfit for that matter.

I looked the gray suit up and down, pausing briefly to take in the bright red clogs. "Sharon, what are you—?"

"Wearing?" she finished for me, her smile returning. "I have a meeting with the show's publicist, and I had no idea what they wanted from me, so a nice lady at the store helped me select this business suit. I hate it, but hopefully it will show I'm good at taking direction. She gave me shoes, too, but they were terribly uncomfortable. Luckily these clogs from my visit to New Amsterdam paired nicely." She paused to suck in a quick breath. "I know Chessy is the star, but I'm the one who signed all the papers, so..."

"You look great, Sharon," Charles said with a friendly grin. "Very professional."

She blushed mightily. "Why, thank you, kind sir."

Charles shifted his weight on the bed, jostling me in the process. Sharon sat opposite us on Octo-Cat's bed while he worked on his fish filet on the floor.

"Hey, Sharon," Charles said, balling up his burger wrapper and tossing it back in the bag. "While we have you here, maybe you can help us with something."

Sharon straightened her posture and placed her hands in her lap. "Anything." She was batting her eyelashes again. Oh, brother.

"You said you found some information about Marilyn's trials," Charles reminded her.

"Yes, but the records were sealed."

This didn't deter Charles one bit. "I may be able to get around that, if I find the right people to ask."

Sharon and I both looked to Charles askance.

He waved off our concern. "If I can find out where any of the cases took place, I can contact the prosecutor's office and let them know I'm working on a family case. See what they can tell me."

"Sure, let me just email you my notes," Sharon said, pulling out her phone. When that was taken care of, she leaned toward me. "Not only is he handsome, he's brilliant, too," Sharon confided in me with a whisper more than loud enough for Charles to hear too.

This time Charles was the one to blush mightily.

Octo-Cat's muffled voice rose to meet my ears. "And here I

thought you were the only one crazy enough to join the UpChuck fan club," he said around a mouth full of food. "Looks like you aren't even the president, anymore."

This was getting ridiculous. I wasn't threatened in the least, but I still scooted closer to Charles on the bed and rested my head on his shoulder.

"You are a lucky, lucky girl, Angie Russo," Sharon said. "Now don't you forget to invite me to the wedding. It is my new life mission to land myself an uncle or a cousin. If they're half as perfect as your Charles, I'll die a happy woman... Now let me see that beautiful ring of yours again."

"Um, actually, it disappeared while I was taking a nap," I admitted with a frown.

"It's missing?" Sharon's eyes widened and she let out a huff. "Well, it's got to be around here somewhere. Want me to help you look?" she offered, sliding off the bed and onto her feet.

I stood, too. "Yeah, we searched everywhere, but—"

Sharon nodded sympathetically, then glanced toward the digital clock that hung on the wall opposite. "Oh, shoot! I can't stay to help, or I'll be late! Call me later! We'll find that ring—and that grandmother—yet. Don't you fret!"

And then Sharon ran off so fast that I didn't even have a chance to say goodbye.

14

"That was weird," I said, watching as the glass door bounced back open following Sharon's sudden departure.

"You don't think she…?" Charles let his words trail away as he got up to push the door shut as best he could.

I tilted my head and scowled at him. "Are you actually suggesting she stole my ring?"

"She doesn't seem to have a problem entering without permission, and well…" His words fell away again, and he shrugged.

"She has a big, fat crush on you. Is that what you wanted to say? That she is so smitten for you that she stole the ring so she can fantasize about being your bride?"

"Smitten *with,*" Charles corrected with a sigh. "And, well, it sounds stupid when you say it like that, but it's not like we have any other leads to go on."

"Sharon is my friend," I reminded him. "If anyone stole my ring, it's that nasty Millicent." True, Sharon had only been my friend for a week, but she'd made up for her bad first impression, unlike the owner of this bed-and-breakfast who just kept making things worse every time we ran into her.

Charles sat back on the bed and placed an arm around my shoulders. "We'll find it. I promise, but let's try to figure this thing out with your grandma first, okay?"

I nodded. "You're right. One thing at a time."

"Exactly." He got up to retrieve his work bag.

"So, I guess, you see what you can learn from what Sharon gave you, and I'll check her social media."

"Mommy!" Paisley let out a sharp bark to get my attention. "May I please go outside to play?"

"Right, okay." I opened the door for her and watched her frolic toward the sandy beach. "I think I'll go out, too. Keep an eye on her," I told Charles. "Come get me when you're ready to head back out?"

He gave me a hearty thumbs-up. He'd already pulled his laptop out and situated it onto his lap. You can take the guy out of the office, but getting the office out of the guy was a whole different story. Charles's lawyer skills had come in handy many times before, and they just might be the thing to save the day now.

I'd be gutted if we had to leave Katahdin without ever meeting my grandmother. We just had to find her. We had to, and we would.

I approached the lake and found Paisley digging a hole in the sand. She didn't even notice me as I approached.

"What's that?" I asked when she pulled her head out with a small, black object in her mouth.

"It's a pretty rock," she mumbled, accidentally dropping her prize when she did. She yipped in surprise, grabbed it back up, and ran off with tail wagging. I was fairly certain my nan's dog had just unearthed a clam but had no idea what she was actually doing with it. It's not like she'd be able to crack open the hard shell and get at the meat inside.

I shrugged and continued cutting a path toward the dock. Well, whatever Paisley was up to, at least she was happy about it. Sometimes I envied her, how easy it was for her to see the best in every situation.

Me, on the other hand, I had a hard time not worrying about what would come next. Especially now.

I'd told Charles I would check Grandma Marilyn's social media. Mostly it was because I'd have felt guilty if he dug deep into research while I sat around twiddling my thumbs.

Of course, I'd already checked her social media as soon as I knew her current name and location. I'd tried to find her before last night, but Jones wasn't exactly an uncommon surname. I finally managed to find the correct profile yesterday evening while I was supposed to be relaxing in the tub.

Unfortunately, my grandmother hadn't posted a single photo of herself during all her years on the site, assigning a simple stock-image daisy to serve as her profile picture.

She also rarely updated her status. When I checked last night, the most recent one had been made about eight months ago—commentary on some TV show she'd just started watching on some cable channel I'd never heard of.

I navigated to her profile now, expecting to see the exact same feed.

But no.

My grandma had posted an update less than an hour ago. We'd probably just left her neighborhood at the time. *Whoa.*

"Nothing beats sunny skies and sandy beaches! Hello, San Francisco!" she'd captioned a photo of the Golden Gate bridge.

Wow. Was she really clear on the other side of the country?

What dumb luck.

Of course, California made sense. Her phone had a Cali area code. Hey, maybe she was planning to move back and change her name again.

Then I'd never find her.

I scrolled through my newsfeed idly, completely frustrated with this turn of events and wondering how I would break it to Charles, especially considering that we'd lost my engagement ring because of our trip out here. And it hadn't even been a full week since he'd proposed.

Ugh. I was the worst fiancée ever.

Tears stung at the edges of my eyes, and I didn't try to hold them back. Stupid San Francisco, I thought, looking for someone to blame other than myself.

Then, for whatever reason, I navigated back to my grandmother's profile to look at that picture again. Perhaps it was just to wallow in my dumb luck, or maybe I'd subconsciously realized that something didn't quite add up.

That's when I saw it. She'd checked in when she posted the photo, not at the Golden Gate bridge in San Francisco, but at the Golden Wok in Katahdin, Maine.

Oh my gosh.

She was here—here and lying about it.

When she'd tried to pull up the Golden Gate bridge, the social media site must have brought up nearby establishments with similar names. My grandmother hadn't noticed that the geo-tag gave her away.

But why would she lie about being out of town?

"Hi, Mommy!" Paisley called as she rushed past me, then dipped her head and picked up a pink shell, only to immediately take off running again.

"Hi," I called back distractedly. My grandmother was here, and she knew I was looking for her.

She wanted to put me off her scent, but I refused to go home without meeting her first. Maybe she'd never want to see me again after—and that possibility hurt me deeply—but, still, I at least had to try.

I'd rather meet her and have it go badly than never get the chance at all.

Now I just had to tell Charles what I'd found, and we could figure out our next steps from there.

15

When I shared my discovery about the failed social media check-in with Charles, I may have mentioned how much I wished Pringle was there to help us make a plan.

And Octo-Cat took the bait, hook, line, and sinker.

"The dog and I are better than that raccoon fraud could ever hope to be," he growled and then insisted he could handle things from here.

We drove back out to the condominium complex, and I watched as the pets tore away from the car to begin their top-secret recon mission. Octo-Cat had declared the details of the operation to be on a need-to-know basis and then had proceeded to explain that I did not need to know.

Charles reached over and squeezed my knee.

With growing trepidation, I closed the door so that he could drive us around the corner and out of sight.

The part of the plan that I'd been privy to involved Charles and me circling the block slowly while the animals followed through with their mission to track down my missing grandmother.

"Am I wrong for kind of wishing the raccoon was with us?" Charles asked later with a snort. "At least he keeps things interesting."

By this point, we'd driven around the neighborhood at least a dozen times, and the residents had noticed. If we kept this up much longer, we'd soon have a cop car on our tail.

"You know I only brought up Pringle to get Octo-Cat to think helping us was his idea, right?" I reminded him with a laugh. "So, yes, you are very wrong for thinking Pringle's presence would improve anything. You don't have to listen to him prattle on the way the rest of us do. Do you know during our last trip, he decided to pick up trucker lingo?"

Charles burst out laughing. "You're kidding. Why didn't you tell me earlier?"

"I've tried my best to block it out, honestly. He was going on and on about Smokeys and ten fours and whatever else. I couldn't manage to understand the half of it."

"Huh. Makes me wonder if you could understand animals speaking a foreign language. Like—"

"Stop the car!" I shouted as I spotted the waggy black blur of Paisley rushing down the sidewalk barking at us.

"Mommy! Mommy! Mommy! Mommy!" I heard her crying as soon as the door opened.

"I'll park the car and catch up," Charles called as I jumped out of the car.

"What's going on, Paisley?" The little dog leapt into my arms and frantically licked my face.

"We found her! We found your grandmama," the Chihuahua yipped excitedly. "Follow me!"

She leapt from my arms and began sprinting at full tilt. I glanced back to make sure Charles was coming before I started running after the quivering bullet of a dog.

I sprinted after Paisley, thankful for the time Nan had forced me to work out with her friend's dog Cujo for a time. Of course, the husky had moved at a steady, even clip, unlike the wildly darting mini-dog I was attempting to follow now.

My current canine guide also didn't seem to worry much about the obstacles I was having trouble getting around, over, and under. The first thing I tripped over was a sprinkler, and it sent me crashing down onto the same lawn that belonged to that grumpy guy we'd met earlier. Why? Just why?

Staggering back to my feet, very little time passed before I crashed headlong into a raspberry bush.

Meanwhile, Paisley remained blissfully unaware of my challenges and of how far I'd fallen behind. The little dog's legs were almost invisible with her sprinting, hopping gait.

Trying to focus on Paisley meant not paying enough attention to the road ahead of me, and I thumped into a set of garbage cans, then jammed my knee into a fence post.

Maybe we should have followed her in the car. Too late for that now, I guessed.

Off-balance and disoriented, I was overwhelmed when I saw that Paisley was no longer surging forward. She now ran tight circles behind one of the condos.

"Mommy! Mommy!" she yelled. "It's right here! This is the place!"

And there was my grandmother, sitting at a small patio table with Octo-Cat, who was happily munching on a shrimp cocktail. I stood there, woozily, my mouth opening and closing without any sound coming out. It would so leave the wrong impression if I threw up now.

Octo-Cat looked up at me and yawned before licking the sauce off his paw.

"Angela," he purred. "This is your grandma Lyn. Lyn, Angela."

"Hello, Angela," Lyn said, almost as if she were responding to Octo-Cat. "Sorry for giving you the runaround, dear. I'm... Well, I was afraid you'd be disappointed, and I couldn't stand the thought of you rejecting me."

My heart felt like it was breaking for her. She had been just as worried about meeting me as I'd been about meeting her.

But before I could find something to say, she continued. "I was tipped off that you were heading my way when your friend... Um, what was her name again?"

"Sharon," Octo-Cat replied.

"Ah, Sharon," Lyn said as if prompted by Octo-Cat. "The reality star that was looking into me wasn't the subtlest of people. So I knew you were coming here. When I saw you and your fellow sitting out in your car for so long, I knew it just had to be you."

She poured more iced tea into her glass and added a few more shrimp to Octo-Cat's cocktail.

"Of course, the moment you got out, I knew for certain. The family genes are extremely strong. You look so much like my sister did when we were growing up. But I'm sure that's not why you made the trip out here."

"Of course not," Octo-Cat said, polishing off another shrimp. "We were here to find out why your husband decided to take your child and make a run for it."

I winced at Octo-Cat's bluntness.

"Relax, Angela. I understand how cats can be," Lyn said, clucking her tongue and shaking her head. "And for the record, you're right, Octavius. I lost my dear little Laura because her father didn't believe me when I told him I could talk to animals. Such a shame."

Whoa. I still hadn't even said so much as hello, and already my grandmother had told me her big secret.

It was a secret we shared.

Did this mean...? Could I talk to animals because she could? I couldn't wait to hear more.

16

A few minutes later, Lyn handed me an old photograph and a fresh glass of iced tea. She handed a second glass to Charles, settled back into her chair, and pulled Octo-Cat onto her lap.

I expected him to object, but he simply curled up and began purring.

"That's your mother," she said wistfully. "It was the only picture I had of her for so many years until I found her on the news. There's so much I missed from all of your lives. But I guess I understand. Your grandfather wasn't a bad man. He was just scared."

I nodded along. Gosh, I just loved listening to her voice. She could talk forever, and I'd be her willing captive.

"It all started when I was working at the diner to pay my way through college," Grandma Marilyn continued. "Jimmy, the owner, was a good enough guy, but he was also a cheapskate." She glanced at me over the edge of her glasses, and I laughed. "He wanted to fix every last little thing himself. Said repair shops were all a scam to bilk the working man out of his hard-earned money.

"So when the power cord to our industrial sized coffee maker got frayed, Jimmy fixed it. It didn't work that well, but cheap was better than good, if you asked him. As for me, I ended up taking quite a shock. When I woke up, I found the world a lot noisier than it had been."

"Me, too!" I squealed, standing up and jabbing my thumb into my chest. "Oh my gosh, it was the exact same!"

Grandma Marilyn laughed. "Yes, Every animal was talking and the problem was that only I could understand what they were saying. I tried to keep it secret for as long as I could, but when animals know you can talk to them, they won't leave you alone. I'm sure you understand that.

"William tried to be understanding. After all, we'd been together a short time and he thought maybe it was just overwork or some sort of 'female thing' that was causing me to think I could understand animals. And the doctors, they agreed with him. Claimed it was some sort of pregnancy-induced hysteria. Times were different back then. I didn't have many rights as a young, unwed mother-to-be. William had done right by me and proposed. Our wedding wasn't far off, either, until I started talking to cats and dogs. Then he found one reason after another to delay. And then with the doctors involved, I wound up on bed rest and drugged out of my mind on who knows what kind of drugs.

"I barely remember giving birth to Laura. In fact, for a time, William convinced me that I'd never been pregnant in the first place. I can't really be mad at him. He thought he was helping me. If he didn't really love me, I'm sure he would've just had me committed and taken off. But, though we never did make it official via marriage, he stuck with me through it all. Trying to fix me. Trying to get rid of the voices in my head."

I squeezed Charles's hand under the table.

My Grandma continued on, her eyes dry. As tragic as this tale was, she'd lived it. She'd already come to terms with how her life had turned out.

"For ten years I was in and out of institutions. Bouncing from one diagnosis to another. Schizophrenia, multiple personality disorder, psychosis, detachment from reality. They threw everything at the wall to see what stuck.

"We ended up out in California of all places when I managed to talk to a desert cottontail. He was very different from any of the animals I'd spoken to before, and it sort of clicked in my mind that I wasn't crazy, no matter how long doctors and my beau had been trying to convince me otherwise.

"I broke out of the hospital and went on the run. It was much easier in those days. No cell phones, no electronic credit card monitoring. It took actual phone calls and detective work to track down someone that didn't want to be found.

"Sure, I hit a few speed bumps along the way, a couple of arrests and some close calls with my abilities, but I learned how to hide it from everyone, and I tried to appear normal for a time. Not much of a life, I know, but I was at least out of the hospitals.

"Of course, old William felt guilty and eventually tracked me down to a small town near the Florida-Georgia border. Gave me this picture of Laura, thanked me for letting him go so that he could find someone else. He said he still loved me, but that we weren't any good for each other.

"I never saw him again after that. But knowing that your mother was out there, I had at last found a purpose. I drifted from town to town, doing whatever work I could find and making friends with any animals that might be able to help me track down my daughter.

"That's actually why I've got such a large collection of flamingos out front. Each one represents a close friend I've made along the way. Of course, wild flamingos only live to be about twenty, so sadly, that display is more like a memorial."

She leaned forward and steepled her fingers. "Angela. I don't know how to tell you this, but having this gift is a lonely life. Sure, you can talk to all the animals, but you really miss out on the human connections that give life meaning. And that's why I was so worried you would reject me. No one wants a crazy old woman in their family tree."

"I do," I said, unshed tears blurring my vision. "I want it more than anything."

"I do, too, sweetie. When Octavius here told me you and I shared more than just a passing genetic resemblance, I thought maybe, just maybe I'd found my family again."

I offered her a smile that started small but then grew to take up a huge portion of my face. I'd sat transfixed for her entire story, and now I just couldn't help it—I threw my arms around her and gave my grandmother a hug.

The first of what I hoped would be many.

"I'm so glad I found you," I whispered, not wanting to let go.

"Thank you for not giving up on me. I can't have made it easy."

"Actually, when you have a moment, I'd like to teach you about social media safety. That way, the next time you want to hide from someone, you don't make the same silly mistake." I explained how I'd determined she wasn't really out of town, and together we shared a great big belly laugh.

We sat at that rickety patio set for hours, sharing stories of our lives, telling her about what Charles and I hoped for with our wedding, and of course, remembering all the weird and wonderful animals who had enriched our lives along the way.

"Do you promise you'll come back tomorrow?" my grandma asked after we all shared a delicious dinner of grilled chicken and vegetables.

"You couldn't keep her away if you tried," Charles promised, pulling me into his side as we both stood.

"I know that," Grandma Marilyn said. "I already tried and failed."

We all laughed again and said goodnight. This didn't feel like a first meeting. It felt like coming home.

Like family.

17

Charles and I returned to the bed and breakfast well after dinnertime, both with huge smiles on our faces.

"What a day," he said.

"Yeah," I said back. It was all either of us needed to express. Our time with my grandmother had said it all.

"I liked Grandma Lyn," Paisley said as I lifted her into my arms and climbed out of the car.

"She reminded me of Ethel," Octo-Cat remarked, drawing Paisley's and my eyes to him.

I didn't say anything because we were no longer in the privacy of the car, and Millicent had already proven she wasn't above spying.

"Hang on a sec," I told Charles and waited.

Luckily, Octo-Cat didn't hesitate to continue. "What?" he asked, stretching in the backseat while we all waited on him.

"She's a nice, old lady. A nice, old, relatively normal lady. Also, she had tea."

"I don't know why I was expecting something more profound," I murmured to myself.

Paisley squirmed within my arms. "What about the *pound?*"

I patted her head. "Everything is perfectly fine. Let's head back to our room," I said while looking at Charles, just in case Millicent was watching.

The gravel crunched at the edge of the lot as another car pulled in. And not just any car—a police car.

"I smell trouble," Octo-Cat said with a grin, hopping out of the car and craning his neck to see better while hiding behind my legs. Always hungry for someone else's drama, that one.

Millicent spilled forth from the entryway, waving her arms overhead. "Officer, officer! This is them!" It looked as if she'd taken great care with her appearance, considering the obscene amount of both makeup and jewelry she now wore. She'd been expecting us.

The policeman unfurled himself from the driver's seat, reaching an impressive height, close to seven feet, if I had to guess. He tucked his thumbs into his belt loop and approached me and Charles.

Paisley shook and squirmed, not because she was frightened but simply because she was eager to say hello to the new arrival.

Clearly a dog person, the cop reached over and scratched under her chin with his thick fingers, then pulled back and glared down at Charles. "You been giving Mrs. Strobel trouble?"

"No, sir," he said, standing in place, far more calm and collected than I could ever be in this type of situation.

"Are you kidding me?" I boomed.

Millicent ran in front of us, shouting, "Yes! Yes, they have! Then they refused to leave when I asked them to. That's why I'd like you to escort them from the property!"

The officer glanced at each of us in turn, finally deciding on Charles as the most rational one among us. "Would you like to tell me what happened here today?" he asked, pulling out a notebook that looked comically small in his oversized hands.

Charles didn't miss a beat. "My fiancée's engagement ring went missing," he explained, taking care not to talk with his hands the way he usually did. "We reported it to Mrs. Strobel immediately upon discovering its absence last night."

The officer bobbed his head. "And then?"

"This afternoon, we returned from meeting a friend when Mrs. Strobel met us outside the bed-and-breakfast, demanding to know where we had gone and whether we'd engaged in any illegal activity. She then accused us of stealing the ring, not realizing that we were the same ones who'd reported it missing. When we pointed this out, she accused us of implicating her establishment in a planned insurance fraud, which I can assure you is not accurate."

The officer raised one eyebrow. "Then?"

"Then she demanded we leave. Naturally, since we had booked our reservation for two nights, we didn't see any reason to check out before said duration. Also, my fiancée was not eager to leave before we could find her missing engagement ring."

"Uh-huh. Then?" He glanced sidelong at Millicent, who stood openly scowling at Charles.

"We had lunch with a friend in our room, went back out to visit the same friend that we'd gone to see that morning, and then returned, leading to present circumstances," Charles concluded.

Millicent shook a finger at us. The sleeves of her oversized mint silk blouse belled in the wind. "You see that? They have too many friends! I don't trust them one bit!"

The policeman shifted his posture slightly so that he was facing Millicent. "Ma'am, what evidence do you have that these two guests of yours faked the disappearance of their engagement ring?"

She patted her stomach furiously. "I don't need any evidence. I feel it all right here. In my gut! Always go with your gut!"

The officer pressed his lips into a firm line. "Unfortunately, that's not how the law works. Without any evidence to go on, I won't be able to follow through on your request. Also, it seems to me that you are, in fact, the one in the wrong here."

Her jaw fell open. "What?" she barely managed to gasp. I was guessing that neither Millicent's brain nor her lungs were getting much oxygen in that moment.

"Quite simply put, you're harassing these people."

She shook her head, apparently too angry to argue. Well, good, because I was more than done here.

"There's something else, too," Charles shot in, finally speaking freely again, hands and all. “A case of gross negligence. You see, there’s this problem with our door…”

I listened with a smug grin as Charles went on to describe our issue with both the front door and the side door for our room. He also filed a formal police report about my missing ring.

At some point, Millicent stormed off. If she hadn’t hated us before, she definitely did now.

Charles and I laughed the whole thing off as we made our way back to the room. Not even Millicent’s ridiculous antics could spoil the wonderful day we’d had with my grandmother.

“That plan backfired on her, huh?” Charles asked with a wink.

“Oh, spectacularly!” I giggled. “And I loved every moment of it.”

Suddenly, Paisley surged forward, barking as she ran. “Get away, you big bully!”

I just barely spotted the flash of orange as Louis scurried off into the night.

“Paisley!” I lifted her to my face and let her lick my cheeks. “I’m so proud of you! You stood up to him all on your own!”

“And don’t come back!” she yelped into the night, clearly very pleased with herself.

“What a strange trip this has been,” Charles said as we finished the walk to our bedroom. The door, as always, was cracked partially open.

“Strange, but good,” I added.

We bobbed our heads in agreement.

“But let’s stay somewhere else next time we come to pay Grandma Marilyn a visit?” Charles wanted to clarify.

I grabbed his hand and planted a kiss on the back of it. “Definitely.”

Next time we came for a visit, I already knew exactly where I’d be staying. Grandma Marilyn had invited us to come soon and often and said we always had a place to stay.

And who needs decently reviewed bed-and-breakfasts when you have family?

18

"For all its faults, there is one thing I'll actually miss about this place," Charles said after we'd both taken a moment to relax following the stressful encounter in the parking lot. Our emotions were ping-ponging all over the place out here, and we just needed a moment to catch up with them.

"Oh, yeah." I turned toward him with an expectant smile. "And what's that?"

His cheeks lifted in that signature smile I loved so much. "Beach access."

"There are a million beaches back in Glendale," I reminded him, wrinkling my nose playfully.

"Yeah, but none are right outside our back door." He stood and offered me his hand. "One more moonlight stroll?"

"Oh, you hopeless romantic, you," I teased. Really, Sharon was right. I was, in fact, the luckiest woman alive.

I followed Charles in a lovesick daze until a short way from our room, I tripped and stumbled forward.

Thankfully my knight in shining armor caught me before I could connect with the ground.

"What was that?" I asked, glancing back but unable to see what had tripped me up.

Charles took out his cell phone and shone the flashlight onto a small pile of assorted beach bric-a-brac.

"Just some random nature stuff," he said with a shrug. "At least I believe that's the technical term for it."

"Wait," I shouted as he moved to slide his phone back into his pocket. "Go back over that stuff again, but a bit more slowly this time."

Charles shrugged and did as I asked, moving the light back and forth until it caught on a shiny black rock.

No, not a rock.

"That's a clam, right?" I asked, remembering the scene with Paisley earlier.

He shrugged again. "Yeah, I think so."

I ambled over and pointed at a pink shell. "And that's a shell?"

"Yes, that one I'm sure of. I'm absolutely certain that is a seashell." He poked me playfully in the side, but I was too focused to return his silliness in kind.

"Paisley," I called into the night, turning back toward our

room, which was still in sight. The little black dog nudged the glass door open and then came bounding toward us.

"Yes, Mommy?" she asked, one ear tall and pointy and the other flopped forward.

"Do these things belong to you?" I said, motioning toward the upset pile.

"My treasures!" she cried, running to them and rolling around. "What happened?"

"Yup, that's what I thought. Case solved. Well, almost. Maybe. C'mon, we need to talk to Octo-Cat," I told Charles.

But Paisley whimpered and refused to follow along, "No, please don't tell him about my treasures. I don't want him to steal them from me like he does at home."

"I promise I won't tell him about your secret hoard," I assured the distraught pup.

She followed, albeit somewhat reluctantly.

"What's going on?" Charles wanted to know as we approached the cabin.

"I have an idea about what might have happened to my ring," I told him right as I pulled the door to our room wide open and the three of us stepped inside.

"What do you want now?" my cat demanded. "I thought I was finally getting a bit of me time, but noooo. Here you all are. Again. Story of all nine of my lives. Ugh." He let out a long sigh, but I refused to fall prey to his dramatics.

"You're a cat. Literally every second of every day is your you time," I told him.

Octo-Cat scoffed but said nothing more.

When it was clear he'd yielded the floor, I said, "Listen, I need your help."

"Yup, there it is!" he spat and flicked his tail. "You'd be lost without me, admit it."

"If I do, will you help?" If my pride was the price of his assistance, I'd happily give it up. I'd lived with a cat for long enough to know how this whole thing worked. Which meant I also expected what came next.

Octo-Cat flopped onto his side and yawned. "I'll think about it. Really, I'm quite tired. Between sleuthing and helping you sort out your cloying human emotion, you've been working me hard all weekend. I need some time to rest and recharge."

"Shut up, you!" Paisley barked and kicked her feet back. "If Mommy needs our help, then we're going to give it to her!"

"Paisley!" I said in shock. She almost never took a tough approach to anything, especially not when it involved the big feline brother she idolized.

Octo-Cat stared at Paisley with large amber eyes.

Paisley stared back with shiny black eyes.

And I couldn't believe what happened next.

"Whatever," Octo-Cat backed down, blinking his eyes slowly as he turned to me. "Just tell me what you need, so we can get this over with."

Knowing better than to waste time questioning the madness I'd just witness, I moved ahead with my original intent. First, I explained the theory I'd developed after stumbling over Paisley's beachy hoard, then I told them what I needed them to do.

Octo-Cat rolled onto his feet. "C'mon, Mutt. Let's go do the thing."

But Paisley didn't follow. "It hurts my feelings when you call me that," she said firmly.

Seriously? What the heck was going on here? Octo-Cat was showing his softer side while Paisley was standing up for herself. Nothing made sense anymore. Perhaps this place emanated some kind of strange magic.

Ha, as if!

Once the animals departed, Charles held his hand out to me. "Now about that walk."

19

"Is every trip with you going to be like this?" Charles asked, kissing the back of my hand.

"Yup, and you're stuck with me now," I laughed.

"I don't mind," he said, pulling me close to gaze into my eyes. "I know your grandmother had a hard time because of her gifts, but I want you to know that I plan to always be here for you, no matter what."

"Thank you," I said. "I can't imagine what it must've been like for her back then. To be so alone and for so long."

"Well, you might have to keep the secret from everyone else, but you've got a lot of us who are there for you."

"Yeah, I know, and I—"

"Mommy!" a little voice interrupted.

I pulled away from Charles and looked out into the night to see Paisley bounding up with Octo-Cat hot on her heels.

Octo-Cat held up a paw, struggling to catch his breath. "We… we…we found it. Which means… You owe me… A lobster roll."

"Okay, so where is it?" I asked, excitement crashing over me. Ahh, what a rush! This was one crime I couldn't wait to solve once and for all, not only because of what had been stolen but also because of who was at fault.

Tugging Charles along, I followed the pets inside and went over to the front desk where Millicent sat grumbling to herself while she read her book.

"Excuse me," I said, ringing the bell on the desk.

Millicent rolled her eyes and moved the bell. "Go away," she grumbled, adding in a few choice words under her breath.

"I just wanted to let you know that we've caught the thief that's been plaguing your bed-and-breakfast," I revealed with a self-satisfied smirk. Okay, so I wasn't being the most professional in that moment, but Millicent hadn't actually hired me, so I was justified in my approach. At least that's what I told myself now.

"You've got a lot of nerve," she said, slamming her book onto the desk.

Instead of baiting the old woman further, I walked over to the antique armoire Octo-Cat and Paisley were patiently sitting by. I pulled on the door, and it swung open to reveal…nothing but an empty armoire.

"Behind it," Octo-Cat whispered.

"Oops," I said, closing the door. "Charles, could you help me here and move the armoire over a bit?"

Nodding his agreement, he got low on the furniture piece and slid it across the floor, revealing a large hole in the wall with a fat, orange cat asleep on a pile of valuables like a flugly—that's fluffy and ugly—dragon. Near the top of the horde sat my ring, shimmering in all its matrimonial magnificence.

"It looks like your cat has been taking things from your guests and stashing them here," I said, triumphantly plucking my ring from the pile and allowing Charles to slide it back onto my finger where it belonged.

The old lady's skin went pale, and she stammered a bit before finding her voice. "I'm so sorry. To the both of you. I had no idea Louis was using his nap spot for something so... so... That's a bad kitty!" She scooped the pile out of the nook, jostling the cat from his place.

"I'm so sorry," she said again. "I honestly thought that my guests were lying and trying to sink my business. A developer had offered to buy the place a year ago, and I thought because I'd turned him down, he was trying to run me out of business. I guess that'll teach me to get too involved in my stories. Oh, I owe so many people apologies, and I've got to make sure all of these things get back to their rightful owners. Thank you so much for helping me out, and after I was so rude to you."

"So can we be friends now?" I asked.

Her face soured. "I still don't approve of your shenanigans. And also your beau scratched my floor when he moved that armoire. Expect the repairs to be added on to your bill."

My jaw dropped. From sour to sweet and back again almost instantaneously. I swear, there was no winning with some people.

"I still don't care for you much, but since you managed to help me, I'll let you stay until check-out tomorrow morning," she said reluctantly. "But I don't want you two back here until you're well and properly married. I run a wholesome business here. Now go, get out of here, before I change my mind."

Charles and I rushed away, laughing the whole time.

Millicent didn't know the first thing about us or our relationship, but she believed what she wanted to—and we had nothing to prove.

Now that I had my ring back, I counted this weekend a perfect success.

20

I always loved getting away, but even more than that, I loved coming back home. My life rocked, now more than ever.

I was surprised to find Nan waiting up for me even though it was quite late. "How was your trip, dear?" she asked, stretching her arms overhead and standing to greet me.

"Did you get my message?" I asked, scooping her up in a hug.

"Yes, all seventeen of them. I'm sorry I didn't return any of them. This felt like a conversation we should have face to face."

Hmm, now where had I heard that before. Sharon. I'd need to call and give her an update since we were unable to meet up before Charles and I headed home again. I had a feeling we'd both be seeing a lot of her in our future, starting with our upcoming nuptials.

"Shall I put on some tea?" Nan offered, hooking her thumb toward the kitchen.

"No," I said, gently lowering myself onto the couch and patting the cushion beside me. If I gave Nan an excuse to put this off, she'd keep finding more and more reasons to put it off further. If we were going to have this talk, we needed to have it now.

I reached forward and grabbed both of her hands in mine, waiting for Nan to share what was on her mind.

"I'm sorry I kept you away from your grandmother all these years. It's the one thing in my life I truly regret," she said with a sigh.

I shook my head emphatically. "I don't."

She lifted her eyes to mine, searching. "What?"

"I don't regret you doing that, and neither should you."

Nan swallowed. "Was she really that terrible?"

"No, she was actually pretty cool." I smiled, remembering the moments we'd shared that weekend.

And Nan's expression pinched.

"But I'm glad I grew up with you," I quickly added. "Marilyn is nice, and I look forward to getting to know her much better, but you've helped shape my life into what it is today. And I love my life. I love you. I wouldn't have wanted anything different."

"Really?" Nan looked so frail in that moment. For the first time in a long time, I really saw her age. She'd lived through a lot and carried one very big secret for most of her life. How did she feel now that it had been exposed and that everyone still loved her just as much as before?

"Really, really," I said in a silly voice.

She laughed at my reference to an old movie we'd watched together countless times in my childhood.

"Will you believe me this time?"

Nan wiped away a tear, then grabbed my hands again and gave them a good squeeze. "I'll try."

"Well, that's the best any of us can do, right?" I winked. "Someone super smart and awesome taught me that."

"Speaking of all those lovely adjectives, how was she? Did you find out why William…?" She let her words trail off, unwilling—or perhaps unable—to voice what her late friend had done. With that single action, he'd changed all of our lives forever. We'd never know exactly why he'd done it, but I trusted Grandma Marilyn's interpretation of events. Of course, it led me to wonder if my missing grandpa would have accepted me for who I am, if he'd gotten the chance to meet me before he passed.

Sometimes I had a hard time remaining serious in serious moments. I knew a joke wouldn't help here, so I called upon my best impression of Charles. "Well, you see, the prevailing theory is that he took Mom away because he believed he was keeping her safe from Marilyn."

Nan's eyes bulged. "Was Marilyn dangerous? Is she now?"

I waggled my fingers. "She's kooky-crazy. Turns out she can talk to animals."

Nan gasped. "You can't be serious!"

I just smiled and nodded. "No one would believe her, including Grandpa. He chose never to see his own daughter again rather than to believe something so magical could be possible."

Nan gasped again. "Oh, that poor old man. He missed out on so much."

"It was his choice," I pointed out. "Marilyn never got a choice. You didn't have much of one, either."

"He made a choice, but it was the wrong one. That doesn't sound like the friend I knew. Still, I'm so incredibly grateful for the life we've shared."

"Me, too," I said, peppering her cheek with a kiss.

Nan shook her head and looked down at her lap. "You and Marilyn must have had a lot of stories to share."

"We did, and I really like her."

What Nan said next surprised me more than anything else had so far that weekend. "I think I would, too."

"Good, because she's coming over for dinner next month. I figured that would give everyone enough time to let everything sink in, and it's still well before the wedding. By the way, I have a new friend that I just know you're going to love. Her name is Sharon, and..."

We stayed up the whole night talking, just like the old days. I had a lot to tell my mom, but that could wait until tomorrow. She had her own feelings about our sordid history, and I'd have to find a way to help her work through them.

But that's what the people in your life were for.

They were there for you.

And it was okay to lean on them when you needed to.

I learned that this weekend, and I hoped with time my grandma Marilyn would be able to learn it, too.

I couldn't wait for her to meet the rest of the family, and I couldn't wait to delve further into our shared ability and what it could mean for us in the future.

Would Pet Whisperer P.I. get a new partner member?

Heck if I knew. But for once, not knowing was actually part of the fun.

DEER DUPLICITY

Lately I've been putting my P.I. business on the back burner in favor of planning my upcoming nuptials. But when my brand-new next-door neighbor turns up dead, I drop everything to investigate—especially since I had a clear motive for her murder and I don't plan on saying "I do" in jail.

The police say her death was an accident, but it doesn't seem so open and shut to me. A frightened buck may be the only one who knows what really happened, but I'm having a hard time getting him to stop running and start talking.

. . .

Another problem? Octo-Cat and I can't see eye-to-eye on how to tackle our newest investigation, which forces me to work with my other, less reliable animal sidekicks to get the job done. Can I not only prove foul play, but also solve the case?

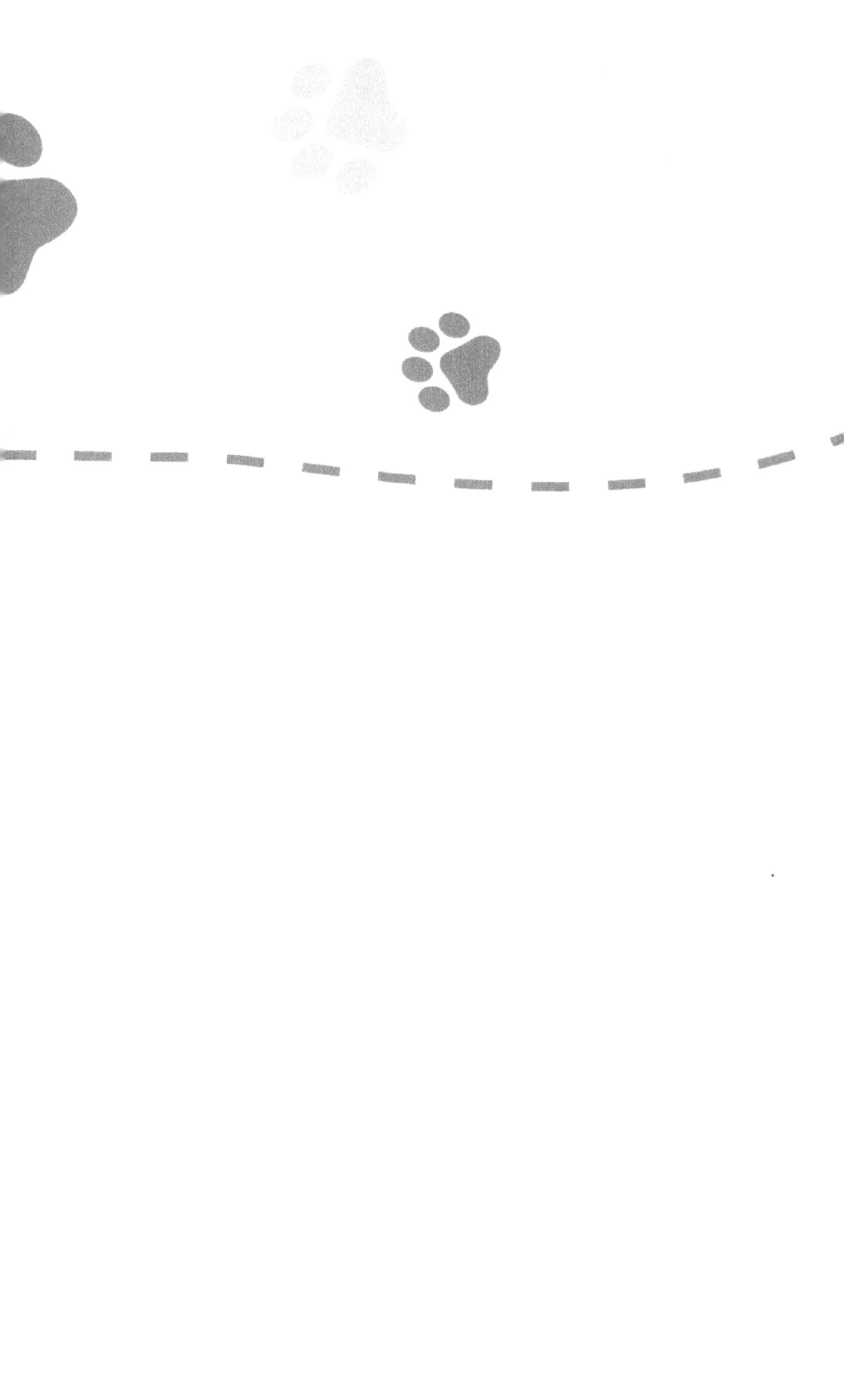

1

My name is Angie Russo, and I live a strange life. Thanks to my charming fiancé and kooky nan, my life is full of love. It's also full of noise... so much noise.

I can talk to animals, and once they find that out, most don't want to shut up. It all started with Octo-Cat. He and I met at a will reading, back when I was still working a temp job as a paralegal. His owner had just passed, and I'd just had an unfortunate run-in with a busted coffeemaker. Put the two together and—bam—our odd friendship was born. The first thing we did together was solve the murder of his former owner, which took some doing since everyone else happily assumed the old lady had died of natural causes.

Once I'd officially adopted my tabby companion, I became the trustee for his rather generous trust fund, and the two of us moved into his former owner's old manor house. I brought my nan along, and she later adopted the most adorable pound puppy, a mostly black tricolor Chihuahua we call Paisley.

Somewhere along the way, our gang realized we had a knack for solving mysteries and started up an official business, which—much to my chagrin—has been dubbed Pet Whisperer P.I. The last thing I want is strangers knowing I can talk to animals, but luckily they all seem to think our moniker is a joke or some misguided publicity attempt.

Whatever the case, they're always happy once we get the job done. Admittedly, most of our cases are unpaid. And usually we're not even formally hired. Mysteries just fall into our laps, and well, what else are we going to do to fill our days?

I don't take kindly to being called an amateur sleuth, mind you. I have an official business with a registered LLC and everything. That makes me a professional, thank you very much.

My fiancé is the senior partner at a local law firm—the same one I used to work at. That place saw tons of turnover until Charles took his place at the top. Now things are nice and steady, and together the two of us make up the small-town Maine version of *Law and Order.*

The last prominent member of our quirky ensemble is our very own trash panda, Pringle. He's a sticky-fingered raccoon who lives in a treehouse out back. He likes cat food and Nerf guns, but he loves reality TV. Most of the time he causes more problems than he solves, but we love him anyway. Well, most of us do.

Even after more than a year together, I'm pretty sure I only register as "kind of like" on my cat's affection scale, and Pringle ranks much, much lower.

Me? I've got all the love I can handle between planning a wedding and getting to know the bio grandmother I recently reconnected with after a lifetime of not even knowing she existed. The best part? My Grandma Lyn can talk to animals too, and believe me you, we've talked about our shared talents until we were both blue in the face.

Nan still feels a little jealous, but she's working on it. I could meet a hundred long-lost relatives and would still never turn my back on the woman who raised me and in the process became my very best friend.

As much as I'm looking forward to tying the knot with Charles, a small part of me is dreading it too. I've lived with Nan almost my entire life—the whole thing excluding a brief period when I tried to establish independence in a crummy rental. Marrying Charles means I'll be moving in with him, and Nan has made it clear that we newlyweds should be granted our space when the time comes.

I guess for now I'll soak up every second with my funny, sunny grandmother. It's not like we'll be moving far away. In fact, I won't be moving at all. Nan has decided to buy her old house back from Charles—what a lucky turn of events that he bought her old place when she moved in with me at Octo-Cat's manor house—and Charles will move in here with me. It's a short drive and one we're all already used to making on the regular.

Things won't be so bad. Just different. I've already told Nan to expect me over for dinner at least five times per week, and I also plan to keep her room exactly as it is in case she ever decides to move back. She's not getting any younger, though I swear she's in better shape than me and will likely outlive us all... even Octo-Cat, who has nine lives to lose before he's through.

* * *

Normally I wake up to the smell of Nan's fresh baked goods wafting from the kitchen. Today, however, a sharp pain on my chest lurched me from sleep.

"Confess or die!" Pringle shouted and sent Paisley scampering over my chest once more.

"Stop! You're scaring me!" the little Chihuahua yipped, tucking her tail tight beneath her as she ran.

"You're scaring us all, kiddo. That's what happens when you keep secrets from the fuzz." Now the raccoon was sitting firmly on my chest as if I were some kind of soapbox for his ridiculous speech. His claws were sharp, and it hurt.

"Pringle," I growled and shoved him off me. "You're not supposed to be in the house, and you're especially not supposed to be in my room."

"Sorry, toots. Didn't mean to wake ya, but you're harboring my main suspect, and that won't do." He shook a little black finger in the air. "There's no hiding from the long arm of the law!"

"But I don't even have arms!" Paisley cried. "I'm a dog. I only have legs!"

Pringle slapped his hand into his forehead and sighed heavily. "Dick Tracy never had to deal with this, I can assure you."

I wasn't sure whether he was talking to me, himself, or an imaginary audience. Whatever the case, I was done with this whole thing. Ever since our resident raccoon developed a taste for old back-and-white gumshoe films, we'd all been short on rest. Lately, he turned everything into a case to be solved. Yesterday we were all treated to the case of "Why is the water bowl empty?" Admittedly, that one was pretty open and shut; Pringle spent more time recounting the glory of his victory than he did investigating.

"Go play somewhere else." I pulled the blanket over my head, praying that this time they might actually listen.

Paisley slipped under the comforter and licked the inside of my ear. "Mommy!" she squeaked so loud it sent me bolt upright. "Pringle says it's my fault there's a big truck outside. He said I've been feeding secrets to the Russians. But I don't even know who that is or why they're in such a hurry."

It was way, way too early for this. Unfortunately, past experience dictated there was no way I'd be getting back to sleep. Besides, poor Paisley had always been too easy of a target for Pringle. He would stay on her until I forcibly split the two of them up.

I groaned and swung my feet to the floor. "Pringle, you are not allowed in my bedroom. Not in the morning. Not ever. Understood?"

"Yeah, I understand. The cat and dog are allowed in, but just because I'm a raccoon..." He threw his arms up in the air. "That's profiling. Just because I've got a mask and rings on my tail. Frankly, I didn't take you for the type."

"Outdoor animals need to stay outdoors," I eked out between clenched teeth.

"Whoa, whoa, whoa, sweetheart. Do you even hear yourself?" Something lit in his eyes, and he laughed. "Oh, I get it. This isn't about me at all."

"It's not?"

"No, you're threatened by my investigative prowess. I get it. A failed P.I. like you? Of course you're threatened by a brilliant ingenue such as myself."

"Excuse me," I thundered, then chased the little bandit out of my tower, down two flights of stairs, and through the electronic pet door, which somehow he'd managed to hack once again.

Paisley ran behind me, barking the whole way. "And stay out, you no-good doodoo head!" she ruffed before bolting through the pet door herself.

I pulled back the drapes to watch the two of them fly through the yard where, sure enough, an enormous moving truck stood idling in our driveway.

2

I strode through the door and right up to that big truck, then motioned for the driver to roll down his window. When he did, he looked me over with an odd smile, making me realize I was still barefoot and in my oversized polka-dotted pajamas.

"Hi. Can I help you with something?" the driver asked, tipping his baseball cap cordially.

Suddenly I became very conscious of the fact that I wasn't wearing a bra and crossed my arms over my chest to preserve my decency as much as I could given the situation. "This is my driveway," I offered with a shy shrug.

He stared at me blankly, blinking a couple times in clear and utter confusion.

"I didn't order a moving truck," I added for clarity.

"Oh. Right. Sorry about that." The driver stopped speaking and frowned. After a bit of hesitation, he continued, “We’re helping the old lady next door. My crew is running a bit late, so she sent me away and told me not to come back until we’re all here and ready to clock in for the job. She also mentioned that she’d be reducing her payment.”

“Confess!” Pringle screeched at the top of his lungs as he and Paisley darted beneath the truck, then ran back out again. Luckily it seemed like my companion didn’t notice the rogue animals skittering about.

“Just how late is your crew?” I asked, trying to keep our conversation on topic despite the crazed antics taking place right in my front yard.

The driver glanced toward the digital clock on his dashboard. “Maybe seven minutes now. They had an early morning pack-up across town and agreed to meet me here to unload. That first job ran a few minutes over, but they’re on their way now.”

He sighed, and I inadvertently found myself doing the same.

“Sounds like your day is starting off a bit rough.”

“I’ll say.” He dipped his head and sighed again just as Paisley and Pringle scampered off into the forest that lines our yard. Once again, he missed seeing them entirely. Still, I felt bad for the guy, having to wake up early just to wait.

“Can I bring you anything? Coffee? A muffin?”

The corners of his mouth lifted into an odd smile but then immediately gave way back into a frown. “That sounds divine, but I really shouldn’t. I don’t want to give the old biddy anything else to complain about.”

Hmmm, this couldn't be good. My new neighbor had only just arrived and already she was leaving a sour taste in people's mouths. Then again, maybe she wasn't quite as bad as the mover was making her out to be. He could have fabricated his story to make his crew look better. Whatever the case, someone had finally moved into the vacant manor next door, and stopping by to welcome her would be the neighborly thing to do. Even if I was a bit nervous about it.

I said a quick goodbye to the driver, hoping the animals wouldn't resurface to bother the poor guy, then marched back inside to find Nan.

Normally she kept busy in the kitchen this time of day, but today she was nowhere to be found. She had, however, left a handwritten note:

Out with Grant at Tulip Festival.

Back by Noon.

I flipped the notecard over and found a postscript scrawled on the back:

P.S. These are for the new neighbor. Tell her I'll come by to say hi later!

I swear, nothing happened in this town without my nan first knowing about it. A little heads-up about the new neighbor would have been nice, but at least she'd made up for it by putting together a lovely muffin basket.

I took a quick detour upstairs to make myself a bit more presentable, then grabbed Nan's latest batch of delectable baked goods by the wicker handle and headed for the door.

Octo-Cat lay snoozing in a sunspot by the entryway. The tabby hadn't been there when I passed by a couple minutes ago, but now he was in such a deep sleep that he appeared dead to the world. *Best to let sleeping cats lie,* I reasoned, choosing not to disturb him until after I had some gossip to share about the new neighbor lady.

When I stepped out onto the porch, the big moving truck was still idling in my driveway but Pringle and Paisley had made themselves scarce. I hoped the wily raccoon wasn't being too hard on the poor little dog. Although past experience told me that would be just the case.

I'd go and find them after saying my quick hello next door and put an end to this game once and for all, even if it meant putting some kind of child lock setting on Pringle's streaming services. He'd eventually become obsessed with another film genre, but at least it would buy us some down time while he browsed.

One thing at a time, though.

As for my current task, the fastest way to the old Harlowe estate was via the woods that separate our lots, so I pushed my way through the thick canopy of trees, taking care not to upset my muffin basket.

When I emerged from the forest, I found an old woman with

short white hair and a sour expression yelling into the cell phone she held out in front of her on speaker phone. I saw her profile as she paced her wide porch, but she didn't seem to notice me standing at the edge of her property with my basket of goodies.

"I already told you," she spat. "Wild dogs are roaming my property, and they're upsetting the local fauna. They already scared off a mother doe and her fawn when they tried to pay me a visit."

"Wild dogs?" the dispatcher on the other end responded skeptically over the speaker phone. "That's not a very common problem in Glendale, not since Pearl took over at the shelter."

"Are you suggesting I made this whole thing up?" the woman fumed.

The dispatcher immediately fell in line. "No, no. Of course not. Can you please describe them?"

Pringle came up beside me and placed a hand on my lower leg, making me cringe with fright. "Hey, toots. Whatcha got there?" he asked, gesturing toward the basket with his furry chin.

"Huge beasts," the neighbor continued as she motioned wildly with the hand that wasn't holding onto her phone. "One was black like a hellhound. The other had stripes."

I glanced down at Pringle and his big, fat striped tail. No. She couldn't possibly…

"Mommy!" Paisley let out a high-pitched bark, running across the lawn toward me and Pringle.

"There they are now!" the neighbor cried, finally looking up and spotting me.

I offered an uncomfortable wave and held the basket of baked goods out before me as a gesture of peace. "These are for you."

"Miss, Miss, are you still there?" the dispatcher asked after several moments of silence on the old woman's part. "Have you been hurt?"

She turned her back to me and continued. "Send someone immediately. My address is…"

I stood frozen to the spot in disbelief. What could Paisley and Pringle possibly have done to upset this woman so much in such a short period of time? And just whom had she called to issue her complaints? She wasn't even moved in yet for goodness' sake!

"Animal control is on the way," she turned to inform me with a steely gaze after finally hanging up the phone.

This startled me even more than Pringle's sudden appearance at my side. "Animal control? What? Why?"

"Seems you can't control your animals. Shame, but someone has to do it. They should be here within the next ten minutes. I suggest you take your two dogs and leave unless you want to have them taken to the pound… or worse." She let the implication linger between us.

"It's just one dog. A Chihuahua named Paisley." I bent down and snapped my fingers to call the dog to me. "She's really very sweet. I'm sorry if her playing disturbed you."

Paisley came running. Once she reached me, I shifted the muffins to one side and scooped the Chihuahua up with my free arm, tucking her into my armpit. "I'm your new neighbor, Angie. I live right next door with my nan. If you ever—"

"Can it, Angie. You only get one chance to make a first impression, and your hellhound already did it for you. I think it's best if we both just leave each other alone."

"But—"

She pointed toward the forest with a shaky finger. "Now go! Get off my property, or I'll call the police."

I briefly debated leaving the muffins, but you know what? She didn't deserve Nan's little bites of heaven, and I sure wouldn't mind scarfing down a few to help me forget this horrible start to the day.

Good riddance!

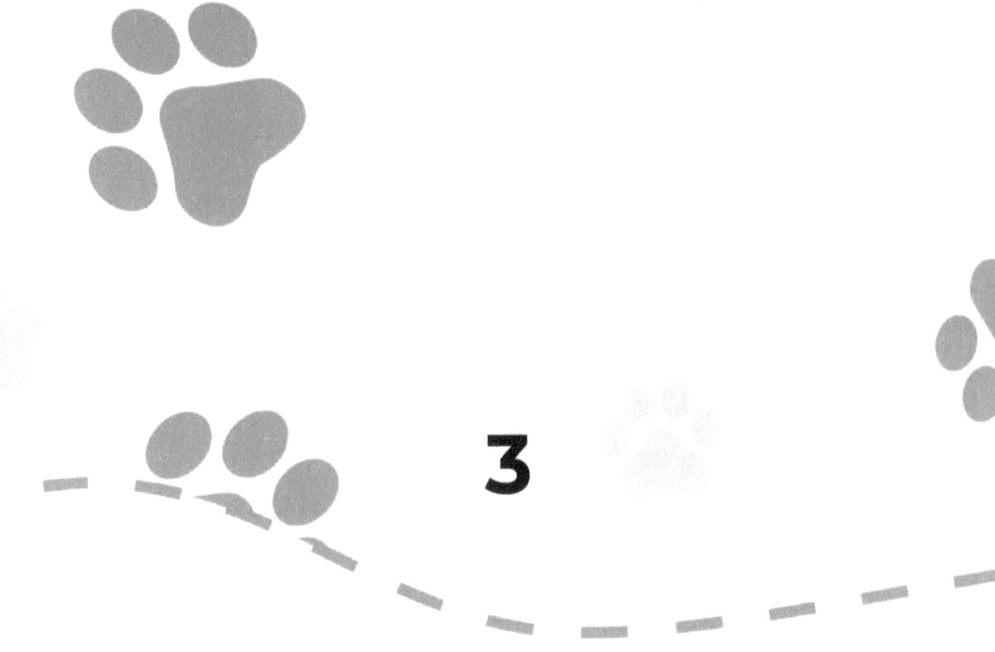

3

"Where were you?" Octo-Cat asked drolly as I strode back inside and all but slammed our heavy front door. "And hey, why the attitude? It isn't very becoming of you, Angela."

I stopped mid-stomp and turned to face my tabby where he sat idling on the coffee table. "I just met the new neighbor."

He flicked his tail and stared at me with large amber eyes that gave nothing away. "I take it things didn't go well."

"She was horrible. A monster!" I cried, throwing myself into the nearby armchair and sifting through the muffin basket until I found the one I wanted—a nice big cinnamon crumble.

I took a big bite right off the top, then continued speaking around my fresh mouthful of sweet and spicy mush. "She called Paisley a hellhound. And she called animal control on us!

Wouldn't even let me say hi before she shooed me out of her yard." I swallowed my first bite and took another.

Octo-Cat pulled his ears back flat against his head until they almost seemed to disappear. "Has anyone ever told you that you eat very noisily and with far more saliva than necessary?"

I groaned. "Yes, *you*. And at least half a dozen times at that. Are you even listening to what I'm saying right now?"

"Believe me, I'm trying. It's just hard to make out your words over all the smacking and snarfing. I'm trying to lend a sympathetic ear, but you're being very rude, Angela." His tail began to wag wildly, suggesting that if I didn't give in to his demands, I may find myself on the receiving end of a serious hissy fit.

"Me? I'm not the rude one here, but never mind." I placed my partially eaten muffin on top of the others in the basket, then brushed off my hands and opened my mouth to show that it was now empty.

Octo-Cat nodded his approval. "You may proceed."

I repeated the whole thing again, becoming angrier and angrier as I did. Seriously, what was this new neighbor's deal? Did she just hate dogs, or did she hate all living things as a rule?

Octo-Cat held up a paw to silence my tirade. "You need to keep your voice down. Did you know cats can hear three times better than humans? Right now, you're little more than a noisy siren blaring right in my ear." He looked me up and down. "In fact you look like one too with that red face of yours. Did you wake up on the wrong side of the litter box today, or what?"

I grabbed the muffins again and hoisted myself from the

chair. “Forget it. I’ll go tell it to Paisley. Or Pringle. Or, hey, maybe the new neighbor isn’t quite as bad as I thought, after all.”

My cat said nothing as I marched away. His hot-and-cold attitude always kept me guessing, but I wasn’t in the mood for games this morning. I needed a sympathetic ear and something worthwhile to distract me. Besides, I’d promised myself I would save Paisley from Pringle’s pretend interrogation just as soon as I’d checked in next door.

Hmm. Now where could they be?

I stashed the muffin basket in the kitchen, keeping one in my hand to nourish me on my search, then headed back outside. Thankfully, the moving truck had now pulled away. Presumably they’d gone next door to finish their job of sticking me with the world’s worst neighbor. *Bah.*

I wasn’t often in a foul mood, partially because I hated who I became whenever rage flew through my veins. Maybe I could ask Nan to lead me on one of her guided meditations when she got back home. Or heck, maybe I’d hit the town and engage in a little retail therapy. True, considering my P.I. client load was light, my funds came directly from my cat’s trust fund—but if he’d simply been willing to extend a sympathetic ear, I wouldn’t need to find some other way to lift my spirits.

Yes, shopping. That would be a good way to keep myself busy today. Just as soon as I rescued that poor little dog of mine.

“Paisley!” I cried, trotting down the porch steps and sweeping my line of vision across the yard.

But she didn't come running. Didn't even bark in acknowledgment. Weird.

"Paisley!" I tried again, eyeing the forest for any sudden flash of movement.

When I still didn't receive any response, fear began to claw at my quickly beating heart. The new neighbor hadn't hurt her, had she? Honestly, after our rude encounter, I wouldn't put it past her. Oh no.

I broke into a jog, rounding the house, calling out for Paisley at the top of my lungs.

"Yeesh. Will you quiet down already?" Pringle poked his head out of his tree house and stared down at me with shining black eyes. "Raccoons have hearing that's at least a thousand times better than humans. True fact. I heard it on the Kardashians. Anyway... you're giving me a headache, and you're interrupting my interrogation. Not a winning combo, toots."

"Mommy," Paisley whimpered softly from somewhere above me. What? *Noooo.*

"Pringle, did you...?" But I didn't even need to finish asking the question before I was tossing my muffin to the ground and launching myself up the ladder and into the trash panda's tree fort. Sure enough, the little dog sat cowering in a live trap. And every time she shook, the entire cage rattled in response.

"Pringle," I fumed, unable to tear my eyes away from the terrified pup. "How could you?"

He appeared unmoved by the whole thing as he settled

himself comfortably in the window. "The dog wouldn't submit to questioning, so I had to bring her in."

"He said he would gag me if I answered you when you were calling, Mommy." Paisley spoke fast and in a higher pitch than usual. "I don't know what that means, but I was so afraid."

"Open the cage," I commanded between gritted teeth. "Open it right now."

"All right, all right. So dramatic. She's not hurt. See?" Pringle deftly unlatched the cage, allowing Paisley to bolt out straight into my arms.

"He dognapped me!" The little dog barked and whined, burrowing into me. "I've never been so afraid in my whole life, Mommy."

I stroked Paisley and cuddled her to my chest while glaring daggers at the raccoon. "Pringle, you're losing your TVs and your Nerf guns, and if I ever catch you inside my house again, I'll turn you into Davey Crockett wearable memorabilia."

Pringle brought a hand to his chest and gasped. "You wouldn't."

"Don't try me." Of course I would never hurt him or any animal, but he'd gone too far in kidnapping and trapping Paisley, all because of some imaginary role-playing game. I'd just about had it with this day already and was close to calling it off altogether. Would it really be that unforgivable if I went back to bed before even fully finishing my breakfast?

I tucked Paisley under my arm and then began to slowly descend the ladder. Halfway to the ground, a question popped into my mind and I retraced my steps. "Pringle? Where did you get that live trap?"

He shifted to his haunches and smiled at me with pointy teeth exposed. "Oh, I found it on the porch next door. It looked handy, so I swiped it."

A wave of anxiety crashed over me. "You stole this from our new neighbor?" If she found this thing on my property, she was going to be livid.

Pringle shrugged. "Steal is a harsh word. More like I borrowed it."

Now I was really torn. If that cruel woman actually managed to trap an animal, there's no telling what she might do to torment it. Then again, the last thing I wanted was to encourage Pringle's thieving ways.

"I'm coming back for it," I told him with a stern look before making my way back down the ladder. I'd have to find someplace to hide it from the both of them. Yes, stealing was wrong, but animal cruelty was far, far worse.

Let's just hope I had a bit of time before she realized it was missing.

4

I deposited Paisley in the second-floor bedroom she and Nan share, then closed the door so that Octo-Cat wouldn't come in and bother her. "Try to get some rest. I'll be back in a little while to check on you, and Nan will be home before you know it too."

"Mommy, can you stay with me until I fall asleep?" the little dog begged, and I didn't have the heart to say no.

I waited as she arranged herself on the pillow with the silk case that Nan kept on the bed especially for her doggie soulmate. Once she was cuddled into a tight little ball, I began to slowly stroke her fur, waiting for her breaths to come more slowly as sleep took her.

Soon I'd be getting married to Charles, and that simple act would change all our lives. Even though Paisley and I shared a close bond, she was actually Nan's dog, and she would be leaving with her when she moved out. My heart clenched as I realized just how much I would miss the little thing. Sure, we'd visit each other all the time, but it wouldn't be the same.

Even after Paisley dozed off, I could have sat there loving on her all day. But no, I had a live trap to hide. With a soft sigh, I let myself out of the room as quietly as I could so as not to disturb Paisley, then headed back outside.

Octo-Cat followed along without comment, which in itself was odd. He only spoke when I put my hand on the first rung of the ladder that led up to the treehouse.

"What are you doing?" he demanded with a cool, uninterested voice.

"Taking care of business," I mumbled as I focused on raising one hand over the other. The ladder wasn't built with humans in mind, and I worried that if I wasn't cautious enough, the whole thing might collapse on me.

Thankfully, I made it up without incident, grabbed the live trap and almost threw the darned thing down to the ground. Then my rational brain woke back up just in time to warn me that the noise might further attract the new neighbor's ire—and reveal the theft. I couldn't exactly blame the situation on the raccoon without sounding like a crazy person, so I did my best to climb down one-handed while holding tight to the cage with the other.

"Why was that up there?" my cat wanted to know when I'd finally made it to the ground. Of course he didn't offer to help, but at least he didn't criticize.

"Pringle stole it from the neighbor and then used it as a makeshift prison for Paisley," I explained, upset all over again as I recalled the horrific scene.

Octo-Cat shook his head. "Someone should really make Davey Crockett memorabilia out of him."

"That's what I said," I exclaimed, then realized I was really having a bad day if I was starting to sound like my cranky cat.

Octo-Cat exposed his claws and stretched into a complicated yoga pose. "Just say the word. As you know, cats are the most elite hunters in any biosphere."

I chose not to point out that his elite cousins were all big cats, not house cats. I also didn't say that I was almost positive Pringle would win in a fight—what with his superior intellect and opposable thumbs.

"No more fights," I said instead as we rounded the house, side by side, just in time to see a white van with the county insignia pull into our driveway. Well, this couldn't be good.

A uniformed officer stepped out of the car and waved at me. "Good morning!" he called brightly as the day around me dimmed further.

"Hi," I called back, swallowing down a fresh lump of anxiety. I set the live trap down onto the grass and hurried my pace to meet him.

"What's that for?" the officer asked, motioning toward the live trap.

I stopped in my tracks, just a few paces away from him.

"That? Oh, there was a raccoon in my house this morning. I thought I might be able to catch him and take him back outside."

"Is the wild animal still in your home, Miss?" He reached for the radio looped onto his belt, sending a cold bolt of fear straight through me.

"No, he's gone now," I insisted just as quickly as I could, then shrugged, attempting to appear casual. "This is just in case he comes back."

The officer frowned and dropped his hand from the radio. "Well, regardless of that situation. We received a complaint at animal control, and I was sent out to investigate."

"Yes, I was at the new neighbor's house when she called your office. I was trying to welcome her to the neighborhood. Lot of good that did." I laughed bitterly despite myself.

"Judging from the call we received, I don't think that's a very good idea." He shook his head and fixed his eyes on the driveway. "That new neighbor is quite the ornery sort. I'd steer clear if I were you."

"Duly noted. Anyway, how can I help you, officer?"

His eyes floated up to meet mine and a sad smile filled his face. "Listen, I'm an animal lover too, and I know how hard it is when you're in close quarters with someone who despises your pets. But the woman who called us was hysterical. It's our job to follow due diligence in cases like this."

I nodded along the whole time he was speaking, eager to send him on his way. "I understand. What do you need from me?"

"I'm going to need to check the tags and licenses for all your animals."

I tipped my head toward Octo-Cat who sat silently watching the full exchange. "I don't have that for my cat, but I can show you vet records if that helps."

He eyed Octo-Cat for a moment before saying, "We really just need the paperwork for your two dogs."

"Who is this clown?" Octo-Cat meowed and lifted his leg over his head to groom his kitty bits. "Should I claw him up for you?"

"No," I shouted, eliciting a strange look from the animal control officer. "I mean, no, that's not right. I only have one dog. Actually it's my grandmother's. She lives with me too. Um, do you need to see her paperwork also?"

My attempt at a joke was completely rebuffed.

Now the previously sympathetic officer wore a scowl as he regarded me. "The caller was quite insistent that there were two."

"You can come look inside if it helps, but I only have one dog." I needed to try harder to play nice. It wasn't this guy's fault that my new neighbor was certifiable.

"Is this the striped one, or the large black..." He paused to check his notes. "Hellhound?"

I smiled despite myself. "Tell you what, I'll go get her along with the paperwork and you can see for yourself."

When I returned with Paisley, the officer had a good long laugh. "Huge? She couldn't be more than five pounds soaking wet." He continued to laugh as he examined the Chihuahua's tags and looked over her paperwork.

"Everything's in order here, so I'll let you off with a warning today," he declared at last.

I let out a huge sigh of relief before realizing the news hadn't all been good. "A warning for what?"

"Your neighbor asked us to file trespassing charges," the officer revealed, then pressed his lips into a firm line.

"Are you serious? I just went over there to welcome her and offer some baked goods!"

"Not against you." He nodded toward Paisley in my arms. "*Her.* Technically, the charge would be dog at large."

"But that's ridiculous!" I argued, ready to march right over there and give that old crow a piece of my mind.

He sucked air in through his teeth, then shook his head again. "Technically your neighbor is in the right. Your dog shouldn't be on her property."

"Oh, okay." I looked down at the squirming pup in my arms while I spoke. "We're just so used to that property being empty, but okay, I'll make sure Paisley doesn't venture back over onto her side of the woods from now on out."

"It's for the best." The officer reached forward to scratch Paisley between the ears. "I'm sorry you're dealing with this. Hopefully your new neighbor will cool down once she's settled in, but somehow I doubt it. Maybe consider a fence or a dog run?"

The whole thing was absurd. I hadn't had any luck, but maybe Nan could talk some sense into the woman next door. Surely this little squabble was something we could work out ourselves, right?

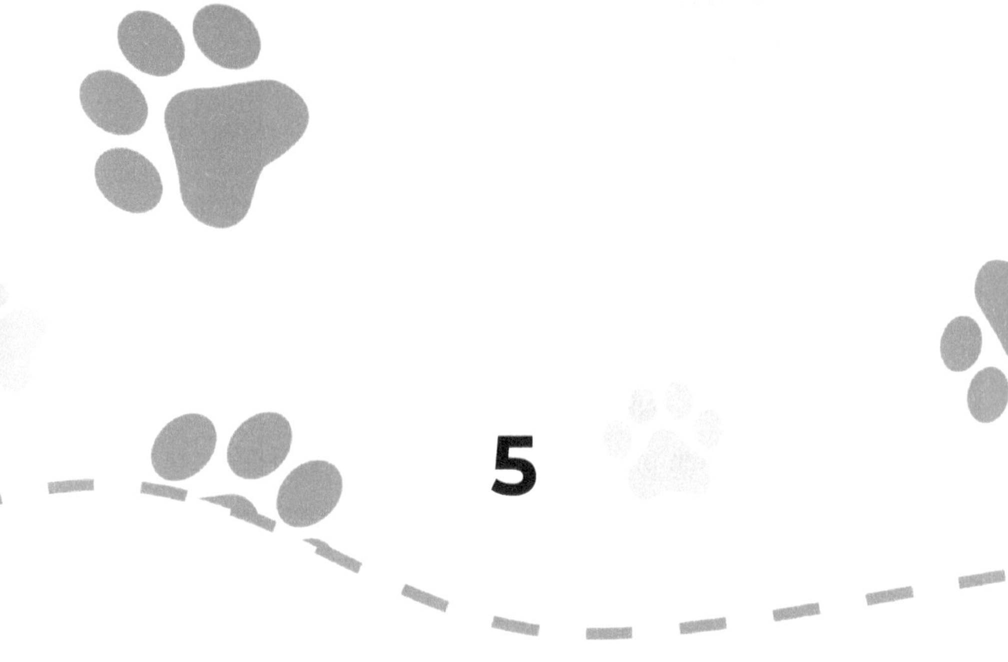

5

As it turns out, the squabble with the new neighbor next door was not, in fact, something we could settle ourselves.

That morning, Nan came back walking on clouds after touring the tulip festival with her beloved. When I told her about the contentious run-in with both the neighbor and with the animal control officer, she fired up her little red sports car and drove straight out to Misty Harbor to pick up some of our favorite lobster rolls from Little Dog Diner.

“The poor dear must be exhausted from her big move,” she reasoned as she held up the white paper bag filled with delicious fare. “I bet she’s famished too. I’m sure it’s nothing a little neighborly kindness can’t fix.”

I tried to warn her off what I considered to be a doomed plan, but she wouldn’t have it.

Nan told me to be more compassionate, leashed up Paisley, then disappeared next door while Octo-Cat and I sat together at the dining room table and got to work on our lobster rolls.

I was just licking my fingers clean when Nan returned holding up a banged-up, crumpled-up bag covered in dirty smudges.

"In all my life..." she huffed, slamming the bag into the kitchen trash. "I've never met such a bitter, such a detestable, evil old witch."

Paisley followed close behind with her tail tucked between her legs and body cowering low to the ground.

"That bad, huh?" I asked sympathetically.

"Worse," Nan said with a giant pout on her wrinkled face.

I resisted the urge to say "told you so," and that was that.

I did make a mental note to check the yellow pages for some local fencing contractors and to set up a quote or two. Other than that, there wasn't much I or anyone else could do, other than hope and pray the neighbor—whose name we still didn't even know—would see herself out of the neighborhood.

And that she'd do so sooner rather than later.

Nothing more happened for the rest of that day, which would later prove to be a rare and welcome break.

Because the very next morning, we received a second visit from animal control. This time a different officer stopped by with photos in hand as irrefutable proof that Paisley had crossed the invisible boundary that divided our two properties by at least three full inches.

Said boundary ran through the forest and was completely ensconced by trees. I didn't even know where our yard ended and the neighbor's began, but *she* did apparently. She'd even set up trail cameras to capture any movement along the border. I argued that my right to privacy had been violated, but apparently I was once again on the wrong side of the law with that one.

I tried to put it out of my mind, but the rest of that day was spoiled same as the one before.

The next day I didn't get any unwanted visitors, but I did receive a letter in the mail explaining that my refusal to keep track of my dog had led to a deer being scared off her property. I, for one, couldn't understand how this person could hate dogs so much while being seemingly desperate to make friends with the deer.

The note was handwritten but signed with only her address in lieu of a name. Even more off-putting was the fact that the envelope sported a stamp and postmark, meaning the bitter old woman had sent it through the post office rather than simply walking it over—or heaven forbid, trying to talk with us.

After that little surprise delivery, I drove straight to the pet store and invested in a hefty supply of pee pads. Paisley would just have to do her business inside until we managed to get that fence up. It wasn't ideal, but it was the best option we had available to us, all things considered.

* * *

Animal control came out for their third visit a couple days after I received the letter in the mail. This time they shared pictures of Octo-Cat helping himself to the bathroom on the neighbor's porch.

When I confronted him about it, my cat grinned wide, obviously pleased with himself. "Someone had to give that woman her due. She peed you off, so I peed on her porch. Justice."

Part of me was touched that the cat had decided to defend my honor, but a much larger part was upset he had created even more problems for us.

We sealed up the pet door then, because even with a fence, Octo-Cat could easily slip over or under to gain access next door. I'd already learned the hard way—and many times over at that—if I gave the tabby a direct order, he would go out of his way to do the opposite.

I prayed the fence contractors would be able to squeeze us in soon, but so far I was getting nowhere with any of the companies I'd contacted. They all claimed to have huge waiting lists now that the weather was warm. And somehow I doubted this was a job Nan and I could pull off on our own. Not with such a large property and not with such intensive labor required to get the job done right. Maybe Charles could find the time to help once he finished his current case. Whatever the matter, I was quickly becoming quite desperate.

* * *

Poor Paisley became notably depressed at having to spend her days indoors. Octo-Cat preferred being inside as a general rule, but the moment it stopped being his choice, he took to complaining loudly and doing so ceaselessly throughout the day. My home no longer felt like mine, thanks to the ridiculous expectations of our new neighbor.

"At least you'll be moving away in a month. Everything will be back the way you like it in your new house," I told Paisley to try to cheer her up. Of course that only reminded her that we would be splitting households after the wedding and sent her into an even greater state of despair.

My heart broke for the little dog, but honestly I didn't know what else I could do to help her. Especially since each time we'd encountered animal control, they reminded me that the new neighbor was technically within her rights, just that most people never minded about these things. I did receive a fine for Octo-Cat's little act of defiance, although I still don't understand what exactly I'd been charged with.

Like anyone could control the comings and goings of a cat!

* * *

After a full two days without incident, we received a visit from the police. A noise complaint that seemed to stem from Pringle watching television at too great a volume. I'd forgotten my threat to remove it from his treehouse after all the drama with the neighbor that took over the week. We were told to turn it down and be more mindful in the future. The thing is I couldn't hear his TV from our house, so how on earth had the neighbor heard it from hers?

* * *

Animal control came again the day after that. This time they were in search of the second dog the neighbor swore was patrolling her yard and upsetting her trash cans. Seriously, that woman really needed to have her eyes checked.

I helpfully let the officers investigate the entire house to prove we weren't hiding a secret second dog and gently suggested that maybe they charge the neighbor with something for wasting so much of their time.

Honestly, the more we tried, the worse it got. Not even my sweet, lovable grandmother could charm her way into that woman's good graces.

Nan, of course, became absolutely incensed after this exchange and even went so far as to hire her Realtor friend to see if, for the right price, we might buy the house next door right out from under the neighbor. "I can sell my old home and move in next door. Then we'll be as close as close can be and also rid of the world's biggest nuisance."

But the transaction was a no go, and the next day we received another post-marked letter:

I know it was you.

Signed,

House #304

6

Over the course of the next week, we received visits from animal control and the police more days than not. At this point, I had half a mind to go pee on that cantankerous old woman's porch myself. If I was getting repeatedly punished for things I hadn't even done, I might as well actually get reprimanded for something I had.

It was fun to think about, but not something I'd ever do in real life. In fact, I didn't really do anything at all. Other than complain ad nauseum to Charles, effectively ruining what was supposed to a romantic evening.

I'd also asked my lawyer fiancé if I could reasonably sue her for harassment or emotional pain and suffering or literally anything that might stick and get her to leave us alone.

Charles said he would research precedents but that it probably wouldn't be worth the time and expense it would take to fight her in the courts. He also promised to help with our fencing project if I couldn't find a contractor by that weekend.

This, of course, was provided I survived until then, which at this point seemed like a pretty big expectation of myself.

I returned from my date that night both exhausted and angry with myself for letting this new rival take up residence beneath my skin. My agitation skyrocketed when I noted police lights flashing outside the neighbor's house.

Ugh. What could it possibly be now? I guessed I'd find out soon enough whenever the police came over to discuss the issue with me.

This neighbor was driving me out of my mind, and frankly I'd had quite enough. Perhaps that's why I was raring and ready to go when I spotted those police lights next-door.

Rather than wait for the officers to make their way over to my house, I was going to go over and find out what was going on for myself. And instead of traipsing through the woods, I decided to track back down my driveway and then march right up hers.

I wasn't usually a combative person, but the lady had never even given me a chance. Nan liked to say you caught more flies with honey than vinegar, but at this point, vinegar was the only thing I hadn't tried. Watching my morose animals laze about the house this past week with no reprieve in sight had filled me past overflowing with both spit and vinegar aplenty. I had to do something to defend my household and get our lives back on track. Otherwise, what kind of a pet owner would I be?

As I stormed up the driveway, I noticed that multiple cars had arrived on the scene along with a red-and-white ambulance, meaning whatever complaint the old witch had cooked up this time was a real doozy.

Thankfully, I spotted my old friend Officer Bouchard among the crowd. He'd saved my life when we first met. Maybe today he could save my sanity.

I waved and shouted a greeting, pushing myself into a jog to close the space between us. Strangely, I didn't spy my neighbor, even though she was typically right in the thick of whatever was happening.

"Listen," I told Bouchard, unable to hide my scowl. "Whatever complaint that horrible woman has cobbled together this time, I assure you it's completely off-base. She's done nothing but make my life miserable since she moved in, and she—"

Officer Bouchard placed a heavy hand on my shoulder, silencing me. "She's dead," he revealed with a soft wince.

I balked at this, unable to believe it. "Dead?" How could she be dead? Surely this was just another of her tricks. At this point I wouldn't put it past her to fake her death and then frame me for it.

"As a doornail," my friend in blue confirmed. "C'mon." He motioned for me to follow him around the house to where a little shed stood out back. The entire area was sectioned off with bright yellow crime scene tape.

Hmm. If this was a ruse, it was a mighty elaborate one.

"We still need to get an official report from the coroner, but we're reasonably sure this was an accidental death," he said, then pointed straight ahead. "Look."

I ventured closer to the shed and found my neighbor lying on the ground with her feet pointing straight up and a giant burlap bag covering her face and chest. Whatever was in that bag, it sure looked heavy.

"What happened?" I murmured, unable to tear my eyes away.

"Looks like this bag of deer feed fell off the top shelf when she wasn't expecting it, hit her clear on the head, and knocked her out." He pointed to the sharp metal frame of the shelf opposite. "She caught the edge there on her way down, sustaining a major head wound, then bled out before help could arrive."

Sure enough, a sticky puddle had flooded the small shed, staining the wooden floorboards red. The nauseating tang of iron filled the air, making me feel like I was going to be sick. If I had been home, would I have heard the crash? Would I have come to check in on her? No, I realized with bleak certainty, I wouldn't have even bothered to think twice.

I stepped back and turned away from the grisly scene, clutching a hand to my chest. Officer Bouchard followed me and offered his condolences, even though my words upon arriving at the scene should have made it clear I'd never been a fan of the old lady who lived next door.

"May I ask you a question?" I said, once I managed to get the bile in my stomach to stop churning. When he nodded his assent, I continued, "What was her name? I never knew it." Somehow it seemed important that I know now.

He checked his notes and let out a chuff. "Looks like this was a Ms. Miller. Ms. Angela Miller."

We had the same name? How was that possible?

It's not as if Angie was an overly unique moniker, but still, the revelation that my sworn enemy had shared my name hit me in an odd way. Somehow, despite all the strife she'd caused me in the last two weeks, this simple revelation humanized her. And suddenly I felt very sad.

What had happened to make this Angela's life so terrible? To make it easier for her to mail a letter next door than to simply stop by and talk? She must have been miserable and lonely—very, very lonely.

I don't know what I could have done differently, other than to be more patient, to give her a bit of time to open up to us. Maybe. I mean, if such a thing were even possible.

"Was it a quick death?" I asked, raising my hand to chew on a hangnail that had been bothering me all day.

"Probably not, I'm afraid, but it does appear she was unconscious, so probably not too aware of the pain."

"Oh." I glanced back into the shed at the unlucky corpse, the heavy bag on top of her, and the pooled blood beneath her. Farther back, the shed was lined with a smattering of gardening tools, bags of fertilizer, and several more burlap sacks like the one that had knocked old Angela unconscious but much smaller. Why had she been reaching for the largest one when there were others she could have grabbed instead? Such a simple decision—choosing the big bag instead of the little one—had ended her life.

I couldn't even be happy that my problems were now over, not when it had cost someone their life. I was just about to thank the officer and head home to share the news with Nan and the pets when a terrible thrashing sound tore through the air followed by a panicked braying of some kind.

Officer Bouchard grabbed his gun and pointed it in the general direction of the sound, motioning for me to get behind him until he'd cleared whatever threat lay in wait.

But instead I dodged his attempts to shelter me and ran straight for the forest...

7

I chased an odd pair of yellow streamers as they trailed deep into the woods. The police and paramedics stayed back, but they didn't know what was going on—I did.

"Wait," I called as I stepped carefully over a fallen branch but still snagged my foot anyhow. "Let me help you!"

But I couldn't keep up, and soon the object of my pursuit disappeared from view, taking the dancing yellow ribbons with him.

"What was that?" Officer Bouchard asked when I returned to the small crowd in my now-deceased neighbor's backyard. "And why in God's name would you run toward it?"

I leaned down and put a hand on each of my knees, woefully out of breath after the short burst of exercise. Nan would have my head if she knew how much I'd let myself go after we stopped our morning jogs.

"A big buck," I wheezed. "He wandered too close and got the crime scene tape tangled up in his antlers. The poor thing was scared out of his mind."

Bouchard tsked and shook his head. "A frightened animal is a dangerous one, which means you could have gotten yourself seriously injured back there. Think your nan would ever let me live it down if something happened to you on my watch?"

I rose to my full height and sighed. "You're right. I'm sorry." Apologizing was easier than explaining why I knew I'd be safe. Nan may have enjoyed blabbing about my secret abilities to all who would hear, but I preferred to keep mum.

Officer Bouchard gave me a friendly nudge on the shoulder. "Nothing bad came of it, but take a little better care with yourself, would you? We only have one Angie Russo in this town, and I'd kind of like to keep her."

I liked the officer, but I'd already seen more than I was comfortable seeing here. I'd happened upon more than one corpse in my day, but somehow Ms. Miller's irked me more than all the others combined. Maybe it's because we shared a name. Or maybe it was because of how I hated her, how I couldn't shake that this was somehow my fault.

Whatever the case, I just wanted to get home.

"I suppose I'll let you get back to it," I said with a tight smile, unable to summon an authentic one. "Please let me know if there's anything Nan or I can do to help with the investigation."

The policeman stretched both hands over his head and yawned. "There's no investigation. Seems like a pretty open and shut accidental death. Just as soon as we finish following procedure, we'll be ready to turn things over to the next of kin. Provided we can find some."

"Oh." I didn't know what to say to that. The whole thing was just very sad and unfortunate. "Well, good luck."

I hung my head and walked away, wondering if I'd somehow inadvertently contributed to the other Angie's untimely demise. I'd sure sent a lot of angry thoughts her way this past week. Maybe even wished she'd just disappear once and for all. But I never would have seriously wanted another human being to die just because she irritated me. Okay, maybe she did more than simply irritate me, but still... Of course, I knew it didn't help anyone now, me feeling sorry for myself, but I just couldn't help it.

I kept my gaze lowered to the ground as I traced my way back around the house, ready to head home, toss on my favorite PJs, and share the news with the others. If I'd been walking normally, I probably wouldn't have spotted the dusty tracks that led up to the basement egress window. I stopped abruptly, facing directly in toward the house. Maybe the old woman had locked herself out at some point and was looking for another way in, but somehow I doubted that. For starters, these tracks were enormous—far bigger than my own feet and definitely larger than the dainty ones I'd seen peeking out from the shed in the backyard. Someone—a man probably—had been spying on the neighbor. But why?

It couldn't have been the movers she'd mistreated. The rain

we got a few days back would have already washed their prints away. No, whoever these belonged to had been here recently.

Animal control certainly came around frequently, but they had no reason to go peeping in her windows. Hmmm.

For a moment I wondered whether I should go share my findings with Officer Bouchard, but he had already told me Ms. Miller's death was an accident. Still, doubts continued to nag at me. If the new neighbor made enemies of me and Nan so quickly, how many other enemies might she have accrued over the years? Judging by the way she'd treated the moving company she hired, I'd guess that not many people had positive run-ins with the old woman, which made the string of suspects impossibly long.

I didn't even know where to begin. I knew nothing of Angela Miller's life before she moved to town and really knew nothing about it since. She'd only lived next door for two weeks, which meant if I were going to investigate, I'd be flying more or less blind.

No, I needed to tell the police what I'd noticed about the bootprints. They at least had a few more channels available to them, channels that weren't always open to novice investigators like myself.

Already past the point of mental exhaustion, I returned to the backyard and found Officer Bouchard chatting with one of the paramedics gathered at the scene.

"Forget something?" he asked with a knowing glint in his eyes. He'd known me long enough to guess that the wheels in my head were now spinning wildly out of control.

A slight breeze blew past, sending a shiver straight through me. I wrapped my arms around my torso and said, "I found something odd. I was wondering if you could check it out."

He murmured something to the woman beside him, then followed me around the house.

"See." I pointed at the boot prints in front of the egress window. Now that he knew everything I did, I could take myself off the case. Ms. Miller had hated me. She wouldn't want me investigating her death anyway.

"What are we looking at here, Angie?" Officer Bouchard squinted, then squatted down to get a closer look.

"Bootprints facing in toward the window. Someone was either trying to look inside or trying to get inside." My eyes went wide as I voiced this revelation aloud.

But he seemed neither curious nor bothered. He simply shook his head and said, "Mmm. I don't think so."

Odd. Why was he so quick to dismiss my concerns? I knew Officer Bouchard well enough not to suspect foul play, but not even being willing to consider this new evidence? Definitely odd.

"What makes you so sure it's not a clue? I mean, really stop and think about it. Maybe her death wasn't really accidental after all." I bit my lip, waiting to see what he would offer in response.

My friend raised one foot and showed me the sole of his shoe. "The pattern matches, see?"

I studied the mix of straight lines and swirls stomped onto the ground, then compared the marks on the bottom of the officer's shoe. Sure enough, it was a match. Except for one small detail.

"But yours is much smaller than that pair," I pointed out, hoping it wouldn't offend him. Men were sometimes funny like that.

"They might not be mine exactly. But they could have been left by any of our team here. We all wear the same kind." He set his foot back down and furrowed his brow. "I'm afraid you're looking for smoke where there isn't any fire, Angie. I know it's scary, but I can assure you, what happened to your neighbor was nothing more than good old-fashioned bad luck."

"Well, if you're sure." I wrapped my arms around my torso again, needing that small bit of comfort. Whether or not Officer Bouchard agreed with me, something felt very wrong here.

He just shook his head and offered me a kindly smile. "I happen to be surer than sure. Nobody uses a bag of feed as a murder weapon. Can you imagine?"

Unfortunately, yes, I could.

8

"Date night go that poorly?" Nan asked me when I appeared in the foyer after a sluggish walk home. "Don't tell me the wedding's off!"

"Everything's fine with me and Charles," I mumbled, sloughing off my shoes and leaning back against the door with a heavy sigh. "With the neighbor, not so much."

Nan was at my side in an instant. "Oh, what did that evil witch do now? I have half a mind to go over there and slap her silly. It's just our—"

"Nan," I interrupted, then took a deep stuttering breath before revealing the harsh truth. "She's dead."

A strangled noise escaped Nan's throat, telling me she now felt quite similar to how I had at receiving the news.

Octo-Cat came trotting gaily down the stairs, his tail held high with a jaunty twist. “Well, that’s one less problem in our lives. Will you break out the catnip or shall I?”

I turned on him so fast, I almost lost my footing and had to reach out for the banister to steady myself. “Octavius Maxwell Ricardo Edmund Frederick Fulton Russo, soon-to-be Longfellow too, how dare you talk like that? A woman is dead!”

He plopped down on the bottom stair and regarded me stonily. “One, I am not taking UpChuck’s name. Try that again, and I will be removing the Russo from my formal title as well.” He paused so long, I almost spoke again, but I also knew better than to interrupt a cat mid-list.

“Two, that hag made our life miserable,” he continued after nearly a full minute stretched in silence. “You and Nan can act all lovey-dovey if you want, but I know the truth. You hated her, and you’re glad she’s gone.”

“That’s it!” He had me in a proper rage now. I was so angry that I was shaking. How could he act so cavalier? This was beyond the pale even for him. “Go to your room and think about what you’ve done.”

Octo-Cat hung his head and laughed mirthlessly. “My house, my rules. Or have you forgotten that all of this is mine?” Another long pause punctuated this rhetorical. “I get that you’re having some trouble processing this all right now, but there’s no reason to take it out on me. Now if you’ll please, I need my Evian topped off.”

“I take it he just said something nasty,” Nan mused from her place beside me. Sometimes I really envied her for not being able to hear the cat's constant stream of commentary on our lives.

I scoffed, continuing to stare daggers at the bad kitty before me. "When does he ever say anything else?"

He shifted his weight from side to side, looking bored with the whole thing. "You humans are weakened by your sense of moral purpose sometimes. A cat, being the superior intellectual creature he is, can see the world for exactly what it is. Humans always like to complain that life isn't fair, but it seems to me that justice was served. The lady next door simply got what was coming for her. Got it? Now don't at me." Having said his piece, he lifted his tail up high and sauntered away while I watched in silence.

"I told you to stay off Twitter!" I yelled after him. It was definitely not to my benefit that I'd taught Octo-Cat how to download apps on his iPad. I doubt he was able to type out his own tweets, but it was bad enough he'd begun adopting the lingo. If he and Pringle ever put their heads together—and realized the cat had the tech while the raccoon had the agile fingers—they could cause some real damage on the interweb.

Unfortunately, this wasn't my most pressing problem at the moment. "The police said it was an accident," I told Nan, speaking hardly above a whisper lest Octo-Cat overhear and add more of his garish commentary.

Nan raised an eyebrow at me. "But you're not so sure."

"You know me too well," I said with a sigh when usually these words would be accompanied by a laugh.

"I found large footprints in front of the basement window. Someone was looking in. Possibly planning a break-in."

"Do you think that maybe—?"

"Angela," my cat yowled, interrupting quite rudely. "Evian! A cat could die waiting, and we both know I'm already light on my remaining lives. I'd hate to lose one of the precious few I have left to dehydration."

I groaned and threw up my hands. "Be right back. His royal pain in the butt needs me."

"I heard that!" he mewled in protest.

"Good!" Sometimes it really felt as if I was the mother of the world's most unruly teenager. At least when Charles and I had children one day, I'd be ready for their worst.

I stomped into the kitchen. Octo-Cat waited in cold silence as I hand-washed his favorite china teacup, fetched a fresh bottle of Evian from the pantry, and poured. Next time he'd be getting toilet water, the little scoundrel.

When I left the kitchen, I rejoined Nan, who had moved to the living room and was now sitting with a sniffling Paisley on top of her lap.

"I take it you overheard what happened to the new neighbor?" I asked the little dog with a curious glance.

She looked up at me with huge, glistening eyes. "Is she dead because of me?"

"No!" I answered emphatically. "Absolutely not."

Paisley shook and whimpered. "Maybe she got scared to death when she saw me."

"She got knocked out by a huge bag of feed, hit her head, and then bled to death," I stated bluntly. We all liked to pretend that Paisley wasn't a teeny-tiny thing, mostly because she saw herself as a big, scary dog—the way all chihuahuas do. But I couldn't let her go so far as to blame herself for something that had absolutely nothing to do with her.

"Ouch. That doesn't sound very nice," Nan interjected. I'd shared the cause of death for Paisley's benefit, but this was her first time hearing it too.

"I'm sure it wasn't." I shrugged, needing to be strong for the two of them even though inside I was still reeling.

"Mommy, what's hell?" the pup asked in that sweet, sing-song voice of hers.

Of course, Octo-Cat chose this precise moment to make his grand re-entrance on the scene. "It's where that old—"

"Octo-Cat, shush!" I yelled before he could complete that thought aloud. Narrowing in on the frightened dog, I murmured softly, "Why are you asking about hell, Paisley?"

"The lady. She called me a hellhound. I know what hound means, but not hell. So what is it, Mommy?"

"Oh, dear." Nan scratched Paisley's head while wearing a worried expression. "I didn't want to bother the animals with religion, but if they can talk, I guess they can also understand. Was this an oversight on my part? Is it time we took Octo-Cat and Paisley to church?"

"Touch me, and you're dead," Octo-Cat growled before running off.

"Mommy?" Paisley asked pointedly again. "Are you going to tell me about hell?"

Honestly I didn't know which of my companions to address first. We had a possible murder on our hands, and the shock of it had worn on us all. Now hardly seemed like the proper time to ponder such existential questions as they pertained to our house pets.

I moved to sit beside Nan on the loveseat and placed one hand on her shoulder while using the other to scratch Paisley's head. "We'll talk about this some other time, okay?" I told them both, hoping that would be enough for now. I already worried about the state of my cat's soul after the remarks he'd made, and I just didn't have the energy to follow this particular train all the way to the station.

Not now. Probably not ever.

I hardly had the energy to consider what happened to old Ms. Miller, but maybe after a good night's rest I'd be able to see things a bit more clearly.

9

My sleep came long and troubled that night. I was surprised when I awoke late in the morning the following day; normally the animals rousted me from my sleep hours earlier.

I tiptoed downstairs, finding only a quiet house to greet me. Nan and Paisley must have gone out somewhere, but where was my cat?

Feeling some minor hesitation, I unlocked the pet door. There was no sense in keeping the animals cooped up inside now that Ms. Miller was no longer around to issue complaints for every minor perceived infraction. Still, it felt weird, moving on so quickly. For the last two weeks, the neighbor's complaints had dictated so much of our lives, and now they just didn't matter anymore.

"Octavius?" I called into the seemingly empty lower level of our home.

When I was met only with silence, I moved to the kitchen to see what Nan had left for my breakfast.

There I found a note tucked under the edge of a blue ceramic plate—and on top of that plate, three fresh-baked vanilla bean scones. I grabbed a pasty hungrily, sweeping my eyes over the note as I chewed.

Flash mob in the park. Took Paisley.

Ah, that was right. Nan had started taking hip-hop dance lessons a few months back and had been over the moon when their class was invited to participate in a sneak dance number. It didn't exactly seem like Paisley's type of thing, but I imagined she'd be standing on the sidelines with Grant as they both lovingly watched Nan twerk and grind.

I glanced down at my baggy T-shirt and shorts with a snort. My grandmother was so much cooler than me. That probably should have bothered me, but it didn't. Not when I had so much else on my mind.

I still hadn't found my cat, so I decided to mount a search. I grabbed a bag of treats from the pantry and made the crinkling noise he adored, hoping it would draw him to me as I made my way through the house.

He wasn't downstairs, nor was he in my bedroom or even curled up in his own. I finally found him in the office, tucked away under the desk where a dark shadow kept him mostly hidden from view.

"Those for me?" he mumbled and crept toward me on four shaky feet to demand sustenance.

I shook three out of the bag and placed them flat on the palm of my hand. "What are you doing in here?"

"Couldn't sleep," he snuffled despite the fact he was still chewing—and the fact that he'd given me guff for doing the very same thing just last week. He must have been really out of it to do such a thing.

"Nightmares?" I offered with a supportive frown.

He shook his head.

"Regret?" I tried. My frown deepened as I recalled our conversation last night.

Octo-Cat stopped munching and met me with odd eyes. "Why would I ever feel regret? I'm a cat, remember?"

"Yes, I know you're a cat, but you were also kind of a brat when you heard the news about that poor woman next door."

He laughed bitterly, then began to choke, then coughed up a bit of food, then continued, "A brat? How dare you call me such a detestable name? And how dare you for even one second accuse me of being fallible? Besides, are you sure the old woman is even dead?"

"Of course I'm sure. I saw the body." How could he even be questioning this? We'd both seen enough bodies in our day to recognize the strange waxiness of a dead person versus a living one.

"Not dead, pah. Then how do you explain the lights that were flashing over there late last night making it nigh impossible for me to catch any shut-eye?"

This caught me off guard. "Lights? It must have been the police."

Octo-Cat snarled but knew better than to take a swipe at me while I was feeding him. "Do you think I'm a moron? I know what police lights look like, and these weren't them. They were much smaller… More treats."

"What do you say?" Sometimes I wished I could snarl, but the best I could settle for in response to his lack of decorum was a frustrated groan.

"Now." His tail flicked and swished.

I groaned again and shook more of the tiny meat bites into my hand for him to nosh on. "You're welcome," I added pointedly.

A low growl rumbled in his throat. "Torches, I think they're called," my cat then offered before digging back in.

I blinked back my surprise, immediately picturing an angry mob wielding pitchforks and torches. But that didn't make any sense, unless…

"Hey, Octo-Cat. What have you been watching on TV lately?" I asked, knowing how impressionable and how theatric he could be. His viewing habits could very well tell me all I needed to decode his slang now.

His ears perked up at this. "Why, Angela, I'm so glad you asked. Usually you don't show interest in my viewing habits, considering my taste is so much more highbrow than your preferred media consumption."

"Uh-huh." I didn't have it in me to argue with him now, not when he seemed to have some information that I needed.

Octo-Cat straightened and met me with large, glowing eyes. "Lately I've found myself rather engrossed with this cheeky little drama set in London. The premise is—"

"Got it. You've gone BBC on me."

"Yes, but what's that got to—"

"You spend time on Twitter, you pick up that lingo. You spend time in front of BBC, you adopt Britishisms into your everyday speech. It makes perfect sense now."

He narrowed his eyes, giving his fuzzy countenance a sinister effect. "The Queen's English is the correct English."

I shook my finger at him. "Don't even get me started on that whole argument, or the fact that you've never once stepped paw outside of the US. My point is you're saying torches, but you mean flashlights."

"Beg pardon?" Now that it had been pointed out, he was really playing up this whole British angle—God help me.

"Wait there," I instructed, sprinkling a few more treats out onto the ground to assure he would do just that.

I grabbed the flashlight we kept in the hall closet in case of emergencies, then clicked it on before returning to my erstwhile feline companion. "Is this what you saw?" I asked, sweeping the tiny spotlight around the room.

"Yes, that's a torch, Angela. Brilliant. Very nicely done." He rolled his eyes in derision. The smarmy part of me wanted to offer him a spot of tea and ask after his mum, but I had more important things to focus on than my cat's penchant for theatrics.

"What time did you see the lights? Are you sure they were coming from next door?" I pressed.

"Very late. Or rather, quite early. Maybe two, three o'clock. And they definitely started next door, but then they moved to the woods."

"Did they ever come to our yard?" I asked, a fresh jolt of fear striking me dead in the heart. The neighbor and I shared a name. What if whoever was out there had meant to come for me, but somehow got their wires crossed? And what if they were still coming?

A woman was dead, and still the vultures were out there picking at the crime scene. Who were they, and what could they possibly want?'

Octo-Cat finished devouring his treats, then began to groom himself as he liked to do post-meal. He paused thoughtfully after several strokes of his tongue across his tail. "I must say, my dear Angela, it seems that something odd is afoot."

"Why yes, Octo-Cat. I couldn't have said it better myself." I smiled at this. While he was being rather annoying today, at least I had his interest. That meant he would help me, despite his lack of sleep the night before. And as they say, two heads are better than one, even when one of those heads is adorned with whiskers.

10

After opening a fresh can of Octo-Cat's preferred cat pate and pouring him a teacup of Evian, I spent the next ten minutes waiting while he took his time with breakfast. In the meantime, I polished off all three scones and made a mental note to have my wedding dress refitted just in case all this stress eating was having an effect on my waistline.

Upon finishing his meal, Octo-Cat then had to tend to his morning ministrations. The small amount of grooming he'd managed while we talked in the office was nowhere near enough to satisfy his habitual self-care.

As he tended to his hygiene, I composed a lengthy text to Charles to catch him up on everything that had gone down since I saw him for our date last night. The poor guy had been working overtime—and then some—to ensure he'd be able to take a full two weeks off for our honeymoon. I hated to bother him with my problems, but I also knew I'd never hear the end of it if I failed to inform him of something so major going on in my life.

I explained the situation as succinctly as I could, finished my message, and hit send.

Less than a minute later, I received notification of his reply. Just enough of it popped up on screen to tell me I shouldn't open it to read the full thing—at least not yet.

Whatever you do, don't disturb the scene to—

Yeah, nope. If I opened that, he'd know I saw his message and then consciously chose to ignore it. Charles knew me well enough by now to know exactly what I planned to do, which is why he was trying to warn me off it.

Maybe if I called the police with this new intel, they'd head over to investigate, but that wasn't a chance I could afford to take. Not when they'd dismissed my concerns about the shoeprints so quickly yesterday.

Besides, I just had a hunch that Ms. Miller's death wasn't as open and shut as it seemed. Something strange was going on over there, and I intended to figure out what.

"Are you ready, Angela?" Octo-Cat asked after one last lap at his paw. Like Charles, my cat also knew exactly what I planned to do. That's part of the reason we made such good partners—at least when we weren't bickering and nitpicking each other.

I nodded. "Let's go check it out."

"Tut, tut. Cheerio." This whole English act was quickly

draining on me. I needed Octo-Cat to be wearing his detective hat, not one that belonged to a misguided thespian. Luckily, I knew just how I could shut this down while making it seem like the whole thing had been his idea.

"Cheerio, funny. You know, that reminds me of the time Pringle knighted himself and decided to vanquish forest monsters in the name of the queen. What was it he would say? Oh, right." I put on my most horrible impression of an accent combined with my most horrible impersonation of Pringle to seal the deal. "Pip, pip, cheerio, my good lad."

I glanced down to Octo-Cat and found his face filled with derision.

"Gag. Could we not talk about the trash panda?" he begged, reverting to his normal East Coast polish. "I'd rather die choking on a hairball, thank you very much."

I smiled to myself as we exited the house side by side and trekked through the woods.

"So remind me again why we're investigating?" the tabby asked as our feet crunched over fallen leaves that had been left to decay since last autumn. We couldn't exactly rake up the entire forest.

"Because the neighbor is dead, and it might have been murder," I reminded him, surprised he had forgotten our mission so quickly today.

"Right, but we hated her. Also aren't you busy enough planning your wedding?" He stopped to sniff the base of an old tree, and I waited.

"Hate is such a strong word," I reasoned.

He smirked. "But it's the correct word, isn't it?"

I groaned in acknowledgment, unable to address his pointed comment with actual words. "I am busy with the wedding, but I can't just let a murder go unsolved." The truth was I'd already finished the hardest part of planning my nuptials—figuring out the guest list and sending out formal invitations. As it turns out, I know a lot of people, making the rest of it far easier by comparison.

"Why not? The police do it all the time," he commented rudely, once again making me wonder how much time my cat spent browsing Twitter.

Just like I hadn't wanted to talk religion with the pets, I also didn't want to get into something so political. "Don't talk like that. The police do their best, but not every case is solvable." Debating Octo-Cat never went well, no matter what the topic. He didn't consider facts valid unless they proved the point he already wanted to make.

He left the strange-smelling tree behind and began moving forward again, leading us both through the woods. "So what makes you think this one is? Solvable, I mean?"

I was getting nowhere by assuming my cat had something akin to a human conscience. At the end of the day, he was a coldly logical being who would always put himself first, no matter the circumstance. As a result of our years together, I'd learned that my cat had two tragic flaws—pride and curiosity. Right now he was tagging along because of the latter, but the moment he lost interest, I'd be left on my own again. Unless... I needed to find a way to channel his pride to make sure he saw this through to the end.

"I don't know if this one is solvable," I admitted with a practiced look of consternation. "But I do know we have a much better chance of solving it if we work together. You know I'm nothing without you, Octavius."

He nodded along, completely unaware of how already I was playing him like a fiddle. "This is true. You need me, Angela. You've always needed me."

"I do," I agreed emphatically. "And what's more, this crime happened right next door. What if the killer comes back and tries to break into our house next... tries to break into YOUR house?"

Octo-Cat reared back and thrashed his front paws in the air like a tiny, unskilled ninja. "Then he'll have another thing coming when he meets the business end of these claws. Nobody comes into my house without my say so."

Now I was the one nodding like a broken bobble head as I brought my final argument home. "I don't know for sure a murder happened. That's why I need you to come check it out and make sense of things for me. We need to protect our home, and I'm not confident I can do that without your help, Octavius."

"Well, of course you need my help, dear Angela. Why didn't you just say so in the first place?"

I shrugged nonchalantly while inwardly beaming with confidence in a job well done. I'd played to my cat's hubris so many times, it was no longer difficult for me to put my pride aside to bolster his own. He was the one who had seen the flashlights last night, and he was the one who could get in and out easily without being spotted or leaving any fingerprints behind. And as much as I liked to puzzle out the clues, Octo-Cat was the one with a truly obsessive mind. Once he gave headspace to a case, he didn't stop until he found the answers he was looking for.

Maybe the new neighbor hadn't been murdered, but I couldn't risk the chance that she had been. Not when this had all gone down so close to home. The police had been quick to rule Angela Miller's death an accident, but I still needed more proof.

11

Octo-Cat and I finished our trek through the woods and approached the neighbor's large front porch. Potted plants flanked the steps on either side, and vibrant flowers dripped down from hanging baskets, creating a welcoming entrance so at odds with how the woman herself had treated visitors. It felt eerie to be in her space when she had so clearly not wanted us here.

"Okay, where do we begin?" I asked my feline companion as I took stock of the porch and yard. The police had already cleared out, which meant we were alone.

"You could go to the door. See if it's unlocked," Octo-Cat suggested in a snooty tone that seemed to imply I should have been able to think of that on my own.

I flexed my fingers demonstratively. "It would leave prints."

Octo-Cat scoffed. “Since when do you care about that? You leave DNA evidence behind all the time.”

“Yes, but normally I don’t have a motive that could peg me for the murder.” I hadn’t really considered this until now, but suddenly it became a very real concern. My troubles with the neighbor were well documented. What was I doing trying to prove foul play when the police were happy to leave it alone?

“The police said it wasn’t murder,” Octo-Cat reminded me even though I was already thinking the exact same thing. It was probably time to admit that I had quite a bit in common with my cat. I was too curious to leave this alone, even though I probably should have. I was curious, but I could still be careful.

“They say that now, but what if they change their tune?” I shrugged. “I’d rather not incriminate myself, if I can help it.”

Octo-Cat jumped up on the porch railing and paced back and forth. “Fine. Then what do you want to do?”

I thought for a moment. “Let’s head around back. I’ll show you the shed where I saw the body.”

That was all I needed to say for him to leap down and take off running toward the back of the house far ahead of me, forcing me to do a light jog to catch up.

“It smells awful,” he said as soon as we made it to our target location.

“Well, there was a lot of blood.” I sniffed at the air but couldn’t pick up anything unusual beyond the acerbic taint of chemical cleaners hanging in the air.

"No, that's not the smell. Blood, I don't mind. I am a carnivore, you know. For me, blood is a bit like a delicious gravy."

I cringed at the thought and briefly reconsidered becoming a vegetarian, as I so often had since gaining my strange gift. "Right, then what do you smell?"

Octo-Cat shuddered and shook out his fur. "No clue what it is. Only know I don't like it." Well, this was getting us nowhere fast.

"It's not exactly helpful when you—"

"Angela, silence." Octo-Cat lifted his head, ears alert and body rigid.

"What?" I paused and glanced around in a panic but saw nothing out of the ordinary.

But Octo-Cat remained tense and frozen. "Shhhh, there's something out there," he insisted.

I turned in the direction he was looking, back toward the forest. I couldn't see or hear anything. "What is it? Is it something dangerous?" I whispered.

"Will you just keep quiet already?" my cat bellowed, forgetting his own call for silence.

At last, a strange, garbled noise rose from the edge of the forest, and a flash of yellow caught my eye. "I... I... I... I am being as qu-qu-quiet as I can!" an unfamiliar voice declared before its speaker had moved fully into view.

"It's you!" I exclaimed, unable to hide my sudden burst of excitement. "You were here yesterday. You saw what happened to Ms. Miller." I didn't know for sure that he had, but something had spooked this buck, and I intended to find out what. I held out both hands to show I meant no harm and took one slow step forward.

"No!" he brayed and shook his head, whipping the yellow tape around in a blur. "Leave me alone!"

And just like that he ran off into the forest, the tangled crime scene ribbon twisting in the air behind him.

"Nice one, Sherlock," Octo-Cat quipped, making me feel even worse about scaring off our witness. At least he was calling me Sherlock. Usually he referred to me as Watson, the lovable side-kick rather than the hero.

"Do you think he saw what happened?" I asked, chewing on my lip as I considered the same question.

"I don't know about that, but I do think he's the bad thing I smelled. Yuck." He kicked back his hind legs in the same way he did after using the litter box.

"We need to get him to talk to us," I said.

Octo-Cat shook his head, immediately dismissing my suggestion. "He's prey, Angela. Chasing after him is only going to make him run farther away from you."

"Okay, then what do you suggest?" Seriously, why did I even bother to put forth my own ideas when Octo-Cat was just going to boss me around anyway?

He sighed. "Well, I don't see anything useful in this shed. My guess is the cops cleared it out as part of cleanup. Meanwhile you're not willing to open the door to let us into the house, so I honestly don't know where that leaves us."

"Wait, I have an idea. Follow me." I only turned to make sure he was following me as I turned the corner of the house. Thankfully, he'd fallen right in line, so I led him to the side of the house where I'd spotted the prints leading up to the basement egress window. The prints were no longer visible, but I wondered.

"Hop down there," I ordered, pointing to the window well that sported a patch of gravel before the window. "See if the window is fully latched."

"Oh sure, send the cat. Just because I'm faster, lighter, and smarter. Uh-huh, I see." Octo-Cat complained but he did so with a smile, and when he'd finished saying his piece, he dutifully hopped down to investigate.

"There's no screen," he called back up, then began to paw at the edge of the glass. "It opens out rather than pushing in. I need you to try it."

"No. Can't leave prints," I reminded him.

"Then we're not getting inside. It's as simple as that."

"I'll think of something," I assured him. "Now come back up."

He hopped out to join me, offering a withering glance my way.

"I'm hitting a dead end," I admitted.

He rolled his eyes. "No, you hit a roadblock, and for some reason you refuse to move around it."

Was I being too cautious when it came to leaving my fingerprints behind? I wasn't up to any wrongdoing, and Officer Bouchard knew me well enough to already know about my amateur sleuthing. Plus I was about to be married to the best attorney in town. I probably wouldn't get in much trouble—if any—but still, something about the situation gave me pause.

And as a P.I. it was important I listened to my hunches... And to rely on my partner for help.

"Can you think of anything else we might be missing?" I asked him.

He nodded as if deep in thought. "We only knew her for a couple of weeks, so think back to all of your encounters with her."

"I only met her that first day. Every other time I communicated with her was via animal control or the police or the post office."

"I never met her face-to-face, but I did enjoy peeing on her porch," he said with a self-satisfied smirk.

"Wait." We were close, I could feel it in my bones. "If she didn't see you, how did she know?"

He cocked his head to the side and regarded me suspiciously. "Know what?"

"That you'd peed." That's when I remembered that the animal control officers had come bearing photographs more than once. I ran back toward the porch and began to search the rafters.

"What are you doing?" he asked in a sing-song voice.

I turned to him briefly to explain. "Looking for a hidden camera."

"It's there," he said, motioning with his nose.

"What? Where? And how do you know? You didn't even know there was a camera."

He crinkled his nose. “It’s got a weird shimmer to it. It just stands out like a sore thumb. Don’t you see it?”

I shook my head, then moved to the side and pointed. “Hot or cold?”

He plopped his butt down and wagged his tail wildly in response. “I don’t know what game you’re playing here, Angela, but I don’t like it.”

I growled and stamped my foot, growing very frustrated with this. “Am I close or far away?”

Finally he got it and was able to direct me to the camera. I grabbed it down, forgetting for a moment about my reluctance to leave prints. *Shoot.*

“We’ll take this back to the house, but I think she had more of these set up around the property. There were other pictures, taken from other angles.” I wished then that animal control had left the pictures with me so that I could use them to help figure out the camera placements, but no.

Octo-Cat grinned deviously. “You need me to go find them, don’t you?”

“I do, but first let’s get this one home and see what we can find.”

12

Back at home, I did a quick web search on the make and model of the trail cam we'd found on Ms. Miller's porch. Once I understood how the thing was intended to work, I began taking it apart in search of evidence. Even though I followed the directions exactly, I couldn't find the memory card that was meant to store the video feed.

"Am I overlooking it?" I asked Octo-Cat in frustration, but he didn't find anything either.

A scrabbling at the window drew my eye across the room. Pringle stood waving with one hand and pointing at the door with the other. As much as I still hadn't forgiven the raccoon for taking Paisley hostage last week, I did want to hear if he had any theories about what happened next door. His mind was always running at a million miles per minute. Usually that was to my detriment, but occasionally his penchant for overthinking could prove beneficial.

I set the camera down on the table, then moved toward the front door and carefully let myself out onto the porch, blocking the way so Pringle couldn't squeeze past me into the house.

Octo-Cat followed through the pet flap. Even though he wasn't a fan of Pringle, he was a fan of drama. He'd also become invested in this case.

"You got some new tech?" the raccoon said as soon as were standing on the porch with him, all the while rubbing his hands together as if he were washing them in a stream. "I wanna see."

That was right. Our resident raccoon was obsessed with all forms of technology. Gossip too. Which made him the perfect spy whenever he managed to focus on the task at hand. It also meant he had a lot in common with the deceased. He might actually understand what had made Angela Miller tick, because I certainly didn't get it.

Dang it, I needed his help.

"I've got a job for you," I said, praying I wouldn't later come to regret this.

"It'll cost you." Pringle rubbed his hands together faster and faster, an addict on the verge of getting a fix.

I'd given into his insane demands many times before, but now that I knew Pringle a bit better, I knew I could get by with much less. "I will let you play with my cool new tech, if you do me a favor first."

"Favor, favor, yes!" he cried, his eyes growing wide as if he could already see a future in which he had taken possession of his prize.

There were three things I needed his help with, but if I told him the full list at once, he'd get distracted and forget to do any of it. If I told him in the wrong order, he could abscond with the evidence before actually handing it over to me. It was like a strange logic puzzle with only one right answer.

I thought it over for a few minutes to make sure I was happy with my plan of action before revealing said plan to the hyperactive raccoon. I also needed to give him enough details to explain the task without providing too much and making him bored.

"There's a big buck out in the woods," I began, speaking slowly and making sure to enunciate each word. "He wandered into the neighbor's backyard last night and got crime scene tape stuck in his antlers. We need him to talk to us, but both times I've tried, he's gotten frightened and run off. Can you get him to talk?"

"You need a confession? Roger that." He nodded vigorously. "I can torture him with—"

"No!" I screamed so loud, the house behind me seemed to shake. "He's a potential witness, not a suspect, which means NO interrogation, okay? I just need to know what he saw. It may be the clue to cracking this case wide open."

He paused, suddenly becoming stock still as he raised his eyes to meet mine. "What's in it for me?"

"I'll let you check out the new tech, and when we're done using it as evidence, I'll even let you keep it."

He took a step back, considering my offer. "What is it? What does this new tech do?"

"That's part of the fun." I made my eyes wide and my smile wider. "It's a mystery surprise. So are you on board?"

Pringle raised his hand to his chin and rubbed it as he thought, then jumped straight up into the air and shouted, "I'll do it," before turning tail and running off in pursuit of our witness. I just hoped he took it easy on the poor buck who was already scared half out of his mind.

Octo-Cat pawed at my leg to get my attention. "Why didn't you ask him to go into the house and find the missing memory thingy?"

I shuddered. "I'd rather leave my prints all over that place than unleash that little bandit on a big empty house full of potential treasures."

"Good point. So are we breaking in?" A smile stretched between his whiskers, and I could tell he looked forward to a little recreational B and E.

"I already told you—"

He hissed when he realized I still wasn't playing into his paw. "Just put on a pair of gloves, Angela. Seriously, it's not even that hard. We also have more cameras to find. Get with the program."

"I'm having a hard time moving past that deer. It keeps coming back to the yard even though it's clearly frightened. Why do you suppose that is?"

Octo-Cat let out a low, long groan. "I told you. The guy's prey.

They aren't the sharpest tools in the shed, if you know what I'm saying."

"In the shed. That's it!" At last he'd given me a lead I could pursue without worry of looking guilty later.

He tilted his head, regarding me with large golden eyes. "What's it?"

"Ms. Miller died in her back shed. She was knocked out by an extra-large bag of deer feed," I reminded him.

"And?"

"She'd only been in town for a couple of weeks, yet somehow she'd definitely managed to make good friends with that buck. She also complained more than once about Paisley scaring off the deer from her yard." I watched Octo-Cat's face the whole time I explained, but rather than appearing enlightened, he looked downright confused.

"So? So what has that got to do with any of this?" he asked with another savage flick of his tail. "Do you think the deer killed her for being late giving him his dinner?"

Okay, now I was irritated too. "Be reasonable," I whined, unable to help myself. "I already said the buck wasn't a suspect. But her apparent obsession with the local deer is the best lead we've got."

My cat rolled his eyes yet again. We may have hit a new record for how many times he could dismiss me that way in a single day. "I thought the best lead we had was the treasure trove of evidence already waiting literally right next door."

I thought about this for a second. Logically, his point was

sound, but something inside me was begging me to follow this new hunch.

"Let's split up," I decided at last. "I'll pursue the deer thing, and you work on finding the other cameras and locating the missing memory card."

"Great, but you still have to let me inside." He yawned. If I didn't act fast, I'd lose him to yet another afternoon spent napping in the sun.

"I'll go grab my gloves..."

13

Nan returned from her flash mob right as I was about to climb into my clunky old sedan and pay a visit to the pet store. "Where are you headed in such a hurry?" she asked, coming out of the garage with Paisley trotting happily at her heels.

"I'm investigating a case," I explained, unable to hide the smile that crept across my face. I really did feel most like myself when I was in the thick of a mystery.

Nan narrowed her gaze and stared at me pointedly. "You're snooping after the neighbor, you mean."

I gasped in alarm. Nan had always approved of my investigative ways. Had she somehow suddenly changed her tune?

My fears were quickly abated, however, when she looked me up and down with a huge smile and said, "And I approve wholeheartedly. Take Paisley with you for a second set of eyes and ears."

At hearing her name, the little dog began to bark excitedly and run quick zooming circles around Nan.

"What will you do here all by yourself?" I asked, giggling at Paisley's playful antics.

"I'm working on a surprise for Grant, and I don't trust you not to go blabbing." She shook her finger at me then laughed good-naturedly. "Actually I'm surprised I've managed to keep it secret for this long. We'll catch each other up when you're back, okay?"

I smiled and nodded before plopping down into my car. "C'mon, Paisley. Let's go to the store!" I called, then lifted the little dog into the car with me when she showed up outside my door. Even though my sedan was close to the ground, Paisley was too frightened to jump into it by herself—a point which Octo-Cat teased her about whenever he got even the slightest chance.

"What store are we going to, Mommy?" Paisley asked once I had her settled on my lap and the car headed down the long driveway.

"I'm not sure. I'm thinking maybe the pet store to start and then we'll just go from there. I'm hoping to get some info about the local deer, just in case her connection to them somehow got our neighbor killed," I explained, turning onto the main road and letting the steering wheel maneuver back to center beneath my fingers.

Paisley braced herself for the turn, then popped back up on

four feet and wagged her tail until it was a blur. "Oh, yes. The deer here are very nice. They wouldn't hurt anyone."

I slowed the car and looked down at the pup on my lap. "Do you know the deer, Paisley?"

"Sometimes they talk to me even though I'm a predator. They don't think I'm very scary since I'm so small." Typically, Paisley would do anything to prove she was a big dog, but now she seemed almost proud that her tiny stature had afforded her some new friends.

Funny how Angela Miller had complained more than once about Paisley scaring off the deer when the Chihuahua was in fact friendly with the local herd. And shame on me for not thinking to ask Paisley about them earlier.

"Do you know a big buck who lives around here?" I slowed the car to nearly a crawl, wanting to stay on the quiet backroads while I was so immersed in our conversation.

"Sure I do," Paisley nodded and yipped. "That's Irving. We used to talk a lot, but lately he's been too scared to say hello." Yes, we were definitely talking about the same deer I'd seen earlier.

Now I stopped the car completely. I could save myself the errand if Paisley already had all the information I needed. "Scared? Why? What did he see?" I asked, pulling the car over to the shoulder.

Paisley hopped up and put her front paws on the car door, peering outside with open joy. "I don't know. He's not talking to me, remember?"

"Right." Well, it was worth a shot. I rolled down the window for my doggie friend and got back to driving.

We drove to a new pet store that had opened up across town, preferring to avoid the scene of a grisly murder that we'd helped solve a couple years prior. This town was filled with too many memories of past cases, and we had a fresh mystery to focus on now.

My phone buzzed from its spot in the cupholder, then it buzzed again. I resisted the urge to check the new messages until Paisley and I pulled into the pet store parking lot and parked.

"What is it, Mommy?" Paisley asked, her paws back on the side door and her tail wagging furiously. She loved car rides, but even more than that she loved visiting new places—or really any place we were willing to let her tag along.

The missed texts were from Charles. Rather than opening them up, I called instead. If he had time to text, then perhaps he also had time for a chat.

"There you are," he said by way of greeting. I could hear the grin underlying his words.

"Here I am," I answered with a lovesick smile as I sighed and laid my head back against the seat rest.

"So," Charles prompted with a soft, breathy laugh. "Tell me about it."

"About what?" I let out a soft chuckle, as if that would somehow prove my innocence.

"I know you went to investigate, and I know you left my text unread on purpose." His words were firm but not angry. He sounded more bemused than anything else. Still, I'd been found out despite my best attempts to be slick.

Oops. "Yeah, sorry about that."

"Hey, your intellectual curiosity and steadfast commitment to justice are both part of what I love about you. Just be careful, okay? And tell me if I can help."

"I love you too," I said, brimming with joy at the thought this man would be my husband in just a few short weeks. "And what was that you just said about me? Can I use it on my business website to attract some new clients?"

"What's mine is yours, including my words. Have them."

I chuckled and made a mental note to update my site once I'd wrapped the investigation. I then took time to explain the scene last night in greater detail than I'd given him earlier. I also told him about our investigation so far that day and my hunch that somehow the deer were important.

"I don't know, Angie," my fiancé said after a long pause. "She fell and hit her head? That sounds like an accident to me. The police may be right on this one."

"Something just seems off about it all. I can't shake the feeling, you know?" I sighed. I'd really been hoping he would pick up on some small detail I'd missed, that by simply confiding in Charles I'd crack the case wide open.

"I do know. I just don't have any suggestions on where to look next." His response was earnest, but he also seemed a little disappointed in his inability to assist with this one. "Think of all the clues you've found. The camera didn't have film. The bootprints matched the ones Officer Bouchard was wearing, and the flashlights at night were only seen by your cat. We know he's not the most reliable. What if he made it up to have some fun at your expense?"

"He wouldn't do that," I said, even though we both knew he would—and had many times before. Was I embarking on a wild goose chase here? And was the gut feeling I had more of a guilty conscience than a detective's hunch?

Charles seemed to think so. "Well, then maybe he got confused about what he saw? Maybe it was all a bad dream?"

I picked at the skin on my elbow. Even though everyone else seemed quick to brush this case aside, I still knew something wasn't right next door. Something had happened, and I wouldn't rest until I found out whether or not that something was murder.

14

I clipped Paisley onto the leash I kept in my car, then the two of us headed inside. This pet shop was much smaller than the bigger chain store a couple cities over. The only adoptable pets it sported were various types of freshwater fish, seeing as the retail shop mainly seemed to focus on pet supplies and not pets themselves.

The storefront was narrow with three long aisles that stretched toward the back. An empty counter stood in front of a large tropical fish tank, an old-fashioned cash register stationed on top.

Paisley tugged hard at the lead, and I followed her down the center aisle, right to a display of dog treats. “Can I have one, Mommy? Can I?” she begged, standing on her hind legs and waving her front paws at me repeatedly.

“Yes, once we find what we came here for,” I promised,

hoping she would at least choose something size-appropriate this time. While it was adorable watching the little dog gnaw on a bone twice her size, I ultimately had to throw away her last chew when it started to stink up the house.

"Can I help you?" A man I hadn't seen before popped his head out from the far aisle and beamed over at me. For a moment I worried he'd overheard me talking with my dog, but then I remembered I was in the company of another pet person. Pet people never questioned someone talking to their animals, and I also hadn't said anything that made it too obvious that Paisley was talking back. My secret was still safe, at least when it came to this particular stranger.

"Hi," I answered with a friendly wave. "I'm Angie. I noticed your shop was new in town and thought I'd come in to check it out and say hello." The store had popped up several weeks ago and I was pretty sure Nan had been in, but I hadn't yet made it by. Judging by the lack of any other customers, things weren't going too well. I'd need to make more of an effort to support local businesses—being as I was a small business owner myself.

"Hello," the man replied with an overenthusiastic wave back. "I'm Frank, and before you can ask, yes, Beans is most definitely around here somewhere."

"Beans?" I asked in a higher pitch than I liked.

"Yes, that's why the store is called Frank and Beans. My mother said it would only confuse people, but I think it's cute. Don't you?"

"Yes. Oh, yes, definitely. Drew me right in." Truthfully, I

hadn't even noticed the name of the shop before entering. Some shrewd detective I was.

Frank joined me in the dog supply aisle, and I got a good look at him for the first time. He wore a graphic T-shirt over a long sleeve collared shirt with checks. He also had on khakis that were just a little too long, judging by the bottoms that were torn up and covered in dirt. I didn't recognize the anime on his T-shirt, so I couldn't say for sure, but the busty character with pouted lips and a flirtatious wink hardly seemed appropriate work attire. I shuddered for the single women of Blueberry Bay.

"Is Beans your dog?" I asked conversationally, unable to tear my eyes away from the cartoon cleavage splashed across his chest.

"Nope, Beans is a cat!" Frank caught me looking and blushed, then placed both hands on top of his shirt to hide the graphic. "His full name is Toby Toe Beans McGillicutty. He's a little shy, but I can go get him if you want to say hello."

"Actually I'm a bit short on time, but I was hoping I could ask you a quick question before I go. I will definitely be back to meet Toe Beans though, I promise." It seemed the friendly thing to offer. Whether or not I liked his T-shirt, Frank still seemed like a nice enough guy. There was absolutely no reason to be rude, especially since I had my diamond engagement ring to show off my status as a taken woman.

"Just Beans," Frank corrected, drawing my attention back to his face.

"Right." I nodded once, twice.

He dropped his hands from his chest and used them to make

big sweeping gestures as he spoke. “Okay, yeah. So what’s your question? I’m happy to help however I can. Mom says it won’t be easy competing with the big national chain, but I say that nothing worth doing is ever easy.”

“Yes, totally agree with you there.” I reached down and grabbed a bag of treats for Paisley, and she immediately began whimpering in anticipation. “I’m getting this. And I was also hoping to pick up some deer feed. I live by the forest and have quite a few wander through my yard day to day, so I thought it would be nice to make friends.”

“Ah, yes, deer are such remarkable creatures.” He waved his arms around wildly and knocked a small bag of treats from the shelf. “I’d love to help. And if you come back closer to Christmas I’ll be able to. Haven’t got any feed in stock now, what with the regulations and all.”

I raised an eyebrow as Frank bent down to scoop up the fallen merchandise. “Regulations?”

“It’s hunting season, which means feeding the deer is not allowed until the season is over. Otherwise we’d have a whole gaggle of gunners baiting the poor things and then blasting their heads off.” He made finger guns and pointed them at me, then frowned and shoved his hands into his pockets.

“Not a fan of hunting, I take it?” I ventured.

“No sirree. Or rather, no ma’am. I’m a proud vegetarian. Although I do make an exception for Beans. It’s not healthy to force a carnivore out of its natural diet. He’s a pescatarian.”

That poor cat. Octo-Cat did enjoy his shrimp, tuna, and

lobster rolls, but he'd have my head if I tried to restrict his diet in any way. The one time I bought him reduced calorie food, he made it a point to puke at the foot of my bed every single day until I switched him back to the full-fat stuff.

"Do you know where I might be able to pick up some feed?" I prompted, attempting to steer our conversation back to where I needed it to go.

"Oh, perhaps I didn't explain myself very well. Mother says I'm always talking too fast and going off the rails, which is a pretty weird expression, right? What have conversations got to do with trains? Anyway, I can't sell you any deer feed right now. No one can, as buying and selling the feed is currently illegal." Frank sniffed and ran a hand through his longish hair. I couldn't tell if he was actively growing it out or if he'd just missed one too many haircuts.

I had to think for a minute to decide how much of my case I was willing to share with this new acquaintance. Despite being a touch odd, he was definitely friendly, but he was also incredibly talkative. I couldn't risk him sharing private details with just anyone who walked into his shop. I had to play this cool.

I laughed it off. "Oh, weird. I had no idea. My neighbor asked me to pick some more feed up for her but didn't mention the regulations. She had a burlap sack filled to the brim with I don't know what. Some kind of grain maybe."

He narrowed his eyes at me, suddenly suspicious of me and all my questions. "She must have gotten it before the season started."

"Maybe she did. Do you know where she might have gotten it? Are there any other shops in town that would sell deer feed during the off-season?"

"The big chain place doesn't have it, let me tell you. Their stores are crowded with a hundred types of dog food, but don't even have this one essential. As far as I know, there aren't any others offering it. You'll have to rely on Frank and Beans for all your deer feed needs. In fact, I already have a nice stock waiting in the warehouse seeing as my supplier accidentally sent the shipment months ahead of time. Silly mistake, but at least he's provided free storage space so we don't have to send the full lot back. Anyway, that will be ready to put out the second those regulations are lifted, but for now can I interest you in some wild bird seed?" He began to head for the next aisle, and I dutifully followed along.

"You can feed the birds all year round. You just have to be careful that it's not stolen by squirrels," Frank explained as he motioned toward his supply. "Although I do have some squirrel feeders too, if that's up your alley."

"Thank you. You've been very helpful." I selected a small bag of bird seed, then put it back. "I'll just take a little time to browse around. I'll let you know when I'm ready to check out."

He nodded enthusiastically. "Oh, yeah, sure. I'll let you browse in peace. I've got some new inventory to sort through anyway. Just holler when you're ready."

When Frank at last disappeared through the swinging doors that separated the front of the store from the back, I scooped

Paisley into my arms and whispered, "Now let's go pick the treats you really want."

15

"Psssst," a strange voice called from the next aisle over. I ducked my head and went to check it out but found no one.

"I smell a cat," Paisley chimed in just as a little paw reached out from behind some boxes of treats to tap me on the arm.

"Psssst," the voice urged again. "I heard you talking to that dog earlier. I know you can understand me." A pair of green eyes glowed at me from the back of the shelf, but the rest of his small body was ensconced in shadows.

"Beans?" I asked, craning in an effort to get a better look.

"Shhh!" The cat moved forward on the shelf, revealing a long, lanky body covered in orange and white stripes. "Not too loud or my human will come back and ruin everything. Just listen, all right? Nod to show you understand?"

I zipped my lips, nodded, and waited for Beans to say more.

He kept his voice low, which made the whole encounter even more eerie. “I heard you were looking to buy some off-season feed, and let’s just say I can hook you up.”

I nodded again and offered a spirited thumbs up.

“Great, great. I’ll give you the info you need, if you give me what I need.” This was feeling more and more like a black market transaction. Who’d have thought that the neighbor’s penchant for feeding the local wildlife would lead me down this strange rabbit hole?

“What do you need?” I asked, eager to follow the lead, no matter how strange the trail.

Beans growled and reared back on the shelf. “Shhhh, no talking, remember?!”

I sighed but nodded all the same. As annoying as Octo-Cat could be, Toby Toe Beans McGillicutty was proving to be far worse.

“I overheard Frank tell you about my little problem. You know, the whole fish-only diet? Man, I am dying for a steak. You stop by later and bring me a nice cut of New York strip, I’ll see what I can do about getting you that feed.” With that, he turned tail and disappeared back behind the shelved goods.

I wanted to call after him to get a little bit more detail about the suggested arrangement, but Frank returned then carrying a big case of canned cat food.

“Still finding everything okay?” he asked, even though it had only been a few minutes since he’d left me on my own.

“Yes, I think I’m ready for you to ring me up,” I said, hoping the treats I already had in hand would satisfy Paisley seeing as Beans had interrupted us before she could pick something out for herself.

Frank sang an old rock tune under his breath as he scanned the two items I'd selected, then offered a closed-lip grin and wished me a good day. "Come back often and buy more," he called after me just as I was headed for the door. "Help me prove mother wrong about the viability of my business choices!"

As soon as we were in the car, I opened the bag of treats and offered one to Paisley, which she happily accepted, wagging tail and all.

"That was pretty weird, huh?" I asked.

"Cats are always pretty weird," she mumbled as she licked at my hand. "But I still like them anyway!"

I waited for her to finish before putting the car in drive and heading to the grocery store. I hoped Beans would be willing to accept a raw steak, because I didn't have time to waste preparing it, especially when any seasoning choices I made could upset the feline and cause him to demand fresh payment. I may not know Beans well, but I knew cats.

I had to leave Paisley in the car while I ran into the grocery store to secure the bribe. Once purchased, I wrapped the meat in a bundle of napkins I pulled from my glove compartment and jammed it in my purse, then drove straight back to the pet store.

Frank had apparently seen me pull back up and stood waiting at the shop door. He held it open with a giant grin, forcing me to squeeze past him to gain entry. "Welcome back. I knew I'd see you again. I just didn't realize it'd be so soon!"

"Well, I thought more about it and realized I would definitely be needing a larger bag of bird seed, what with all the feathery friends who come to roost in my yard. I didn't want anyone to miss out, so I decided to stock up a bit better before putting anything out."

Frank bobbed his head enthusiastically. "Oh, yes, good idea. I'd recommend the Parks brand. Here, let me show you." He began to stroll down one of the aisles and motioned for me to follow.

"Actually, I'm going to spend some time comparing each brand to its online reviews to make sure I come to an informed decision," I countered, having to think quick to buy some alone time. "I hope you don't mind."

"As long as you're buying something, you can go about it however you please. If you need a real expert's opinion, though, you know where to find me." He turned back toward me and winked before heading to the front of the store. Luckily, the bird seed was in the far back of the store, giving me a small semblance of privacy as I worked on my exchange of meat for information with the ravenous Beans.

I stooped down on the floor, tilted so my back was facing the front of the store, fished my cell phone out of my purse, and raised it to my ear. This position would afford me some secrecy as I unpackaged the steak, and the phone would give me a ready excuse if Frank overheard me talking to the animals.

I clucked my tongue and whispered, "Here, kitty, kitty, kitty."

Paisley wagged her tail and let out a sharp bark.

"No bark," I told her plainly, more or less certain her cry had drawn the store owner's attention.

"Psssst, I'm over here."

I turned my head toward the source of the voice, but Beans yelled at me. "No, don't look. Just listen."

I nodded, wondering if every time I interacted with this cat, he'd demand I shut off another one of my senses.

"You got the goods. I can smell it. Now here's what I need you to do. Unpackage the steak and place it on the floor in front of you. I'll come inspect to make sure everything is good, and then I'll tell you what you need to know."

I nodded and reached into my purse, freeing the offering from its foam and plastic packaging and then wrapping the trash in the bundle of napkins before jamming the wad back in my purse. I set the steak on the floor as instructed and waited.

"Mommy?" Paisley cried with joy. "Is that for me?"

I had to pick her up one-handed so that she wouldn't gobble down our payment before it could be collected.

I glanced to the side even though Beans had warned me not to and saw him creeping forward, slow and close to the ground.

He stopped in front of me to inspect the New York strip and give it a couple licks. "Yes, this will do quite nicely."

I tapped on my phone and said, "Hello. Yes. What did you want to tell me again?"

Beans appraised me for a moment and nodded. "Ah, a clever

ruse. Although you don't need to be all that clever to outsmart Frank. Do you think it was his idea to start this store? No. It was all part of my plan to get some variety in my diet so I'm not stuck eating fish food my entire nine lives. Anyway, the warehouse guy is named Steve. He comes here twice per week to deliver stock—in fact, he was just here yesterday, which means he probably won't be back for a few more days. The man you're looking for drives a big white truck with a picture of a crab and a lighthouse on it."

"Yes, I'd be happy to arrange a meeting," I told the imaginary speaker on the other end of my phone. "What days work best for you and Steve?"

"I can't say. He's never consistent. Something doesn't quite smell right about the guy, if you catch my drift. But if he's got Frank's deer feed in the warehouse, I'm sure he'd be happy to sell it to you for a tidy profit."

"Thank you," I said, then stuck my phone in my purse and reached down to pat the orange tabby on his head.

He grabbed the giant hunk of meat and ran off to hide somewhere, and I grabbed the largest bag of bird seed the store had on offer, ready to hightail it out of there and put the next stage of my plan in action.

16

"Okay, my friend, what have you got for me?" I asked my web browser as I pulled up Google and input my search terms: *Crab, lighthouse, warehouse, Blueberry Bay, Maine.*

The first few results were for actual lighthouses, fish markets, and local restaurants, but on the second page of the completed search I found a link to Scotch on the Docks Storage Services, owned by one Steven Scotch. That had to be it, although I hadn't the faintest idea how the crab on the logo related to the name of the company. It was definitely a match though.

The business address given online was for a post office box rather than a physical location, and trying to call the number listed resulted in a prerecorded message that informed me the number had been disconnected.

Very strange for someone I knew from a firsthand account

was still actively in business. In the absence of any better ideas, I decided to drive down to the docks and see if I got lucky.

As I drove through town to the bay that gave this region its name, I wondered how Octo-Cat was faring in his search of the neighbor's homestead. Had he already found the missing memory card and remaining cameras? Or had he gotten bored and decided to take a nap? Either was just as likely, but I'd find out soon enough, I supposed. My thoughts also drifted to Pringle as I wondered whether the raccoon had managed to get the frightened buck witness to speak yet. It was a bit odd that the three of us were pursuing this case from entirely different angles, but it also gave me confidence that we'd have it solved in no time. Even if both cat and raccoon had slacked off, I was still making good progress on my own—or rather, with Paisley at my side.

I pulled into a large, mostly empty parking lot, took several deep breaths, and made my way down to the water. I didn't love being back on the wharf, considering my last visit here had led to my near drowning at the hands of a pistol-wielding madwoman. This time, however, I'd come during daylight hours and of my own volition. I also had Paisley to help keep me safe. Sure, the little Chihuahua couldn't do much in a fight, but she had a habit of barking at even the slightest perceived threat. More often than not, she sounded the alarm for minor things like blowing leaves or an approaching mail carrier, but still, it was good knowing she'd be watching my back, my front, and really all sides of me as I investigated the area.

After a short walk through the area, I found a crew actively unloading a large ship on the quay and marched right up to say hello. "Hey, hello! I'm looking for Steve Scotch, Scotch on the Docks Storage. Do you know where I might find him?"

At first it didn't seem as if any of them had heard me. The handful of burly men and women just kept moving goods from the ship to the land. They made a tiny, efficient army of sorts in their matching dark blue coveralls and heavy steel-toed boots. I'm sure I appeared ridiculous to them with my polka-dotted maxi dress, foam flip-flops, and Chihuahua companion, but I made no apologies for my fashion choices. I only felt sorry for bothering them when they clearly had so much work to do.

"Hi, excuse me," I tried again, raising a hand to better attract their attention. "Do any of you know where I can find Steve Scotch?"

This time they definitely heard me. A couple of the men grumbled to one another while staring daggers in my direction and making me decidedly uncomfortable. I was just contemplating how far I should push my luck when one of the female crew members set down her load and jogged over to speak with me. "Careful who you go asking for around here. Steve Scotch is persona non grata after he stiffed us on our last job."

I winced at this revelation. "I'm sorry."

She dragged her forearm across her brow and let out a heavy breath. "Not your fault, but as far as I know the guy's gone out of business. We haven't seen him around here in close to a month."

I nodded. "Okay, thanks for letting me know." No wonder the other workers had seem irked by my presence. I'd come out of nowhere to remind them of a bad memory. For all they knew, I was looking for the prodigal warehouser because the two of us were friendly. Not because I suspected him of murder. They didn't need to know all the details, especially since they didn't know where Steve Scotch had disappeared to. On all fronts, it seemed the man had gone out of business, yet Beans had confirmed that he still visited the pet store twice per week with new deliveries—and he'd even been there as recently as yesterday. What was going on? And how did it relate to Angela Miller's death? I was so close to solving this case I could taste it. I'd just need to go back to the pet store and talk to Frank or Beans or perhaps both.

But what could I say to explain my line of questioning? Beans was a cat. I was lucky he knew as much as he did and that he was willing to share that information with me for a relatively low payoff. Frank, on the other hand, was clearly uncomfortable with the entire idea of buying and selling off-season feed. If I went back and asked more questions about it, I'd need to explain everything...

Or I could get Nan to go in and specifically ask after the warehouse guy. Maybe she could say she needed to store some things and that Steven had been recommended but she'd had a hard time getting in touch, and then mention seeing his van outside the pet supply store the day prior. Yes, that would certainly beat staking out a strip mall. That was far too conspicuous, considering I didn't want to draw attention to myself or this investigation. Sending in Nan as a collaborative agent made the most sense, which meant I needed to head home now, clue Nan in on the plan, and catch up with the others.

I thanked the dock worker again and then turned back in the direction of the parking lot. Just then, however, Paisley started to growl. I glanced down and found her hackles raised and teeth bared.

Panic shot through me in an instant. I held my breath and asked, "What is it, girl?"

Paisley growled again, then ran forward at a feverish pace. I wasn't sure if we were running toward something or running away, but run I did.

Paisley darted right through a flock of seagulls that had gathered on the pier, barking furiously, then circling back around to chase off the stragglers.

When I finally caught up, I scooped her into my arms. "What was that all about? Is everything okay?"

"They were saying mean things about you, Mommy," she whimpered and squirmed in my arms. "One of them was even going to poop on your head!"

One of the seagulls glided back down and landed on the wooden railing. "I hear you're getting married, Angie Russo," the bird said in an eerily familiar voice. *Alpha!* He was the very same seagull I'd ousted from control of his flock after Charles and Pringle had proven he'd hired a cat to take out a rival flock to expand his territory. Since then we'd become good friends with his successor Bravo and Bravo's adopted daughter Abigull, but I hadn't seen the former head honcho again until now.

"What do you want from me?" I asked, my voice shaky with fright. This guy had murdered dozens of his own kind, and he definitely had an axe to grind with me for revealing his crimes and getting him exiled.

"Oh, you've already done more than enough for me. I just figured it's time I return the favor. See you at the ceremony," he said before flying off.

Paisley barked at him until he was out of sight, and I added another item to my mental to-do list. I'd need to make sure to seagull-proof my outdoor wedding. How hard could that be?

17

By the time I returned home, I was well past exhausted. Still, I had to keep going, especially when I sensed I was so close to finding out what really happened to old Ms. Miller next door.

I'd hardly gotten through the door when Octo-Cat descended upon me, a look of derision etched across his furry face.

"What took you so long?" he demanded, his mouth held partially open to reveal his sharp incisors.

I dropped my purse onto the bench by the door and pushed off my shoes. "First we went to that new pet store in town. Talking to the owner didn't give us any real leads, but then—"

"Can it, Angela. I don't care."

I glanced down to find him glaring at me. Whatever was upsetting him, he clearly blamed me for it. "But you just asked—"

"Again, I do not care." He growled and sauntered away as if I wasn't worth wasting any more time on. "You have already wasted enough of my time. Now follow me."

He led me over to the dining room table where I'd left both my laptop and the camera we'd filched from the neighbor's porch. A third item also sat waiting beside them.

"Is this..?" I asked, unable to hide my surprise.

"Yes, I completed my primary objective in hardly any time at all. Then I was left to wait in agony as you twiddled those opposable thumbs—thumbs I could have made very good use of, by the way. Now turn on the video. I've been so anxious to see what's on this thing that I've hardly been able to eat or nap all day." He sighed heavily and then yawned to further emphasize his point.

I avoided making a sarcastic remark, especially one that involved his weight or activity level. After all, I was genuinely curious what we'd find in this footage too.

I popped the small chip into the SD card slot on my laptop and waited for it to load. Most of the footage was boring, still shots of Ms. Miller's front porch. Occasionally, she'd come out to water the flowers or to yell into her speaker phone—about me, no doubt. I couldn't say for sure since our feed had no sound. I zoomed through the footage faster and faster, about to give up when...

"There!" Octo-Cat shouted and lifted a paw to motion at the screen. "Stop and go back a little."

I did as instructed, then watched in silent horror as my cat appeared on camera, squatted in the center of the porch, and did his business.

"Haha, nice one," Octo-Cat cheered on his past self with clear pride.

"You're disgusting," I said, shaking my head. "If you're not going to take this seriously, then there's no point in even watching."

I zipped the footage ahead again. We'd now made it to yesterday morning. Later that day, the cranky old neighbor would be found dead. Yet again, I was just about to give up and exit out of the feed when something important caught my eye. There on the screen, I watched as a large man strode up the porch steps and knocked on Ms. Miller's front door. He appeared to be the rough-and-tumble sort with a bald head, thick beard, and worn-down clothing.

Could it be...?

I zoomed in to get a closer look, which only made the image grainier. Frustrated, I paused and looked to my kitty companion. "Octo-Cat, can you tell what he's got on his arm there?"

"Of course, I can tell. Feline vision is far superior to human vision, as is our hearing, our intellect, our beauty, our—"

"I'm going to stop you right there, your greatness," I cut in with a snort. "I just need to know what's on his arm. Little bit of help here?"

Octo-Cat chuckled and shook his head. "What would you do without me, Angela? Seriously? It's right in front of your eyes, clear as day, and still you can't tell that the thing on his arm is a drawing of a crab."

"A drawing? Like a tattoo?"

"How should I know? You're not cool enough to get any ink of your own, so I've never seen one in person before."

Well, I couldn't let him get away with that assertion. I rushed to defend myself. "Correction, I am cool enough for a tattoo. It's that I'm not brave enough. There's a big difference between the two."

He just shrugged and turned away, probably rolling his eyes at me. Whatever.

I started the video again and watched as Angela Miller opened the door and appeared to have a heated exchange with the man. He shifted, affording me a better view of his forearm ink, and that's when it all clicked into place.

I grabbed my phone and reopened the web search I'd done earlier from the pet store parking lot. I zoomed in on the logo I'd found on the woefully out-of-date website and held it up to my laptop screen.

"What do you think?" I asked my partner as I too glanced from one device to the other. "Do these two crabs match?"

"Yes, they're the same," he confirmed without further comment.

"Steve Scotch," I said with an enormous sense of relief at having identified the mystery visitor. "He's definitely our man."

Now my cat looked irritated with me once again. "Great, but who's Steve Scotch?"

"You'd know if you had let me tell you about my day instead of interru—"

"Then tell me already," he insisted, the irony clearly escaping him.

I sighed but did as he asked. Even when I was one hundred percent in the right, it wasn't enough to make the cat back down on his opinions. And we had too much to discuss for me to waste time lecturing him on manners. As far as those things went, my words always went right in one fur-lined ear and out the other. For the moment, though, I had Octo-Cat's rapt attention.

"Angela," he gasped when I'd finished. "Why didn't you tell me any of this earlier? These are key facts for our investigation."

"I tried to, but—"

He held up a paw to silence me once more, then hopped off the table and glanced back up at me. "We have clear evidence that connects this shady warehouse guy with the stiff. It's time to go to the police."

"Right. And how will we explain how we happened upon this evidence, or even why we find it significant? My key informant is a cat named Beans, and we illegally secured that footage. We don't need Charles here to tell us that this won't be admissible in court. We have a connection, but not a motive. Not yet. We need to find those other cameras and see what they reveal." I hated the words even as I spoke them. Now we were operating on far more than a hunch, but it still wasn't enough to prove anything to the authorities.

"I already found the other cameras," he informed me with a pointed look.

My ears perked up, and my heart raced with excitement. "You did? Good kitty. But, uh, where are they?"

"Couldn't get them down without you," he said with a snarl. "But now that you've finally decided to show up for the job, let's go."

I swallowed back my retort so as not to waste any more of our time. Once this case was fully solved, I could give my cat an earful about his attitude and how it could sometimes hurt my feelings.

I didn't expect him to care, but at least I would feel a little better.

18

"I found two other cameras," Octo-Cat informed me as I followed him across the front lawn. "Both are in the forest. One points toward our house, and the other points toward her house. They weren't too hard to spot. I'm sure even you would have found them eventually if you'd just tried."

"Great. Lead the way," I said, even though he already was.

My cat made a beeline through the woods until we came upon a thick tree with two cameras mounted on its trunk.

I positioned myself in front of the first and stared out across the forest, trying to determine the visibility of each camera. Despite the thick copse, I could just make out our front porch if I craned my head at the right angle.

I then moved to the other side when a flash of bright yellow caught my eye. It was coming from the neighbor's backyard. Our witness!

I crept closer, not wanting to startle the buck away before I had a chance to speak with him.

"Um, excuse me! What about the cameras?" Octo-Cat hissed but then fell into step beside me anyway.

The buck didn't notice our approach, not when he was so focused on whatever was in front of him. His massive brown body blocked it from view, but my ears soon revealed what my eyes could not.

"Tell me what you know, or it's venison for you!" Pringle shouted and lifted his arms high above his head to make himself appear more threatening.

Irving shook his head back and forth, the yellow tape still tangled in his sizable rack. "Please. Please. I don't know anything."

Oh no! I never should have trusted the raccoon to do such an important job. This deer was already terrified enough without Pringle threatening to eat him. Besides, I happened to know the masked critter had a strong preference for processed food. He'd never eat fresh game, not so long as there was a steady supply of trash cans by the curb each week.

"Pringle, get out of here," I commanded through clenched teeth, careful not to raise my voice and make the situation even worse. I softened my voice when speaking with the buck. "Irving, I'm sorry about him. Nobody is going to hurt you."

"H-how did you know m-m-my name?" he stammered.

I smiled to reassure him that I was friendly. "I believe we have a mutual friend in Paisley."

"The little dog? Yes, I like her, but I don't like him." Irving turned to Pringle with wide eyes as if he'd suddenly frozen and was now caught staring into oncoming traffic. "I do not like him at all," he finished, hardly moving his mouth as he spoke.

And that was when Paisley came zooming onto the scene. "Did you call me, Mommy? Oh, hi, Irving."

The buck still stood staring in fright at the raccoon.

"Is this guy bothering you?" Paisley asked with a ruff. Irving didn't say a thing, but his doggie friend still charged at the trash panda, teeth bared, hackles raised. "Get out of here, you no-good meanie!" she cried and yipped and just generally created a huge ruckus.

"I was just trying to help!" Pringle ground out as he scampered off into the trees.

"Wow," Octo-Cat said flatly, his expression bored. "You actually did a dog thing, Paisley. I'm impressed."

She wagged her tail happily and gave her big brother a kiss on the cheek, unaware that he'd actually been insulting her.

"Ick. How many times do I have to tell you? No kissing the cat!" The tabby tensed at her affection, but Paisley was undeterred. She gave him a good lick-down, then trotted off to roll in a fresh pile of deer droppings. Gross. I'd have to hose her off once we got back home.

But first I had a witness to question.

"Irving, I know you're frightened, but I promise none of us will hurt you," I said, finally breaking him of his whole cliche deer-in-headlights thing. "We're just trying to figure out what happened to your friend who lived in this house."

"She died," the buck whispered reverently. "I saw the whole thing. It was terrible."

"Is that why you've been so afraid lately?" I ventured gently.

He shook his head, waving the tattered crime scene tape around some more.

I approached slowly. "Do you mind if I untangle this for you while we talk?" I asked, raising a tentative hand toward his rack.

"Please, it's been bothering me so much, but nothing I've done has gotten it unstuck."

I lifted both hands and got to work while Irving continued to open up.

"And to answer your question, I'm afraid because it's hunting season. Each year I manage to evade the hunters, and each year I'm an even bigger prize for them as my antlers grow. They all want to turn me into a trophy… or dinner. It's a horrible, barbaric thing." He shuddered and froze again.

I made soft shushing noises and gently patted his flank. "I'm sorry. It must be very hard to live like that, in constant fear that someone is after you."

I waited for him to thaw again before resuming my work on the mess in his antlers.

"I like these woods because there aren't any large predators around," he revealed. "You know, other than humans. I decided to make it my home when I met Angela. She gives me my dinner each night and talks nicely to me. At least she did until—" Irving choked on a sob.

"Until?" I prompted as I continued to work on the mess in his antlers.

"It's all my fault," he bleated. "She was getting me my dinner, same as every night, when her grip slipped. My dinner crushed her to death, and there was so much blood. I tried to help her, but I got afraid and ran away. When I came back, the police were here."

"And you got stuck in the crime scene tape," I finished for him. It all made perfect logical sense, but it still didn't explain all the evidence we'd found.

"I've been running ever since. I keep checking back to see if Angela will return, but I'm afraid she's really dead. I'm going to miss her," he snuffled and wailed, inadvertently jerking his antlers out of my reach. "She was the nicest human I ever met."

My heart went out to Irving. Ms. Miller too. It just went to show that people are incredibly complex and confusing creatures. The same lady was an enemy to me but a friend to Irving. Somehow she was both of those things at the same time, even though it seemed that shouldn't have been possible.

"You said she lost her grip? That it was an accident?"

Irving nodded. "Yes, I'm positive. Oh, it was so terrible. I just hate thinking about it."

"I promise not to bother you much longer." I finally freed him of the torn yellow ribbon. Now I just had one last question to ask. "Are you sure you didn't see anyone else around? Anyone who may have hurt Angela?" I knew I was leading the witness, but we weren't exactly in court here. If Ms. Miller's death had really been an accident, then what was with the dodgy warehouse guy paying her a visit?

Irving raked his antlers against a nearby tree and let out a giant sigh of delight. He seemed to smile as he turned to me, but then his mouth fell open in fear as he revealed, "I did see someone, but not until after she was gone. He came last night with a bright light..."

19

After we finished talking with Irving, Octo-Cat, Paisley, and I returned to the woods. I couldn't dislodge the trail cams from the thick tree trunk, but I was able to open them up and snag the memory cards.

My two furry sidekicks wanted to watch the feed of our house so they could admire themselves on camera, but I put them off in favor of watching Ms. Miller's yard instead.

Sure enough, Irving appeared at the same time each evening to collect his dinner, and the old woman spent a fair amount of time standing with him and speaking words I couldn't hear. The camera didn't afford a view into the shed, but the panicked deer moving back and forth as he investigated the scene confirmed when the death had happened—and that no one else had been around.

"So it wasn't a murder, after all," I concluded with a sigh. I probably should have been happy, but the end result was the same. A woman was dead.

"Well, there you go," Octo-Cat said with an unhappy sneer. "Case closed. I can't believe you had me high-footing it all over thc place for absolutely nothing. I deserve a raise."

"But we had to know for sure," I reminded him. This had happened practically in our own backyard. How could we not investigate?

Octo-Cat remained unconvinced. "Why? Nobody was paying us. We didn't even like the lady. You tricked me into all of this by pointing out how superior I am to you. Lesson learned. Just because you need me doesn't mean I need you."

I put a hand to my heart. "Ouch, Octo-Cat. That really hurts me. I thought we were friends. Besides, if you don't need me, then who is going to open your cans of food? Who is going to take care of you to your exact specifications? Who is—?"

"Mommy!" Paisley barked, and I turned to her with a quizzical glance. "I'm sorry to interrupt, but look!"

I followed her gaze back to the screen. The feed showed nighttime now, but the rear floodlights had been illuminated by motion.

"Just wait," Paisley instructed, her eyes wide and glistening. "He came before, and I'm pretty sure he's coming back again."

Sure enough, a large man stalked across the yard and disappeared into the shed. When he reemerged he was carrying several small burlap bags stacked on top of one another. I couldn't make out his tattoo of a crab, but still I knew we had our guy.

"That's why the shed had been cleaned out," I remembered. "We thought it was the police, but no. Steve Scotch came back to take the deer feed. But why would he steal deer feed? Was it just so he could sell it again?"

Octo-Cat scoffed. "That hardly seems like a profitable venture."

"Something weird is definitely going on here. We know now that it wasn't murder, but think about this for a second." I really felt like I had all the pieces of the puzzle and just needed to see how they fit together. I racked my brain for everything I'd learned about Steve Scotch and the deer feed to put all the clues on display for my companions.

"Go on. I'm listening," Octo-Cat droned impatiently.

Paisley stayed quiet but wagged her tail, which was all the confirmation I needed to continue.

"Okay, here goes," I said, holding up my hands so I could tick off each detail on my fingers. "Angela Miller was feeding the deer next door. But right now there aren't any local shops that will sell deer feed since it's illegal to do so during hunting season."

"She could have brought the feed with her when she moved," my cat argued with a flick of his tail. He liked to be the one to put all the clues together, but this time I had him beat.

I shook my head. "She could have, but I don't think that's what happened."

"Okay, genius," he hissed. "What have you got?"

"She went to the pet store hoping to make a purchase, but Frank probably gave her the same lecture he gave me. Knowing how she was with us, she probably gave him an earful, creating quite the scene."

He nodded. "Right. I'm with you so far."

"Okay, here's where we have to join our two threads. The cat Beans mentioned that the warehouse guy had been at the store yesterday. That's the same day Angela died. My guess is he overheard her yelling at Frank and then approached her once she'd left the store offering to sell her some feed at a significant markup."

"But you said she hadn't brought feed with her when she moved." Octo-Cat grinned at having caught me up, but he hadn't. Not really.

"I think maybe she brought some but ran out quickly when a huge buck started showing up for dinner every night. She needed to replenish her supply or risk losing her friend."

"Oh, that's sad!" Paisley chimed in, her ears drooping. Honestly, I hadn't even been sure she was listening since she still had her eyes glued to the footage on my laptop.

"It is sad, but more than that it's unlucky. When I was talking with Frank, he mentioned that his supplier had accidentally sent the feed several months early but was paying for it to be warehoused because of the mistake. Frank promised he'd have some for me to buy the second it became okay to sell again. Here comes a third thread."

I paused, but neither animal had anything to say.

"Once I figured out the name of the storage company, I looked it up online. The address was a P.O. box and the number had been disconnected. I went down to the docks to ask after Steve Scotch, but one of the workers told me that he'd pretty much disappeared a month back after refusing to pay them for a job. All signs point to him being out of business..."

"Except he's still going to the pet store twice per week and he came by our neighbor's house at least one time," Octo-Cat pointed out.

"Exactly."

Octo-Cat yawned. "So where does that leave us?"

"I think Steve Scotch quit his job because he found a better offer. But he still needed a front so he kept up the whole Scotch on the Docks facade."

"A front for what?" He yawned again. If I didn't hurry, I'd lose him entirely.

"That's what I'm trying to figure out. Whatever it is, it involves the pet store though."

"Do you think Frank is a bad guy?" Paisley whined. "He seemed very nice to me."

"Maybe, but it's also possible he simply doesn't know what's going on. If he were to blame, then I doubt he'd have been so forthcoming with the details. Also wouldn't he have tried to sell me the feed under the table when I came in asking about it?"

"What's under the table?" Paisley wanted to know, squirming to get a better view.

"It's just an expression for when people do things the wrong way," I explained with a laugh.

Her tail drooped in disappointment, softening my heart.

"I have an idea. Let's all go to the pet store. Do you wanna go on another car ride?" I asked in a hyper babyish voice that always got Paisley riled up.

"Hard pass," Octo-Cat said, hopping down from the table and sauntering away. "I need a nap. But let me know how it goes. Also don't forget about my raise."

20

When I arrived at Frank and Beans a short while later, I found a police cruiser already sitting in the parking lot outside.

Inside, I found Officer Bouchard standing on one side of the counter and Frank standing on the other. I let myself in, but neither seemed to notice my arrival.

"I already told you, officer. I would never sell deer feed off season. My professional ethics are a point of pride." He spotted me standing in the doorway and offered a broad smile. "Oh, hello again. Three times in one day. I'm starting to think you're addicted to my store."

"What's going on here?" I asked, picking up Paisley to cradle her to my chest and to give her a better view of the scene.

Officer Bouchard frowned. "That's not really—"

"They're accusing me of selling stolen goods," Frank interrupted, all too happy to share. "Can you believe that? Me? I can assure you I follow the letter of the law."

And there it was, that final piece that brought the whole picture together. I turned to Officer Bouchard, unable to hide my excitement. "The big bag that crushed Angela Miller, there was something other than deer feed inside, wasn't there?"

"But how could you possibly—Angie, you've been investigating again, haven't you?" He put both hands on his hips and glared at me.

I shrugged and offered a small smile.

The policeman sighed. "Fine. Just tell us what you know, but don't say a thing about how you know it. I really don't want to have to take you in for questioning."

I nodded and shared all that I had learned.

"So you're saying this Steven Scotch guy used the pet store as a front for his black market activities?" Officer Bouchard summarized when I was halfway through.

"Yes, he quit showing up at the docks about a month ago, around the same time Frank first set up for business. He still comes by this place twice per week, even though all signs point to him having gone out of business."

Bouchard gave Frank a pointed look. "Care to amend your story at all?"

"No," I cut in at once. "Frank's not guilty. Steve was using his products to hide the fenced goods, which is why he's in and out of the pet shop so much despite it not being too busy yet. My guess is Steve overheard Angela Miller when she came in searching for deer feed. When Frank wouldn't sell it to her, he saw the opportunity to make some quick cash and offered to hook her up for a price. But then he must have given her the wrong bags. That's why he came back to her house, asking to get the feed back."

"How do you...?" He shook his head and frowned again. "No, no, don't tell me. Just keep going."

"Then he came back later that night, found the shed unlocked, and took all the remaining feed bags," I concluded, almost feeling like I should throw up jazz hands at the big reveal. Thankfully, I managed to restrain myself

The policeman nodded thoughtfully. "Thank you for telling me just enough to put me on the right path. Looks like I need to bring Steve Scotch in for questioning. Have a good day," he said to Frank, then turned toward me with a raised brow. "Stay out of trouble, you hear?"

Frank and I stood in silence for a few moments after Bouchard left. Finally he shook his head, laughed, and said, "Okay, so what can I sell you this time?"

"Actually," I confessed, feeling a bit sheepish, "I was only here to investigate. The lady who died lived next door to me." I pulled a card from my purse and handed it to him.

"Angie Russo, Pet Whisperer P.I." he read in apparent awe. "You can talk to animals?

I forced a laugh. "Of course not, don't be silly. It's just a gimmick, and an excuse for bringing my cat and dog with me on all my cases." I still hated that Nan and my mother had saddled me with a name that skirted so close to revealing my secret.

Frank's eyes grew wide. "You have a cat? We should set up a playdate with Beans."

"Yeah, sure." I knew Octo-Cat would hate being forced to spend time with another cat, especially one as weird as Beans, but I'd leave the idea in my back pocket in case I ever needed a creative way to punish him.

"I have to get home," I told Frank, who still stood there studying my card. "But I promise I'll be back to do some real shopping."

I wasn't sure he'd heard me since he kept studying my card as if it held the secrets to life, the universe, and everything. When my farewell went unmet, I quietly let myself outside and then drove home to share the news with Nan and Octo-Cat.

* * *

"So it wasn't a homicide," Nan summarized as she sipped at her tea. We were sitting together in the living room now as I went over the encounter I'd had with Officer Bouchard and Frank at the pet store. Octo-Cat was still off napping somewhere, which meant I'd have to recount everything again later, but I didn't mind.

I shook my head. "Nope, but her death revealed another crime."

"Funny that." Nan wrapped both hands around her mug and sighed. "This is why I keep up with my meditation, you know?"

I scrunched my brow in confusion. I was often confused when

it came to Nan, but that was part of her charm. She gave me a knowing look. "That Angela died because of some silly accident. She slipped, hit her head, and then she was gone. That's some majorly bad karma."

"It was just dumb luck."

"Not luck. Karma. It's one of the strongest forces in the universe, and let me assure you, it is anything but dumb. That woman put lots of bad energy out, and all of a sudden it came zipping back at her." Nan took another sip of tea.

I didn't know what to say to that, so I simply shrugged. A gentle knock at the window behind me drew my attention and provided a nice change of topic.

Pringle sat on the ledge holding a bouquet of flowers. When he saw he had my attention, he held them up in offering, then motioned to the door.

"Be right back," I told Nan, who seemed content to sit with her tea and her thoughts as I crept onto the porch to speak with the raccoon.

"These are for you," Pringle said, holding the flowers out to me once more.

"Thank you. They're beautiful."

"I got them from the neighbor's porch. She won't be needing them anymore."

It took great effort to hold back my groan. I tried to focus on the fact that Pringle had brought me a peace offering instead of the fact that he'd filched said offering from the neighbor.

"I'm sorry," he said, hardly above a whisper.

"No, that's not right," he muttered to himself, then got down on one knee and declared with a great sweeping gesture, "I'm sorry!"

I shifted my weight from foot to foot, unable to believe what I was hearing. "You're sorry? For what?"

"For all the times I have hurt you or others because of my actions. I thought long and hard after what happened with that deer."

"And with Paisley," I added with a glower.

"And with Paisley," he confirmed. "I didn't mean to cause any trouble, honest. I just like being included, but sometimes I go about it the wrong way."

I offered him a kindly smile. "That's very big of you, Pringle. I appreciate the apology."

"I'm starting a twelve-step program," he said with a grin. "The seagulls told me about it. When I'm finished, I won't have a drinking problem anymore."

I bit back a laugh. "But Pringle, you don't have a drinking problem."

"Oh, right! The program usually helps people who drink too much alcohol, but the seagull suggested I could do the same twelve steps to help with my behavioral issues. There's a nice group of people who meet every night at a church not far from here. I already scoped it out. There's a perfect spot where I can sit at the window and look in."

"Well, that sounds lovely. Good on you, Pringle."

"Yeah, you know that Alpha isn't such a bad guy, after all."

"Wait, you said the seagulls told you about the program."

"Yeah, well, really just one seagull. Alpha. Remember him?"

Fear enveloped my heart. This was the same bird who'd threatened me earlier that day. Was he using Pringle to get to me? How could getting the raccoon help he so clearly needed ultimately serve to hurt me? What was this bird's big plan?

"Thank you again, Pringle." I raised the flowers to my nose and took a big whiff to show my appreciation. "I'm proud of you."

"Yay, I'm doing it!" he cheered before scampering off the porch and around the house.

I headed inside to put my ill-gotten bouquet in some water. I'd only just closed out one case and already I had another.

What on earth was that devious seagull up to now?

WHAT TO READ NEXT

Ever since Angie Russo woke up from a near fatal run-in with a coffee maker, she's been able to talk to—and even worse, understand—one very spoiled tabby named Octavius.

This collection includes *Scheming Sphynx*, *Honeymoon Hearsay*, and *Animal Accomplice*. Add in a disaster of a wedding, an old house harboring dangerous secrets, and an aspiring social media influencer, toss on your favorite deerstalker cap, and let's go sleuthing!

The *Pet Whisperer P.I.: Books 16-18 Special Collection* is now available.

Get your copy so that you can keep reading this series today!

SNEAK PEEK

SCHEMING SPHYNX

My name is Angie Russo, and in just a few short days, I will become Mrs. Charles Longfellow, III. It seems like ages since that first day our eyes met across the office and I instantly fell head over heels for the handsome new law associate from California. Really though, it's only been a couple years.

And even though I immediately fell in love, it took Charles a little longer to figure out I was the one he'd spend the rest of his life with. It all started when he blackmailed me into helping with a difficult double homicide case. He was the second person to learn of my strange ability to talk to animals, and rather than gawk at me, he decided to put me to work.

Now we've solved many cases, both together and apart, and in the process we've fallen irrevocably in love. He's now the sole partner at the firm, and I've moved on from paralegalling to working as a full-time private investigator… in theory.

In reality, I primarily live off my cat's trust fund, but I do try my best to find new mysteries to solve, whether or not my help has been requested. Why, just this spring, I solved the murder of my next-door neighbor. Oh, was that one a doozy!

Luckily, we've been light on work in the weeks that followed, giving me plenty of time to focus on wedding planning.

So, that's me. Former paralegal, current private investigator, future bride. And oh, you wanted to know more about the whole talking to animals thing?

Well, it all started when I met Octo-Cat at a rather unusual will reading. This was before Charles had even joined the firm. He was the first one to really trust me to help research our cases. Before that, I was mostly a glorified secretary. And that day, it was my job to make the coffee. Things didn't exactly go well, and let's just say I've had a completely rational fear of that particular appliance ever since.

The unexpected zap messed with something in my brain, and when I regained consciousness, I was met with big amber eyes and stinky tuna breath. Yes, the estate's primary beneficiary was a cat, and when he realized I could understand everything he was saying, he recruited me to help solve his owner's murder.

And thus a lifelong *something* was born. Most days Octo-Cat and I get along fine, but sometimes he can be a real stinker. Still, I wouldn't trade him—or really any part of my life—for the world.

My true best friend is my nan. She's the main one who raised me while my parents focused on making the most of their careers. She's not even my biological grandmother, a fact I discovered only quite recently. And after months of searching and with a little help from a militant flock of seagulls, I was recently able to meet my Grandma Lyn—the one who gave birth to Mom.

Both will be at the wedding, which will definitely be awkward. But we'll have lots of other guests to help keep the two mostly apart.

Nan's dog Paisley, a mostly black tricolor Chihuahua she rescued from the pound, is going to be the flower girl at our wedding. Pringle, the raccoon who lives in a treehouse in my backyard, is not invited but will probably crash the party anyway. Our seagull friends Bravo and Abigull have told us they'll be watching from the trees. Another seagull I know, Alpha, has threatened to ruin the whole affair. He's also recently befriended Pringle and encouraged him to take part in a twelve-step program to help with his behavioral issues. I'm not sure I trust his motives on that one, but the group therapy has definitely been helping Pringle to turn over a new leaf.

He's still not invited to the wedding, though.

I'll be plenty busy hosting all the guests we have coming from out of town. Even my old frenemy Bethany Peters is coming up from Georgia along with my cousin Mags to take part in the happiest day of my life to date.

Charles's family is coming out from California, of course, and our friend Sharon is taking a detour on her RV tour of the country to swing on by too. Basically, everyone who's anyone to us will be in attendance—past clients, old friends, distant family… Even my cat's girlfriend's owner is coming all the way from Colorado to pay her respects.

In lieu of a bridal party, our three cats will be standing at the altar with us. I've found adorable bowties for Octo-Cat and Jacques and a miniature lace veil for Jillianne. Charles hasn't been owned by cats as long as I have, but he's a sucker for the two hairless Sphynx he inherited from my first dead next-door neighbor, Senator Harlowe.

Over the last several months, I've been giving the two speech lessons to help them overcome their strange accents—not out of the goodness of my heart, but rather at Octo-Cat's demand. He made it very clear that neither Charles nor his cats would be welcome in our house unless the two kittyfolk stopped communicating in only riddles and rhymes.

It was a tall order, but I'm fairly accustomed to my cat bossing me around, and this demand wasn't particularly unreasonable as far as Octo-Cat goes, which meant I was happy to comply. Plus it gave me a chance to bond with Jacques and Jillianne ahead of us becoming one big happy family.

They weren't too sure about me at first, but now I'm fairly certain I've won them over…

ABOUT MOLLY FITZ

While *USA Today bestselling* author Molly Fitz can't technically talk to animals, she and her three feline writing assistants have deep and very animated conversations as they navigate their days.

She lives with her child and their own private zoo somewhere in the wilds of Alaska. Molly will occasionally venture out for good food, great coffee, or to meet new animal friends.

Learn more about Molly and her books, and be sure to sign up for her newsletter at **www.MollyMysteries.com**.

ALSO BY MOLLY FITZ

Learn more about Molly's collected works, so that you can decide which book you'd like to read next...

PET WHISPERER P.I.

Angie Russo just partnered up with Blueberry Bay's first ever talking cat detective. Along with his ragtag gang of human and animal helpers, Octo-Cat is determined to save the day... so long as it doesn't interfere with his schedule.

Start with book 1, ***Kitty Confidential***.

MERLIN'S MAGICAL MYSTERIES

Gracie Springs is not a witch… but her cat is. Now she must help to keep his secret or risk spending the rest of her life in some magical prison. Too bad trouble seems to find them at every turn!

Start with book 1, ***Merlin Takes a Familiar***.

PARANORMAL TEMP AGENCY

Tawny Bigford's simple life takes a turn for the magical when she stumbles upon her landlady's murder and is recruited by a talking black cat named Fluffikins to take over the deceased's role as the official Town Witch for Beech Grove, Georgia.

Start with book 1, ***Witch for Hire***.

THE MYSTERIES OF MOONLIGHT MANOR (WITH TRIXIE SILVERTALE)

Sydney Coleman has it all—until she doesn't. No sooner does she launch her bed and breakfast, than a trio of ghosts turn up oppose her at every turn. They insist she solve the murder of their mistress, but Sydney is desperate for cash. If she can't book some guests fast, her haunted mansion is utterly doomed.

Start with book 1, ***Moonlight & Mischief***.

CONNECT WITH MOLLY

Sign up for my newsletter and get a special digital prize pack for joining, including an exclusive story, *Meowy Christmas Mayhem*, fun quiz, and lots of cat pictures!

Sign up: **MollyMysteries.com/subscribe**

Now, if you ever wished you could converse with cats, here's your opportunity! This is me officially inviting you into my whacky inner world as part of my Cozy Kitty Book Club.

For those who just can't get enough of my zany cat characters and their hapless humans, this book club will provide new content to devour and the chance to get to know my best author friends.

From exclusive stories, behind-the-scenes trivia to never-before-released bonus content, and monthly giveaways, there's a lot to love about the Cozy Kitty Book Club. Join today to find out what we're reading next!

Join: **MollyMysteries.com/club**

www.ingramcontent.com/pod-product-compliance
Lightning Source LLC
Chambersburg PA
CBHW030626310726
48979CB00003B/904

* 9 7 8 1 6 4 4 5 1 5 3 3 4 *